MW00464647

WRONG MAN DOWN

WRONG MAN DOWN

Jerry Masinton

Anamcara Press LLC

Published in 2020 by Anamcara Press LLC
Author © 2020 Jerry Masinton
Illustrations © 2020 by ©Volodymyr Shcerbak - stock.adobe.com
Book design by Maureen Carroll
Georgia, Timeburner, and Salvation.

Printed in the United States of America.
Book Description: Millie Henshawe—intrepid, smart-talking, gay
ex-GI—is the field agent (hired gun) for Continental Removals, LLC,
in Boston, a niche firm catering to very special clients. Millie's well-
honed skills are tested when the unexpected happens and the hired
gun becomes the target!

ANAMCARA PRESS LLC
P.O. Box 442072, Lawrence, KS 66044

https://anamcara-press.com/

Ordering Information:
Quantity sales. Special discounts are available on quantity purchases
by corporations, associations, and others. For details, contact the
publisher at the address above.
Orders by U.S. trade bookstores and wholesalers. Please contact
Ingram Distribution.

Publisher's Cataloging-in-Publication data
Masinton, Jerry, Author
Wrong Man Down / Jerry Masinton

[1. FIC050000   Fiction / Crime . 2. FIC060000   FICTION / Humorous / Black Humor. 3. FIC062000   FICTION / Noir.]

ISBN-13: 978-1-941237-38-0 (Paperback)
ISBN-13: 978-1-941237-57-1 (Hardcover)
ISBN-13: 978-1-941237-39-7 (EBook)

Library of Congress Control Number: 2020936257

Dedication

To Martha

Contents

What seems beautiful to me, what I should
like to write, is a book about nothing,
a book dependent on nothing external, which would be held together by the
strength of its style, just as the earth, sus-
pended in the void, depends on nothing
external for its support.

—Gustave Flaubert

Chapter 1

Kansas City, Here I Come

No fucking way was Millie going to shoot the guy in the men's room at Kansas City International.

What the hell was Ralphie thinking? I should just waltz in behind the guy, wait till he unzips, and then pop him while he's thinking happy thoughts? Or get in the stall next to him and fire when he flushes? In a stall a suppressed round would still sound like a cannon. And let's not forget that the place is usually full of guys trying to look cool while holding on to their weenies. Ralphie, she thought, should have canceled when the client asked for last-minute changes.

Millie had agreed to this assignment only because the target was supposed to drive his own car. She knew how to work in airport parking lots. But any other area was impossible. Well, theoretically possible, but why take the risk? The place would be sealed off in minutes. The one rule with airports: only the parking lots.

At first Ralphie had told her: "Our client says the guy always leaves his car in the parking lot across the street from the terminal. Black Lincoln Navigator. Kansas license LOL-555. Follow him to the parking lot, pay him off, walk back to the terminal. Simple."

Now Ralphie calls and says, "The client says the guy decided to hire a limo this trip, I don't know why. So it's your call as to when and where." And Millie says, "Ralphie, are you fucking crazy? The guy has a driver? Where's he going to be while I entertain the subject? Not to mention the added risk if the driver gets a good look at me. Am I supposed to do him too? What the hell's wrong with you, anyway?" No doubt about it, she was getting wound up. "Plus," she said, "it's not professional to improvise. People can get hurt."

So Millie told Ralphie she was out, the contract had been breached. Thirty minutes later Ralph Klammer of Continental Removals was back on the line with her. "Millie, our client appreciates the problem, OK? But he's done business with us before and asks us to make an exception. He's willing to pay double. Just tag the subject, not the driver, he says. The guy has to go to baggage claim, so he'll be open for business a while. You can take a little time, see what the options are. The driver will be curbside waiting for him. Maybe our guy never makes it out the door, know what I mean?"

"Ralphie, Goddammit, let me think." She was calculating how many things could go wrong. She lost track after a dozen or so. "All right: tell the client I'll see what's possible. No promises, though. There's too much play in a situation like this, you know that. We should just cancel and renegotiate."

"Millie, you're right," Ralph said, "but I have to be frank here, I'm in a bind. Our cutout says the client is not someone you can negotiate with, if you know what I mean. Now ditch that phone, OK? Use another one of the burners if you're in a jam."

"Ralphie, wait a sec. We don't do business with the Mob. That's one of our rules."

"I said I'd try not to. This guy, I don't know who he is. He gets in touch with somebody he knows, then that guy contacts one of our cutouts, who puts in a call to

Philly. Then, OK, Philly calls us. That way there's never any direct contact between client and contractor. It's safer all around. I'm not telling you anything new here. So I don't know the client. But no, I don't think it's the goombahs. Why would they call us when they can do their own work in-house? Though who knows, maybe they don't want to leave their signature this time."

"So what the hell, Ralphie? This is our part of the game. The clients hire us, sure, but they don't run the fucking operation. Once they call Philly, that should definitely be that from their end. Just tell the guy I followed procedure for this type of situation and cut off contact."

"Millie, here's what our boy in Philly says: no fucking delays. You just gotta use your ingenuity. So over and out, OK?"

Millie had flown into KCI that morning, taken a shuttle into Kansas City, and removed a package from a storage locker in the bus station at 3rd and Grand. The package was wrapped in brown paper and had no markings on it. She didn't know who'd put it there and didn't want to know. Ralphie had given her the key in Boston and told her that the package would be in locker #33. She considered 33 a good-luck number.

Ralphie had also shown her photos of the guy and told her that he would be arriving at 4:30 from New York on Southwest, alone. He'd pick up his luggage and walk across the street to his car. She'd follow him at a distance but get closer as he approached it. Then she'd whack him when he unlocked his car door or trunk, help him get inside, and close the door.

Earlier in the day, she'd made a practice run to the parking lot. It had two levels, with hundreds of cars on each level. No one would pay any attention to her. That was the plan. Piece of cake.

But now she's supposed to clip the guy at baggage claim? Ralph knows that that would put her at maximum exposure. Plus, the conditions are totally unpredictable. Who knows if a kid might get in the way, or if somebody's baggage might bump against her at the wrong moment? She was successful at her work because she controlled the variables. And now she's supposed to play it by ear? Jesus Christ. This guy had better be worth the aggravation. She knew one thing: she would not—repeat not—use a fucking gun inside the terminal. Can you imagine the number of witnesses there'd be?

She'd been back in the terminal since 2:30. The arrivals board showed that the flight would be an hour late: it was now scheduled for 5:25. They're always late these days, she thought. But 5:25 is no problem. As Millie was turning things over in her mind, the arrivals board said the flight had been delayed another twenty minutes. Still not a problem. It'll be darker by that time, and every little bit helps when you're trying to leave the building without being noticed.

Millie didn't mind waiting. She was patient by nature, and she used her time to go over the details. She always had a Plan A and a Plan B in case something went wrong. Which of course was not unknown. Things did go off-track. Like maybe the target decided to visit his girlfriend instead of going straight home to the wife and kids, or instead of going to the office that day he drives his kid to soccer practice. People's inconsistencies: you had to anticipate them. But, let's be honest, they also made her job interesting.

Anyone looking at her in the terminal would see a young woman with a baby bump reading a book called *Eat, Pray, Love* and sipping a Starbucks across from Gate 39. She'd be wearing a long print dress, a baggy gray sweater, and a ball cap pulled low over her horn-rimmed glasses. Her shoes would be an old pair of gray Nikes. Her brown hair would be pulled back in a ponytail.

On the floor beside her there'd be a brown leather tote and a small black duffel from Walmart. The tote had a change of clothes in it, shoes, a pair of extra-thin black leather gloves, makeup, a spare wig, and a pair of clip-on sunglasses. In the duffel were two white plastic shopping bags, a pistol, a silencer, and an Epipen. Handy for working in close if you wanted to.

If someone decided to look through the duffel, Millie would have delicate questions to answer. But in a few minutes she'd go to the women's room and put her Glock, the silencer, and the Epipen into the baby bump, which had slits on either side for pockets. She'd come up with the idea for the fake baby bump watching the Patriots' quarterback Tom Brady using a hand warmer during a January game in Foxboro. Right then and there she saw the beauty of it: a nice little pouch for her gear. A baby bump with a Glock in it? Get serious.

In any case, after she'd settled the bill, the duffel and everything in it would be tossed. So would the thrift-store clothes and shoes. She'd wear a different outfit for the flight back to Boston. On that trip she'd be a slim blonde with chopped hair and no glasses. She'd be wearing beige slacks, a Navy blazer, and dark slingback pumps. Her Massachusetts driver's license would identify her as Lorna Van Dyne, twenty-eight years of age. Her business cards would read: Van Dyne Fashions in raised black lettering. Except for the startling baby blues that gazed back from the license photo, nothing about her would resemble the woman sipping a Starbucks.

The flight would get in at 5:45. Her own flight left at 7:25. She'd be cutting it close.

Chapter 2

Continental Removals

Millie Henshawe had gotten into the removals business by chance. When she left the Army, two years ago, after two deployments to Iraq, she had had no definite career plans. Her Chrysler 300 was paid off, and she had $12,500 in the bank—not a fortune, but she wouldn't starve while she looked around. She checked in with old friends in Waltham, but the women either had kids or were trying to. Definitely not for her. A total non-starter. The only guys that had stuck around were potheads, part-time Star Market checkouts, or aspiring juco dropouts.

After three weeks at home she drove cross-country to L.A., sold the gas-guzzler, and took a job as a cocktail waitress in a sports bar. The tips were good, the vibe was easy, and she made friends. But their lives revolved around the next big party, and somehow Millie didn't see the point of selling alcohol five nights a week and then consuming as much of it as possible the other two nights. She thought of this time in her life as a strategic pause. She pictured herself as a driver at a red light, gunning the engine, getting ready for the light to turn green.

One of her regular customers, a philosophy prof from UCLA, said she was probably undergoing an existential crisis. "Really?" she said. "How do you think I caught it?" He got the joke but said this was serious. She had to find out who she was and lead an authentic life, he said. Oh, boy. Be polite to the customers, her boss had said.

Millie wondered whether the guy's regular drinking schedule made him authentic. She said, "No offense intended, Professor, but I've known who I am since I could spell my name at four." She touched his hand, poured him another drink. "On the house."

Three months later, back in Boston, she ran into a guy at the gym who offered her a job. She'd noticed him working out there at Equinox for a couple of weeks, not shy about looking her over. She didn't return the looks.

One afternoon he walked up to her and said, "Hi, my name's Kevin. What's yours?" She waited for a beat or two. "Jennifer Lopez," she said. He wasn't sure how to field this. Millie just looked at him, taking her time. Maybe feeling a little off-balance, he said, "You just bench-pressed a hundred and twenty without breaking a sweat." "A hundred and thirty," Millie said. "And if that's your line, you need a better one."

He wasn't bad-looking—six feet tall, slim and well-built, a touch of gray in his short dark hair. Nice smile. But she had zero interest. Not in the market. "I've also seen you practice kick-boxing. You're good. Tell you what I want. A friend of mine has a job you might be interested in." She could guess what his friend had in mind. Millie racked the weights she had been using. Kevin tried again: "I see you've been in the Army." He was looking at the tattoo on her left bicep.

Millie said, "Kevin, I'm glad you can read. Now just check the Yellow Pages for a real job candidate. Look under 'Escort Services.'" Then she walked into the women's locker room, showered, and left the building. Kevin was waiting for her on the sidewalk. He was getting under her skin. He said, "Let's start over, OK? I'm not trying to hustle you. My name is Kevin Stark, and I'm a headhunter. Do you know what that is?"

"Yeah, you run around in the jungle with a blow gun."

"That's pretty close, all right." By this time they were walking down Boylston Street.

Millie said, "First of all, you don't know a thing about me, including my name or my background. Second, you haven't told me what this amazing career is that you're dying for me to start. Tell you what: my car's a block away. If you can convince me in five minutes that this is the job of a lifetime, I might think about it. And, Kevin, one more thing: if you try to jump me, I'll put you in the fucking hospital."

He stopped, smiled. "You know, I think you're going to be perfect for this job."

That was Thursday. On the following Tuesday, Millie went to work for Ralph Klammer, who ran Continental Removals, a small firm in Newton that catered to individuals who would pay serious money to get rid of certain, shall we say, undesirable people in their lives. Continental would do the job and clean up afterwards, if the client wanted. All jobs guaranteed.

Ralph had inherited the business from his mother, Sheila, God bless her, when she had passed away. Ralph explained that he and Millie would be the main actors, though there was also Mr. Moustakas, who drove the firm's tiny white van, cleaned the office, took care of the hardware, and did the special clean-ups after a hit. Best man in his line of business.

Mr. Moustakas cleaned one other office in the same renovated Victorian house that Continental Removals occupied. Parsons McLean, a gently declining firm that handled wills and trusts, enjoyed the garden view out back. Continental looked out onto Cabot Street. Old Mr. Parsons, Ralph said, was long-deceased. Mr. McLean worked two or three afternoons a week. His part-time secretary, Mary Michael Mulloy, came in every day but spent most of her time playing online Solitaire. Sometimes she and Ralph sat out on the front porch and discussed TV shows or real estate. Mary Michael also advised Ralph on his mutual funds and helped him with other odds and ends.

In addition to the business, of course, Ralph owned the grand old house. He lived upstairs and still slept in the same bedroom that he'd used as a child. "I like a set routine," he said. "I don't like changes. Never could understand why people like to travel. Matter of fact, Millie, I hardly ever leave the house, except for my walk down Center Street to buy Dunkin' Donuts for breakfast."

Ralph loved his work because he didn't have to leave the house and he could wear his bedroom slippers to the office. His only other interest was raising indoor plants. "I'm a pretty simple guy, Millie," he said. "I lead a quiet life." And now that she was here, he didn't have to worry about who would do the contract work.

That suited her fine, but she had to ask: "Who's been doing it up to now?" This had been on Saturday, during the second of her two interviews. They'd been sitting in his office, a desk between them, chatting on a first-name basis. Before Ralph could answer, Millie had another question: "Why do you want a woman for this job? I thought only guys did it."

Ralph nodded to himself once or twice. He said: "I'll be frank here, Millie. We had a guy before you, a retired grade-school teacher looking to build up his retirement. Good, reliable contractor. Worked for us five years, never a complaint from any of our clients. Then one time, on a trip to of all fucking places Fall River, pardon my French, somebody drilled him and put him in a fucking dumpster.

"So, I have to tell you, this is what people call an occupational hazard, though seeing as you were a soldier you don't have to worry. You know how to handle yourself. We had to refund the client's money, of course, plus fifty percent. The firm's reputation suffered."

He was being honest. She appreciated that.

"Now the other thing, why I want to hire a woman. Think about it, OK? Who'd ever look for a woman contractor? You said it yourself: Only guys follow this trade. But that's just in the movies. In real life, women sign up for high-grade jobs same as men. Times have changed, Millie, otherwise you wouldn't of been a soldier. Bottom line, you'd be aces in this job. A good-looking girl going about her business? Nobody's going to think a thing about it."

"What if I say no, Ralph? Will you have to kill me?" Saying it with a straight face.

He had a chuckle at this. "Nah, I trust you, Millie. You won't tell nobody. Besides, who would believe you? 'Hey, Ralph Klammer over on Cabot Street there, he wants to hire me to whack people.' What do you think they'd say? 'Gee, thanks for the tip, lady, I'll try to stay away.'" He gave her another little laugh.

Ralph leaned forward across the desk, serious now. "You ain't scared, are you, Millie?"

"Scared of what, Ralph?" She almost called him "Ralphie" because he was wearing his bedroom slippers and—for Jesus' sweet sake—argyle socks. Probably knitted by his mother. "No, just thinking. In Iraq the other side had guns and shot back. The guys here that you want me to pay off? They won't even know I'm around. So no, there's nothing to be afraid of. It's just a big step, is all."

"Take your time, Millie. Give it a few days."

"No, I'm fine. I'm ready to give it a shot. Now: does somebody teach me the fine points, or do I read the instruction manual?"

"You know the guy I told you about, the one who was iced in Fall River? He didn't have your sense of humor. That's probably why he ended up in the dumpster. We don't have a book for this job, Millie. You'll have to learn from Mr. Moustakas. He's the expert."

Chapter 3

Jauncey Chambers

The passengers were now walking out of the jet-way into the concourse, blinking and looking for the baggage area. Millie stood to the side of the group waiting for relatives or friends. She had a clear view of every passenger.

Not far from her stood a limo driver—little guy wearing a black suit, white shirt, black peaked chauffeur's cap—holding a hand-lettered sign that said DR. BLANCHE RUSSO. Not her guy, obviously. Besides, the target's driver was supposed to wait at curbside for him. Millie figured he'd grab his suitcase, walk out the door, and get right into the car. No delay, no problems.

But why had the guy decided not to use his own car? Had he been tipped off that a contract had been taken out on him? If that was the case, why stop at baggage? Why not just get out of the airport as fast as possible? The luggage: did it contain something worth risking his life for? Too many questions, she thought. The job was the same no matter what the answers were.

Millie was ready, her pre-game jitters gone. She could concentrate on what she had to do. This was the part of her job that she liked best: she was cool under pressure. And why shouldn't she be? She usually held all the aces. Today, though, with the client's last-minute changes, there were a couple of wild cards in play. Well, she could always cancel the show if things got too chancy. The added adrenalin, in the meantime, sharpened her reactions.

Keep your mind clear, she reminded herself. Look for a medium-size man with doggy jowls and close-set eyes who resembles Richard Nixon. At least that's who she thought of when she saw the photos: the disgraced president in those old black and white photos looking like a con with mumps. She really didn't know anything about Nixon—that was just her imagination playing around, like the idea that followed for a new line of Mr. Potato Head toys with little arms sticking up from his shoulders and his tiny fingers in a V-sign.

She shouldn't be having any thoughts of any kind at this moment, let alone dumb ideas about Mr. Potato Head. So, OK, she wondered: where's my date for the evening? His name was Sheldon Kukich, and according to Ralphie he was a rough character.

Ralphie had said: "This guy, Millie. This guy is a bona fide son-of-a-bitch, I hear. I don't know too much, but our contact in Philly told me one or two things. He's the type guy with, you know, tendencies, you get me? Acts crazy on general principles. You'll get a kick out of this, Millie: this Kukich used to be a shooter for a gang out of Toronto. Then he got to be the new boss when the old one caught a bullet in the head. Year or two later Kukich disappears for some reason. Not long ago he turns up in Kansas City. That's it. That's what I know. But I ask myself, why does a guy with his juice drop out of sight and then move to Kansas City? Unless he wants to disappear. But I'm just guessing here, right? And like my mother used to say, 'Ralph, don't ask too many questions because what you don't know won't hurt you.'"

"Sometimes that's true, Ralphie, sometimes it's not, if you ask me. No disrespect to your mother."

"No, no, that's fine, Millie."

"I just want to know everything I can when I'm out in the field, that's all I'm saying."

"Well, that's a different question, isn't it? Out in the field you don't want any surprises."

The plane had to be nearly empty, she realized. Dr. Russo had come and gone, barely acknowledging her stubby driver as she strode through the concourse. Maybe that kind of self-confidence helped her to get through medical school, Millie thought. Or maybe the doc just needed to get home and throw down a few. You know what, she said to herself, it's time to be on full alert.

A woman of about sixty came up to Millie and said, "Are you waiting for someone too?"

"I don't think he's going to show up," Millie said.

"Oh, that's terrible, dear!" the woman said. "When are you due?"

"What? Oh, I'm not sure." Trying to keep her mind on the remaining passengers.

"I don't understand," the woman said. "You need to keep track of the date, dear. Oh, here's my husband, Clarence. Look at him: he's like a lost puppy. He's so impatient." She turned and said, "Clarence, come here. This young woman has been abandoned by her husband."

Christ, all I need is a crowd staring at me, Millie thought. She said, "I'm OK, ma'am, really. He's not my husband."

"Oh, my God! Clarence, did you hear that?"

"Noreen," he said, "what are you doing? This is none of our business. Let's go on home." He took Noreen's arm and said, "Have a nice evening, Miss." He looked over his wife's head and rolled his eyes.

Millie was sure she hadn't missed anybody coming out of the jet-way, but she had to settle herself down after the little scene with Noreen and Clarence. This is why you don't accept last-minute changes, Ralphie. Something always happens. Noreen is the kind of woman who will tell everyone she knows about the poor pregnant girl in the airport waiting for the boyfriend who's never going to show up. Well, the poor girl is going to vanish forever in a short time, so no harm done. But the point is, I don't need any fucking distractions.

Two flight attendants, wheeling their little suitcases behind them, walked through the door. They're always the last ones off the plane, aren't they? So our guy missed the flight, Millie thought. He got wise somehow. Well, she'd pretty much wanted to pull the plug anyway. She actually felt relieved, though maybe a little disappointed too. This would be her first unfinished assignment. She'd just have to call Ralph, give him the details, and fly back home.

As she was turning away, wondering where to dump her gear and old clothes, she saw an old guy in a wheelchair, blanket over his knees, head down, being pushed out of the jet-way by an airport employee. When the man cleared the door to the gate area, a woman from Southwest closed it behind him and secured it. The old guy was the last passenger.

"That's pathetic," Millie said to herself. "That's fucking pathetic."

The woman said, "What, Honey?"

"Oh, nothing. Sorry," said Millie. The dumb bastard probably thought he was going to get away with it, too.

Millie followed the wheelchair, staying a few steps behind but not losing the guy in the crowd. She had to step around groups of three or four who blocked the way, and once she ran into an old woman who forgot to signal for a left turn. Casually she slid the empty duffel under a café table. She shouldered her tote so her hands would be free. Then she reached into the baby bump and screwed the silencer on to the barrel of the

Glock. She'd use the pistol only if she managed to get Sheldon outside the terminal. Otherwise it'd have to be the Epipen. They were now at the baggage carousel.

It was crowded. Two flights were picking up their bags at the same place. She lost sight of the wheelchair, found it again, edged closer. She was ready. But people kept pushing in front of her, and the wheelchair moved toward the far end of the carousel. Millie tried to follow but got caught in a knot of travelers that blocked the way. What now? He has to go through the doors. Cover the doors.

Millie almost walked into the guy pushing the empty wheelchair back into the terminal. I gotta move, she thought.

OK now: Pull down your cap. Unbuckle the pouch belt. Stick your hand inside. Grip the pistol.

She walked out the door. Checked right. Checked left.

And there he was, Sheldon Kukich, being assisted into the right-rear door of a Lincoln Town Car with tinted windows. He had a bandaged foot. Explains why he didn't drive his own car.

Before he closed the door, he looked back into the terminal. She saw him for only a few seconds, but she was sure it was Kukich. He saw her too, but his eyes slid over her. He clearly wasn't interested in the drab woman on the sidewalk with the ratty dress and knee-length sweater. It helped that she was in the shadows. She was about eight feet from him. She was close enough to see that he needed a shave.

"Put the damned suitcase into the trunk, Jauncey, I'm in a hurry," he said as he started to pull the door shut.

"Yes, sir, we just got to wait for the car ahead give us some room."

Jauncey tossed the bag into the trunk and closed the lid. He opened the driver's door and got in. Just as he

16

closed it, Millie tapped on the window and gave him the signal to lower it. When he did, he was looking into the barrel of her pistol peeping out of the fake baby bump.

"Whoa, lady, what you got in that pillow? Who are you?"

"Your fairy godmother. Unlock the doors," she said.

He glanced in the rear-view mirror. "Lady, damn, you diggin' yourself a deep hole, you know that?"

She put the pistol against his cheek. "Do it." The doors clicked open.

"The fuck's going on, Jauncey? Don't give her any money." Sheldon sensing something wrong.

But Millie was already sliding in beside him, the barrel of her pistol pressing against his throat. "Stay calm, Sheldon, we're all friends here." Kukich started to move. "Don't even think about it." Millie turned slightly to her left and said: "Pull out slow and easy, Jauncey." Then to Kukich: "The wheelchair stunt, Sheldon, it never works. Whose idea was that?" He sucked in a deep breath: a rasping sound. Millie pressed the gun harder against his throat. "Close your eyes. Move an inch and you're history."

"Take the first left, Jauncey," she said. "We're going to the parking lot. Find a space on the lower level."

Kukich, eyes shut, breathing hard, said, "Who the fuck sent you?"

"What's in the luggage, Sheldon?"

"You bitch. You lousy bitch." He could barely get the words out. He kept swallowing, trying to clear his throat.

"Talk nice, Sheldon. You doing OK, Jauncey?" she said.

"Me? Tell you the truth, I been better."

"You got any kids?" Talking to Jauncey but looking at Kukich.

"You ain't in enough shit, lady? Them two boys eat the bear. You want, I give you they phone number."

What the hell? Millie thought. He's playing with me.

Kukich opened his eyes, tried to move his head. "Sheldon, didn't I tell you to keep your eyes closed?" She pressed the pistol under his chin, forcing his head up. He closed his eyes. "Now put your right hand behind you and lean back."

He whispered, "Gotta pee."

"Oh, for God's sake, Sheldon, we can't stop here."

The Lincoln was now nosing into the down-ramp. "Move ahead a few rows, Jauncey. That's it. See if you can find a dark spot." Millie knew what would happen next. Kukich twisted hard to his left, went for the gun, missed, and barely had time to hear the *fffttt, fffttt, fffttt* of the shots fired into his chest.

Jauncey swerved, almost hit an oncoming car, swung back the other way, then braked hard. The driver of the car gave a long honk, but kept moving. The noise of the horn ricocheted off the concrete floor and ceiling.

"Damn! Goddamn, lady! I knew what was comin', but you snuck up on me. You almost give me a seizure. Put me in some kinda coma."

"Pay attention, Jauncey. Pull the car into one of those open slots down the row there." He did. "Good. Turn off the engine. Now give me your keys." He passed them back to her. "Now your phone."

"My phone? Man, how'm I goin' take care my business?" He gave it to her. "Now what you goin' do? Shoot me? Go ahead, then, only make it quick. I ain't a patient man." Millie found Kukich's phone in his jacket. One of the pockets also contained a fat roll of bills.

"Hand me your wallet, Jauncey."

"Man, I get up this morning, I had a permanition it's gonna be a bad day. Get out of bed, I know it's a mistake. All downhill after that. You ever have a day like that?"

"I'm having one now," she said. She touched the back of his head with the pistol. "Your wallet." He handed it to her. Millie opened it, took out his driver's license, and gave it back. "Where's your chauffeur's license, Mr. Jauncey Chambers?"

"Don't need one. Never been a chauffeur."

"Are you working for Sheldon?"

"Uh-uh, just took him to the airport last week and come for him today."

"How did he know to call you?"

"My cousin Earle work for the man, do his yard. Told him I had a cash-flow problem needed appeasing. So the man call me, say drive to his house. Pay me extra if I keep my mouth shut."

"Did anyone see you pick him up?"

"Nah, no one was around. Neighbors can't see his house anyway, all them trees."

"How much extra did he pay?"

"Five dollars. Man had no respect for me. Prob'bly done him myself, if you didn't do him for me."

"You understand why I want your driver's license and phone, Jauncey? I know who you are. I know how to find you."

"Man, this just like the movies, ain't it?"

This unhinged son-of-a-bitch jerking my chain again. "Keep your hands on the steering wheel where I can see them."

"They already there. I know what to do."

Millie decided maybe he did know what to do. "Do you know how to lose a body, Jauncey?"

"Grew up past Eight Mile, De-troit. What you think the answer is?"

"Have you done time, Jauncey? B and E? Auto theft? Drugs?"

"Did three out of five at Joliet for grand theft auto. Shoulda been lighter but was my second conviction."

"Did you steal this one too?" she asked. "No way," he said. "Got it last year from a friend I know in St. Louis." Maybe, maybe not, she thought. "Get rid of it," she said. "Don't just park it somewhere. It'll have blood stains. The cops will trace it back to you. They'll figure you robbed Sheldon and then shot him. Drive it into the river. Torch it. Sell it to a chop shop."

"You think I can collect on the insurance then? Now you talkin'."

She tossed the roll of bills on to the passenger seat. "Here. This is the big tip Sheldon promised you."

"Man, looks like we partners now, don't it?" Jauncey reached for the money.

Millie said, "Jauncey, I told you, hands on the fucking wheel. Listen up. You remember the tower back there where people catch the elevator?"

"I know where it's at."

"Your keys will be in front of the first car on the right. I'll put them behind the concrete barrier. Wait here for an hour before you go after them. Then drive Sheldon somewhere. And Jauncey? Try not to get a speeding ticket."

As she walked away from the car, she looked back, Jauncey sitting there with his hands on the wheel and a dead man in the back seat. She figured ten minutes max before he popped the trunk and opened Kukich's luggage.

Millie took the elevator to the street level. She was alone. By the time she got out of the elevator, her frumpy clothes and baby bump had been stuffed into the two white plastic shopping bags, along with the pistol, the silencer, and the Epipen. She then tossed everything into a trash barrel in the women's restroom.

Ten minutes later Lorna Van Dyne passed through security and boarded her flight back to Boston with time to spare. She bought a vampire romance with a sexy cover to read on the plane. The title: *Count Ciro's Brides*. After forty or fifty pages she gave up. It was like reading the weather report. When a girl gives herself to a vampire, shouldn't it be interesting? How hard can it be to write something with a little pizzazz? She ended up reading a copy of *USA Today* that someone had discarded. By the time the plane passed over Niagara, she was asleep.

Chapter 4

Ralph's Story

Couple of days later Millie was in Ralph's office on Cabot Street for the postmortem. He had fresh donuts and a pot of coffee. He was wearing white socks with his slippers. She was wearing jeans, white Nikes, and a Patriots football jersey with GRONKOWSKI lettered on the back over the number 87. Her way of hiding in plain sight in Boston.

"Ralphie," she said, "you ought to see the security lines at Kansas City International. They're fast and the people are half-way friendly. When I fly out of Logan, I have to get there an hour and a half early, minimum. And the security people treat me like some kind of criminal. KCI almost spoiled me."

"So you didn't have too much trouble, then?"

"Not with the flight, no. But with the other stuff, yeah, there were a few complications." She gave him a brief run-down of the operation, leaving out some of the less pertinent details, like her conversation with Noreen and Clarence. Also the one with Jauncey, because what could anyone make of that? For that matter, she didn't say too much about what had gone on inside the car, just that she didn't have to do the driver. Also she didn't see any reason to mention the tactical usefulness of the pouch—for instance, the fact that it functioned as another silencer. Ralph wasn't interested in the nuts and bolts of the job anyway, she knew that. Tactics were Millie's business. Mr. Moustakas, sure, he'd like the technical stuff, but he wasn't around today. Ralph's interest was basically the bottom line and customer satisfaction, whether the order had been filled as per contract. So Millie kept her story short. But at the end she added, "I just didn't like the extra risk after the client forced the play, that's all."

"It won't happen again. Promise. I'll tell 'em, 'Once you give us the job, our shooter makes all the decisions, including whether to cancel if things get sticky.' But back to Kansas City: you did a terrific job, Mil. What gets me is you made the fucking guy disappear. No one's found him. No one's heard anything about him. That's what our guy in Philly says. He told me, he said, 'Our client has a connection in Kansas City that says, "No body's been found, no car, nothing. The driver's gone too."'"

Ralph continued: "The client figured at least one or the other would turn up—right?—the body or the driver. Or somebody would call the cops. But nothing happens. So I start to think, if the driver's alive why didn't he call the cops? OK, I can maybe come up with an answer for that. But then how about the other stuff? I run it through my mind, and I ask myself, how the hell did she do it?" He raised his hand. "No, don't tell me, Mil. It's better for me not to know anything. My mother, you know, my mother used to say to me, 'Ralphie, don't ask too many questions because. . .'"

"Because what you don't know won't hurt you," Millie finished. "You already told me."

"Yeah? Good. Here, have another donut." He poured more coffee. She took a glazed. They were her favorite if they were just out of the oven, and these were still a little warm. But she also liked the old-fashioned do-nuts and the crullers too. Tough to choose. Good thing I never gain any weight.

"Ralph," she said after a moment, "Do we have any new jobs lined up? You told me about a possibility in Dorchester two or three weeks ago. Did that ever de-velop?"

"Oh, yeah, the wife-beater. It fell through, Millie. The wife was still tryin' to put the money together when something happened to change her mind. She decided to have her new boyfriend ice the husband instead of us. But get this: the lovebirds end up in jail the same night they whack the guy. Boston's finest on top of the job, keeping the city safe. Not that the cops had to look very far. Those two—the wife and her dumb Southie boyfriend—must of figured, they must of thought, it's easy to clip someone, set up a perfect alibi, and get away with it.

"But that's not what happened. This guy, the husband, is a boozer. He comes home shit-faced one night. He and the Mrs. get into it. As usual when he's on the sauce, he slaps her around a little on general principles before he flops on the bed with all of his clothes on. Well, this time is the last straw for the lady. She decides that she has to whack the guy herself, now, before he kills her. So she calls her boyfriend and talks him into helping her, who the hell knows what she told him. 'Should I bring a gun?' he asks. 'No, that's too noisy. I have a plan.' So he gets there, and they go find the guy stretched out on the bed. The plan is, they're gonna put a pillow over his face and suffocate him. But when they get things going, the guy fights back. He's stronger than they figured. Maybe he sobered up a little when he saw what was happening. It could happen. This is something they don't bother to think about ahead of time, by the way.

"Now things start to get out of hand. The wife has the pillow. The boyfriend has an arm. They're trying to hold him down. The husband's slapping 'em with one hand, trying to kick, hitting back in other words. Jesus, what a fucking scene.

"They all roll around on the bed for a while, there's a lot of yelling and, and before you know it, the bed collapses. Musta been a hell of a racket in that room, Millie. Anyway, the wife stands up and sees that the husband is choking the boyfriend. She's scared, but she's in the soup too and knows she's gotta do something quick. So she picks up a table lamp and smacks the husband in the head with the base. And just like that he's gone. She didn't need her boyfriend after all."

Millie had asked a simple question: do we have any work lined up? She would have been content with a simple answer—yes or no. But Ralph wanted her to have the unedited version, including the footnotes. Millie wondered how he could possibly know all the details he'd mentioned. She asked him: "Ralphie, how do you know what went on? You weren't even there. Did somebody tell you this stuff?"

"This guy I know, Millie, that I see at Dunkin' Donuts in the morning sometimes. He told me. He's good friends with the detective that wrote up the case. I went to high school with him."

"Who, the detective?"

"No, the guy. He's an old friend. Does crime reporting for the *Globe*. He's in pretty good with the cops."

"The cops?" Millie leaned forward. "Wait a sec', Ralph. What are you telling me?" She brought up her hand and started to count, extending a finger for each number: "One, you're friends with a crime reporter for the *Globe*. Two, he's pals with a Boston detective. Three, the cop tells him the story of a homicide where a woman whacks her husband. It just so happens she's the same woman who wanted to hire us to do the guy. And then—this is number four, or is it five?—the reporter tells the story to you. Doesn't that strike you as a little odd, Ralphie? I mean, who would believe that kind of coincidence? I wouldn't. Well, I do because you just told me. But I don't like it. What's going on here?"

"Going on? I don't know. It's a small world, that's all."

"That's it—it's a small world? He's a reporter, for god's sake, Ralphie. His job is sniffing in the gutters for news. Does he ask whether you have any juicy stuff for him? Do you tell him stories about our real-life murder business? You're buddies from high-school days, after all." Millie had run out of breath. She paused, sucked in some more air. "Hey, did you two guys date?" Fucking with him.

"Come on, Mil. He thinks I run a small moving company, do office cleaning on the side. In fact, Mr. Moustakas moved him to a new apartment a couple of years ago. I just thought you'd have an interest in this situation since you asked. Lemme finish, will ya?"

"Sure, just no more surprises, OK? I don't want to learn that the wife had our business card on her when she was arrested, with weekend rates and seasonal discounts."

"Mm-hmm. That's good, Millie. But where was I? Oh, yeah, the murder scene. You can just see it. The husband's layin' there on the fuckin' bed with his busted head. He's tilted at an angle because the mattress is half on the floor, half off the bed. The bed frame has cracked in two. Blankets and sheets are twisted up. There's the bloody lamp too, don't forget that. Things look bad enough for the lovebirds, you know, because anyone sees this place, they're gonna figure the missus and her bozo boyfriend did the guy. What else would you think?

"But they don't stop there. The next thing they do, these two get down on the bedroom floor, right in front of the dead guy, and, you know . . . ." Ralph extended a fist and made a twisting motion. "They can't even wait, see, they gotta go at it then and there." Ralph sat back in his chair and sighed. His lifted his arms and then let them fall to his sides.

"That's why they did the guy, Ralphie, so they could be together."

"You're being cute again, right? Sometimes I'm not sure. Here's what I think. Something about the dead guy layin' there put ideas in their head. Now that he's on ice, they figure, why wait? This is what's meant by true love, Millie. You lose your fucking mind. Naturally they get caught. Neighbors hear screams, people fighting, the bed breaking, who the hell knows. But the woman, when they get her in custody, she says. This is just what I hear, you understand. I wasn't there. She says: 'You think I'm sorry? Fuck him! That was the best sex I ever had!' Try to make the dead guy there feel bad, see." Ralphie explaining the lady's thinking here.

He shook his head. "Amateurs, Millie, what can you do? So the job in Dorchester's down the toilet. Too bad, too, because it would of been an easy night for you. You coulda got home early, popped some popcorn, watched a little TV with Mandy. Mr. Moustakas, he woulda done the removal, like always when it's a local contract. And just like that"—Ralph snapped his fingers—"the wife's problem goes away. Day or two later, she and the boyfriend that she had to rescue check into the Ritz-Carlton for their honeymoon. And as far as the late-lamented is concerned, well, what's there to say? The little lady, she don't know where he's gone. She says he never tells her anything. His boss at the warehouse has no clue, and he doesn't give a damn anyway. It's a mystery to everybody. The wife's all broke up, of course, because she loves the guy in spite of some roughness around the edges. But before too long she moves to a new town with her widow's pension and her classy new boyfriend."

"So we don't have anything."

"No, like I said."

"Good. Maybe I'll get out of town for a few days."

"You need some time off? That's what you want? I know you've had a lot of stress lately."

"Stress? No, that's not a problem. I get a lot of down time with this job. That's what I like about it—I don't have to sit on my tail all day in a cubicle. I work out three times a week, Mandy and I go shopping when we want to, see movies. Go to the Middle East Club to listen to Jared PM when he's in town. What I was thinking, she and I could spend a few days in Boca or maybe Puerto Rico. Her birthday's coming up."

"Sure, go, Millie, you deserve it. The company will pay the bills. But stay in touch in case Philly calls, OK? I'll have Mary Michael order the tickets. Which place you want to go to?"

"Mary Michael? The Mulloy woman? The one who brings you the tuna casseroles? I thought she mostly worked for old Mr. McLean in the other office, just did odds and ends for you."

"Yeah, that's her."

"But why would she buy our tickets? That's your job, isn't it?" A few seconds went by. "What about security?" Millie asked.

"Mary Mike's an old friend, Mil, from my mom's time. She helps out with the business. Orders airline tickets, books the hotels, stuff like that."

"Maybe I'm a little dense here, Ralph, but you're going to have to help me out. She's not even in the goddamned firm. Don't you think you should have mentioned this to me? Dropped a little hint somewhere along the line? We're talking about my ass here. Out in the field I need to know I'm secure."

Ralph's face took on a certain expression. Possibly that of a shortstop who boots an easy one with two men

28

on. "Actually, Mil, she's part of the firm. You're right, I shoulda told you. The subject just never came up, I guess. I can see where you might have some questions."

Millie put her half-eaten donut on his desk. It was an old-fashioned, and she had been enjoying it. She leaned toward him. "Some questions, yeah. This woman knows where I go? Which flights I take? Which hotels I use? Where's your fucking head, Ralph? This business has to be air-tight, as you goddamned well know. You mentioned stress. Here's what I call stress, Ralphie—civilians running around who could have me killed."

"Aw, Millie, take it easy. She and I go way back. Let me tell you a little story, OK? Something nobody else knows. Well, Mr. Moustakas, of course, he knows. But that's different."

"You're killing me, Ralph. A story? You just told me a fucking story. And that was about another old friend who's a risk to our security. I don't want a story. I want an explanation. And make it short, OK? Jesus—something else just occurred to me: does she order the fake IDs too? I feel like a bug in a bottle." Millie was steaming up.

Ralph rubbed his hands on his pants. "Well, yeah, she does the paperwork, keeps the records. Mr. Moustakas buys the hardware, keeps track of inventory, does the clean-ups. Mary Mike, she knows people who produce fool-proof documents. She's a lady with great connections—here, New York, Toronto."

Millie said, slowly and patiently, spelling it out for a slow learner: "So any time she wants, this lady with the great connections, could locate me and have me whacked. Or—here's another possibility—she could give me up to the cops. Not that she would, this nice old friend, this lady with great contacts in New York and Toronto, but she could. And I've been in the dark about her all along. That's a pretty good story, Ralph. I'm

29

trying to figure out how it ends. One quick question, I mean aside from why you didn't tell me about her: why the hell does she work for you?"

He moved his head up and down as he talked. Now his hands were moving too. Ralph Klammer trying to be open and earnest. "She works for us, Mil, for you and me. She's, like, another partner, only you might call her a silent partner. She helped my mom set up the business, way back when. Even did field work for a while. Has some great stories. Tell you the truth, Mil, I think the job brings a little excitement into her life. Reminds her of the old days. That's it. That's the story."

"So she's safe. I don't need to worry, you're saying, she's been here forever, you just forgot to fill me in. Jesus Christ, Ralphie. OK, I'll buy it, but when I get back I want to meet this Mary Michael. In the meantime I won't think about taking her out. Go ahead, tell her to book the tickets. Let's make it Jamaica. Florida's full of ladies with blue hair. I'll tell Mandy. "

"Sure, sure. Mil, can I ask you something?"

"Of course, Ralphie. We're partners, after all."

"Does Mandy know what you do, what business you're in?"

"She knows that I work undercover, that's all. I could be CIA, FBI, anything. She also knows that the secrecy is for her own good. Like your mom said, 'What you don't know won't hurt you.' That's how I want to keep it: I don't want her to know anything that would hurt her."

Chapter 5

Mary Michael's Story

B ack from Jamaica, Millie called Mary Michael to set up a meet. It was time to get acquainted, see what's what. Mary Mike liked Johnny's Luncheonette, said it reminded her of the movie *Diner*, and the burgers were off the chart. Millie said fine, she'd had enough jerk chicken and plantain on Jamaica.

Millie was seated in the back booth when Mary Mike walked in. A tall, angular woman, elbows flapping as she walked. A long bony face with startled dark eyes and Jay Leno chin. A perfect storm of gray and black hair swirling above her head. She was wearing a blue print granny dress with a white collar and pleats down the front. Millie didn't even look for the black lace-ups she knew were there. She was aware that several pairs of eyes followed this—how to put it—this phenomenon, pressing forward toward her booth.

Mary Mike barely said hi before ordering a cheeseburger, home fries, and a chocolate malt. Millie went with a burger and fries, no onions, and Coke.

Jerry Masinton

"So what should I call you?" Millie asked. "Just Mary, or do you want me to use both names?" Small talk, she thought, would be the best way to get started. Probably shouldn't discuss clothes or hair styles, though.

"Everyone calls me 'Mary Mike,' but anything will do, Millie. I want us to be at ease with each other. I know that Ralph just let it slip—didn't he?—that I'm in the firm. Making it look like he'd been keeping me secret. Must have been a big surprise, had to be."

"Well, you know," Millie said, "I wasn't expecting it, that's all."

Mary Mike took a big bite of her cheeseburger, closed her eyes, and sighed. "To die for," she said. Then: "I told Ralphie, I told him at the beginning, when you signed up, 'Make sure this girl knows everything. She's coming into the business. This isn't a nail salon, Ralphie. We do removals. This girl's going to be family. She has to trust us.' Well, I assume he covered the basics with you—the business side, the set-up with Philly, and so on—and then brought in Mr. Moustakas to teach you the operational side."

"Yeah," Millie said, "we did all that. He made sure I knew the drill."

"And he told you about old McLean's office on the other side of the house, right? Because he had to explain who this old guy was who wandered in once in a blue moon. This lawyer with his last few clients, all of them with one foot in the grave. But somehow he didn't get around to my work for the firm. Is that about right?"

The lady wants to get right to the point. OK with me, Millie thought, the sooner the better. "Yeah, and to be honest, I was a little surprised, because I've been in the firm a year and a half now, and I figured I knew how everything worked. Ralph says he just forgot to tell me."

"That's just like him," Mary Mike said. "He thinks about what's right in front of his nose, sometimes, and

32

not much else. That's why I have to do the long-range planning. Millie dear, your fries are getting cold. Mind if I take one?"

"Help yourself."

"You haven't touched your burger, either. Are you OK?"

"I'm good, I'm a slow eater."

"Did you think Ralphie was trying to cover something up?"

"No, no, I believed him. He's so damned transparent, you know, I don't think he could tell a decent lie. Also, you're never around when he and I plan an assignment, so your end of things doesn't come up. He gives me the documents I need, the tickets, the reservations, names, background, what have you, and that's it. If I need to, I talk strategy and weapons with Mr. Moustakas. OK, but at the time, Mary Mike,"—and here Millie leaned over the table—"I got a little nervous, hearing that someone I didn't even know was ordering my tickets, choosing my hotels. Knowing ahead of time where I'd be. I said to him: 'Jesus H. Christ, Ralphie, are you that dumb? Or just fucking careless?'"

"You blew up at him."

"For just a minute or two I thought we might have holes in the operation that needed to be plugged. So, yeah, I might have been a little on edge."

"Plugged. Well, that's as good a way to put it as any, I guess," she said. "In your place I would have felt the same way. You know, I was the first one in the firm to do your job?"

"Ralph told me. He said you worked in the field. I got the impression that you liked it." She put a couple of fries in her mouth. They were cold. She sipped her Coke.

"Liked it, oh, yes, we were pioneers, his mother and me. Here we were, two working-class girls with no education who needed to make a living. In those days, you couldn't find anything better than secretarial work, with the boss putting his filthy hand up your skirt every chance he got. So we decided to set up shop ourselves, Sheila and I, and we decided on the removals business. I went out on the road. She'd have been right there with me, God bless her, but she had little Ralphie to bring up, so she stayed in the office and kept the business end organized." She smiled. "You wouldn't believe how many calls we got. All we had to do was set up our system of cutouts and blinds and we had all the business we could handle. Those were grand old days, Millie, let me tell you. I liked being on the road: every job was an adventure. And, goodness, the money! The problem was where to put it all."

"What did you do with it?"

"I learned from a man I knew how to hide it, move it around, wash it. He showed me how to invest it legally too. You can make a lot of money that way too, Millie, you know that?"

"So I've heard."

"I'm going to tell you a secret, Millie." Mary Mike glanced from side to side, a conspirator with state secrets. "Not even Ralphie knows this. I didn't want to upset him. Everything has to go according to Hoyle for Ralphie, otherwise he thinks the world's ending, and this would have sent him into a tailspin. So, Millie: that fella who showed me how to move money around? He turned out to be a target, and I had to do the job."

This news caught Millie in mid-swallow. Some of the Coke she was drinking came out her nose.

"Oh, Jesus, Mary, and Joseph!" Mary Michael said. "What have I done? Here, hon', let me pat you on the back."

Millie waved her away. "I'm fine," she gasped, "fine." She wiped her nose with her sleeve. "Just give me a sec." She used a napkin to blow her nose. "Honest to Christ, Mary Mike, you and Ralph are killing me. Why the hell were you spending time with the mark in the first place? You know the rules."

"I was dating him, that's why. It was pure chance that we accepted a contract on him. Well, Sheila did, not me. He and I just happened to be involved at that time. It's a small world. Sheila didn't know about us, of course, though it wouldn't have mattered to her. She'd have found another contractor for the job."

"So you were sleeping with this guy, and then you popped him. What were your feelings? What kind of hardware did you use? Help me out here, Mary Mike, I'm in the dark."

"I'll get to that. First, let me start from the beginning—the romantic part. He and I met at La Guardia. We were both taking the shuttle back to Boston. He seemed nice. He was an investment banker in New York. He did mergers and acquisitions. Do you know what those are?"

"Skip the economics lesson. Get to the story."

"Well, his work isn't all that important. We met again the next day for drinks, talked for hours, and one thing led to another—you know how it goes—and soon we were seeing each other whenever he was in town. 'Seeing.' What a word. We couldn't keep our hands off of each other. We had a good time, and he taught me how to make money out of thin air."

Mary Mike sighed. "Now here's where the romantic part ends, Millie. Turns out the son-of-a-bitch, pardon my French, had a wife and two kids. Well, of course. Why was I so surprised? Isn't that the way it usually goes? But I didn't know for a long time. How could I? Andy didn't show me his passport and marriage license before we jumped into bed. When I found out that he'd been unfaithful to me, I wanted to kill him."

"Unfaithful. With his wife. And then you found a way to whack him."

"That's just an expression: I was boiling mad, and, who knows, I might have done it that day if he'd been around. When Sheila told me about the contract on him couple of days later, I was struck dumb. Honest to God, Millie, I was flabbergasted. Which, to tell you the truth, it was funny. If you think about it, there's a humorous side to it."

"I guess so. Who wanted him out of the way?"

"I'm almost there, Mil. This next part, I don't know whether it's comical or sad. Anyway, my boyfriend . . ."—Mary Mike started to laugh—"my guy . . ."—and here she couldn't help herself, she put one hand over her mouth and held the other one up to signal a pause. "My guy—Jesus, I can't stop!"

Now it was Millie's turn to glance around furtively. People were trying not to stare at them. I hope they don't think she's my mother, Millie thought.

It took Mary Mike a few minutes to glide back to earth. She took a deep breath. "All right: I found out about the wife. Janice, her name was. This was another thing that happened by sheer chance, Millie. Andy and I had spent the night at the Ames, where we always did. He got up early and flew back to New York. I had breakfast in bed and a long shower. Just as I was getting dressed, the phone rang. I figured it was Andy, so I answered.

"'Hello,' I said.

"'Who is this?' a woman said.

"'Oh, oh, I thought. 'Thees ees Juanita,' I said. 'I clean the room.'

"'At nine in the morning? Check-out's not till eleven. Besides, maids don't answer the phone. Goddammit, who are you?'

"'Who ees thees, please? Joo hab a message?'

"'This is Andy Greenspan's wife, sweetie, and, yeah, since you ask, I have a message: if you've been fucking my husband, you're gonna be sorry. He is too. You're probably sorry already with that dickhead. Just pray you never see me, Conchita.'

36

"Bang! She slams down the receiver. I think: how could I have been so damned dumb? It never occurred to me to ask Andy if he was married. I didn't snoop through his things while he was asleep. Totally unprofessional. Love does that to you."

"So then what, you went ballistic?"

"What I did is, I calmly finished dressing and left the hotel. I felt like I'd been hit by a truck. In other words, I was numb. By the time I got home and shut the door, I couldn't do anything but scream. But then I calmed down and just wanted to kill him. And in two or three days, my prayers were answered: his wife hired us to ice him."

"Whoa, you're losing me, Mary Mike. I don't get how this guy's wife took out a contract on him with our firm. What are the odds of that happening? Aren't there reliable contractors in New York?"

"Sure, but that's another funny thing, Millie. She didn't know it was us. She got in touch with somebody who got in touch with somebody else, and that guy called our guy in Philly, who contacted us. Who knows how many blind phone calls there were?"

"Lot of stuff happening by chance here, Mary Mike. Are you jerking my chain?"

"Millie, it's just fate, that's all. Karma. It tickles the hell out of me. I sleep with a guy. His wife finds out he's got a girlfriend. She finds out from me, for God's sake! She decides to take out a contract on him. Then, she just happens to get through to our firm. And I just happen to be the contractor who does the work. Everything ties together."

"In my experience, nothing ties together, unless I do the tying."

"I kept wondering, after we got the contract, what she'd think if she knew. You know—if Janice knew that the woman who was sleeping with her husband was the woman she'd paid to take him out." Mary Mike sat up straight and took another deep breath. She blew the air out: "Fwoooo! Don't let me get going again, Millie, I won't be able to stop."

By now the waiter had taken their plates. The check was waiting. Millie picked it up. "I'd still like to know how you did him. What your state of mind was. It's a professional question."

"Well, hon', I called him up and said, 'Andy, get up here, I need you, I don't care about your wife. I just want to be with you.' I poured it on. I cried. I sobbed. 'Please,' I begged. I put on a good act. Next day, he flew up and booked a room at the Ritz-Carlton. We planned to celebrate being together again. I told him I'd be there at eight. Ice down plenty of Dom Perignon, I said. I've got a big surprise for you."

"You had him hooked."

"Oh, yes, he was hooked. I was reeling him in. I told him I'd be his whore for the night and to bring fifteen brand-new hundred-dollar bills to pay me. I said to him: you'll get your money's worth."

"You didn't need all that rigmarole, Mary Mike. Why expose yourself that way? You could've been in danger. You could've blown the assignment."

"No, I had everything under control. You asked how I felt. I felt calm as a cucumber. Cool as a cucumber. You know how it is: you get excited, sure, but you concentrate and keep your mind clear. It was basically just another job to me. OK, a part of me wanted to give Andy a farewell ride, I admit. But I didn't do it. You can be proud of me."

"Oh, I am. Finish the story."

"I told him, 'Sweetheart, spread the bills on the bed. When I get there, we're going to play a naughty little game.' So I show up at eight, on the dot. I'm wearing a scarf pulled down low so if there are any surveillance cameras, they can't ID me. I'm carrying my bag. Under my raincoat I'm in a shorty maid's uniform. OK, he opens the door and looks at me.

"'Jesus Christ, Mary Mike! Christ almighty!' He loves the sexy maid's outfit that I flash him. My blouse is un-buttoned halfway to my navel. Every guy's fantasy, you know. I rip my scarf off, shake out my hair. He starts to say something, but I shoosh him with my finger.

"'Take off your clothes,' I whisper. 'Hurry.' He thinks this is the kinky game I promised, so he takes off every-thing but his jockey shorts. I tell him that's enough for now. The shorts are polka dot, can you believe it, Millie? Blue with little white polka dots. At least they weren't pink.

"Now he wants me to strip too. 'Lay down on the bed first,' I say. 'Grab up a few of those bills,' I tell him. OK, he does that too, but he's a little confused: what's this for? From the time he opens the door till now, Millie, this all takes, I don't know, maybe a minute and a half."

"Mary Mike, I really think you should have just done him in the parking lot. It was a routine hit, a no-brainer. This elaborate set-up, my god, what's the point?"

"You'll see. I wanted to send a message."

"Ralphie was right: you did enjoy your work."

"Whistle while you work, Millie, that's my motto. So: he picks up five or six of the bills, evens them up, and asks, 'What do I do with these?' 'Stick 'em down your shorts, lover.' Oh, boy, oh boy: his eyes light up like Christmas, and he puts the money in his little bank. You can imagine what he's thinking. And then, just as he cracks a smile, I jab the needle into the side of his neck. It takes him a second to figure it out, what the game is, and I tell him: 'Your bitch of a wife Janice paid me to do this, Andy. But I would've done it for nothing.' I'm not sure he heard this last part. I sure hope he did."

"What you said to him as he checked out—that wasn't the message."

"You're a smart cookie, hon'. I had one more thing to do. I took the spare maid's uniform out of my bag. I laid it out carefully over his body, like he was modeling it. Then I picked up a couple of hundreds and dropped 'em on top. In case you were wondering, I used my nails to pick up the bills."

Mary Mike fluffed her hair with both hands, but the storm didn't die down. She was enjoying herself. "Now," she said, "when the cops discover Andy's body, they have to figure out why somebody draped a maid's outfit over him, right? And of course what they find gets back to Janice. She hears about it, too. You see how gorgeous this works?"

"Yeah, I see. Only you and Janice know about the woman who claimed to be the maid. You're telling her that the maid iced her husband. And she already knows that the maid's been fucking him. So you're also saying: 'Fuck you too, Janice.' And she can't do anything about it because she's the one who hired the maid to kill her own husband."

Mary Mike nodded. "Mmm-hmm. But there's more than that, Millie, if you think about it."

"OK, give me a sec," she said. She continued: "That's easy: there's no way Janice can ever find out who the hitter is. She can't go to the cops, she can't ask the guy she contacted in the first place, who has no idea who got hired, and she doesn't know whether the contractor works solo or hires out to some firm."

"And . . .?"

"And then there's the money wrapped around her husband's weenie and scattered all over the bed. That's a message to Janice, too. And it's also for the police. You're telling all of them that the crime was personal, it wasn't for the money."

"That's right, hon'. I have to tell you, though, there's even more angles to figure, if you really look close."

Millie, really in to it now, said: "Well, the cops will think at first that Andy was probably iced by a hooker, because how else do you explain the champagne, the big bills, Andy in his classy shorts? If it was a hooker, though, she would have taken the money. But the killer didn't take the money. Why? She was making a statement, that's why. But she and the victim knew each other from before. Am I OK so far?"

"That's the way they'd figure it. Go on."

"So maybe the killer wasn't a hooker, after all. Was she a maid at the hotel? No, that's just a fish. There *is* no maid. That still leaves the maid's uniform, though, and the cops aren't sure where to go with it."

"They don't have a clue. Well, they do, but they don't know what it means."

"It's tangled up pretty tight, all right."

"Wheels within wheels, Millie. That's what Sister Immaculata used to say. She'd tell us, 'Wheels within wheels, girls. Don't trust appearances.' She'd have made a good assassin, Sister Immaculata."

"OK," Millie went on. "So they'll think: the killer, whoever she was, was pissed off enough to whack him and ballsy enough to decorate him with the maid's dress. Maybe this lady wanted revenge for something. Or maybe she was just a hired gun, with no stake in it one way or another. But a pro would have no reason to play dress-up with Andy. And yet, the whole thing looks like a professional job. No one forced their way into the room. The contractor was methodical. And don't forget the murder weapon: amateurs don't usually carry hypodermic needles in their pocket."

"That's the line they'd follow, yeah."

"The cops figure that all those pieces have to fit together. But they can't see how. But no matter which way they look at it, Janice's number comes up. Either the wife did it and staged the whole thing, or she hired a pro to set it all up. But wait: neither solution holds up. Janice wouldn't be screwing around with Andy that way, not after she discovered the affair. And no pro would take the time for all that hanky-panky. Still, the cops have to question her—Janice—because it's part of their job. But she can't say a damned thing without pointing to herself. In fact, though, she doesn't even know very much. Though she sure as hell knows about the maid. Not who the maid is, but that she exists. Well, all she really knows is that somebody called herself the maid and ended up whacking Andy."

"Don't you just love it, Millie? Let me tell you, I didn't understand all the angles myself at the time. It took a while for me to see the beauty of it."

"I don't see how anyone's going to see the whole picture, Mary Mike. Who's ever going to figure out that the maid and Andy's girlfriend and the hitter are the same woman? Who, besides Janice, knows that the girlfriend lied about being a maid? And who's going to put it together that Janice hired the maid?"

"It's been more than twenty years, and no one has. It's a cold case. Nobody even cares anymore."

"So why did you tell me?"

"I did it so we can get to know each other better. I know stuff about you, now you know something about me. That means we can trust each other. Like I say, everyone in the firm has to trust everyone else. It's a tough world out there."

Chapter 6

Mandy

Millie drove home, enjoying the throaty roar of the rebuilt C10 Vortec under the hood of her old Silverado. When her car guy dropped in the engine, he also gave her a new transmission to handle the V-8's 200-plus horses. Millie liked the deceptiveness of the pickup's rusting exterior hiding the heart of a beast. No one would notice a dinged-up hick ride with sandbags in the bed. And no one could catch her if she had to book.

Mandy was lounging on the couch, watching TV: *Young Frankenstein*. She was wearing a pink t-shirt with black lettering across the front: DUTCH GIRLS LIKE DYKES. The t-shirt was sheared off at her midriff. The black thong she wore—a V of string, a thumbnail of fabric at its point—advertised her slender hips and long legs. Her dark cropped hair matched the thong. Millie remembered some old French guy singing in a late-night TV movie: "Zank Avon forr leetle gulls." Though no one who saw Mandy would consider her a little girl. Millie couldn't think of the actor's name.

Mandy turned off the TV. "Millie." It was a whisper, but it carried. "Where've you been, *Tesora*?" Mandy rolled the "r." She brought her knees up, patted the couch for Millie to join her. "I've missed you."

"You remember: I had to check out this woman at the firm. See if she was legit."

"And . . . ?"

"She's not your average bear, but she's OK. Good at long-range planning." Millie sat at the end of the couch. Still thinking about the strange life of Mary Michael. Mandy stretched her legs over Millie's lap and crossed them. She wiggled her toes.

"Did you miss me?" Mandy licked her lips. Made a kiss-kiss sound. Batted her eyes. Parody of a come-on.

"Don't be kittenish. I don't like it."

"Sure you do. Sometimes you do." She uncrossed her legs and reached for Millie's hand. Millie let it rest on Mandy's thigh. Mandy urged the hand higher. And again higher. "There. That's better."

"We're in a mood today, aren't we?"

"I'm sorry, *Tesora*. I'm disgusting when I get this way. Don't pay any attention to me."

"What's wrong?'

"Oh, nothing. Emerson from the agency called. They postponed the shoot that was supposed to start next Monday. I told you about it. The photographer said he has appendicitis or something and can't work. I had just shaved for the swimsuit shots, too. I told Emerson, 'Why can't you just get another photographer?' and he said, you know how he talks, 'Amanda, darling, we absolutely, but absolutely, must have Jean-Pierre,' or whatever his name is—Jean-Claude, Jean-Jacques, Jean-Merde, I don't know. He said, 'Our readers just adore his sense of composition.' And I said, sweet as spun sugar, 'Emerson, darling, the readers of *Punt*, if they can read at all, don't give a shit about composition. It's a men's magazine. All they care about is tits and ass—the bigger, the better. They'd be happy with shots from my granny's Brownie box, no pun intended.' And Mr. Emerson Lint, all business now, says: 'Amanda, dear, Jean-Pierre will be back on his feet in no time at all, we know this is a terrible inconvenience, but in the meantime would you please ready yourself'—that's his phrase, 'ready yourself'—'for Mr. Oscar's project, which we'll start next Thursday.' So I say, 'I'm already ready, Toots, I'm as slick as an otter. Would you like to see? I can send you a personal snap-chat of me being ready.' And Emerson, you know what a dreary little twit he is, 'Amanda, darling,' he says, 'such a pleasure to do business with you. We'll be in touch.' I was furious. Can you rub a little?"

"What's the Mr. Oscar project?"

"Micro thongs and tops. Less is more."

"How much less?"

"You can hide the micros under your G-string and still have room for your pistol."

"I'll have to stock up. You never can tell."

"Not much bothers you, does it, *Tes*?"

"Some things do. Losing you would."

"That'll never, ever happen, sweets. We're partners to the end. Like *Thelma and Louise*. Or, no," she paused. "Butch and Sundance. You're Butch and I'm Sundance. You ever see that movie? They love each other more than they do the girlfriend."

"We saw it together. We decided it was their coming-out party."

"Remember Etta Place? 'I'm twenty-six, and I'm single, and a school teacher, and that's the bottom of the pit.' I'll never forget that line. Wow, what are her poor students supposed to think? I'll bet she got booted out of the teachers union for that. Don't stop rubbing."

"She's saying that a tough life with two outlaws would be better than what she's had."

Mandy said, "Really, Mildred? That's so sad. You know, I'd have slept with Newman. Those blue eyes? Ohmigod!" She gasped: "Ooooh! I'm getting chills all over. Would you have, *Tes*? Slept with him?"

"Only if he'd asked. We need to get out of the apartment, Priss. Let's go to the gym."

"You know how I feel about exercise, Millie. 'I'd buy cigarettes already lit up, if I could.' Whose line was that?" Suddenly she sat up, swung round, and straddled Millie. "Let's go to bed. We can work out there. I feel a little needy today, *Tes*."

They kiss.

"Mmmm, you smell good." Millie says. "What's that shampoo? I love it."

"Acqua di Parma. I knew you'd like it."

"I want to breathe you in, all of you. Help me with this shirt, Priss."

Millie lifts her arms. Mandy pulls the jersey over Millie's head. Her own t-shirt comes off next. "Oooh! You're so beautiful, *Tes*!"

"You too, Priss." She nuzzles Mandy's hair. "I have a question."

They kiss again, longer this time.

"Tell me."

"Can I use some of your shampoo?"

"Oh, sweetie, that stuff cost me the earth." She draws back: "Well, maybe. It all depends."

"On what?"

"On what you do for me."

"What would you like me to do?"

She whispers into Millie's ear.

"Language, Amanda. What would your mother say?"

"She'd say, 'Amanda Press Bradford, you're filthy in thought, word, and deed.' That's what."

"I do love you, Priss."

"Me too, *Tes*, but hurry, I can't wait."

"Yes, you can. You always tell me it's best when you're so ready you can hardly breathe."

"I stopped breathing ten minutes ago."

"Don't worry, Priss. You'll be breathing hard in no time at all."

Chapter 7

Wrong Man Down

The phone woke Millie from a dream about desert sand getting in her eyes and mouth. In the early-morning light the two bedroom windows appeared to her as soft blobs of gray. Four blobs when her tired eyes started to cross. The phone stopped chirping. From somewhere came the sound of a high E-string breaking. Uh-oh. Headache coming on.

She and Mandy had put away maybe just a drop too much red wine the night before. The grinding hangover explained the dry mouth and scratchy eyes. When will I ever learn? Millie looked over at Mandy on the other side of the bed. Lying on her side, hands folded under her cheek, the picture of innocence. She'd sleep till three or four, Millie knew, wake up fresh and rested.

Millie's hangover remedy was two double-packs of Alka-Seltzer, followed by a mug of hot chicken broth, followed by a scalding shower, followed by a five-mile run. OK, three miles today because of the bass-drum solo inside her head.

She felt a little better after the run. Better, but not great. Mandy was still asleep, one arm thrown over her head like a ballet dancer.

There was a text from Ralph, in caps: WE GOT TROUBLE. So Millie double-timed it to the office. The usual set-up: two cartons of fresh coffee and a box of Dunkin' Donuts. It was ten in the morning. Ralph was wearing pale blue socks with tiny yellow dots. God bless Ralphie. Our very own clothes horse.

He started to say something, but Millie held up a hand. Wait a second. She removed the top of her coffee and drank most of it down. Took a bite of an old-fashioned. Finished the coffee. Pointed to Ralph's: "Are you going to drink that?" He pushed it across the desk to her. "You and the cover girl paint the town last night?"

She shook her head. Mistake. Sucked down half of Ralph's coffee. "Nope. Quiet night at home. Why'd you call?"

"Millie, I never seen anything like this. I get a call from Philly couple hours ago, he says, 'Ralph, I hate to tell you this, but our client says your shooter might of put the wrong man down. The fucking client's up in the air about this.' So Philly says to the client, 'No, there must be some mistake, because we got the best shooter in the business, bar none, and this outfit, you know, you used 'em before, has a perfect record. The shooter worked the guy close-up, confirmed the kill.' Then he tells me, he says to the client, '"Think about it: no body, no witnesses, no cops, nothing. Couldn'a been a better job. Textbook case. Take my word, you got what you ordered."' But the fucking client don't buy it, and he says to Philly, 'I paid you double, asshole, to ice this fucking guy and you fucking didn't do it, and now you owe me my money back for my fucking aggravation. Plus, I expect you to fucking track down this fucking guy and do it right this fucking time.' And then that was the end of the conversation, and Philly called me and said, 'What the fuck are we going to do?' And so I called you."

Millie chewed on a donut. "I told you we should have ditched this operation once the client stepped in, Ralphie. We should have rescheduled."

"I know, you're right, but the client—"

"I know, the client insisted. Paid double. Blah, blah. OK, what's done is done. But I got the right guy, Ralphie. He was the beauty you showed me in those photos. I was close enough to smell his doggy breath. It was him, all right. I also had what you'd call independent confirmation."

"So now what?"

"So the client's got a hair up his ass, that's all. What can he do? He doesn't know who we are, he doesn't know who he's talking to when he takes out the contract. There's too many cut-outs in between him and us. But for the sake of business, tell Philly to get back to him, tell him to double-check: check with his stooge in the Kansas City Police Department. I assume that's where he gets his information. Tell Philly to tell the client, 'we checked. The guy's dead. Period.'"

"OK, yeah, but let me tell you the rest, Millie. Apparently the police out there found a body in a car a few days after the job. This body had some ID on it. You can figure what's coming now, right?"

"I'm ahead of you. The body's a stranger, but the ID belongs to our guy."

"Correct. The ID is our guy's. Only it ain't our guy carrying it, it's somebody else. So the guy that we had to ice, he's somewhere else, and this other guy, the wrong one, is found with our guy's ID on him. So it looks like our guy got away. And that's why the client blew his stack."

"I don't know what the hell this is all about, Ralphie, though I'm starting to get a hunch. But even if the wrong guy ends up dead with the other guy's ID on him, that doesn't prove our client's target is alive. It just proves that the wrong guy has the target's ID. You follow me?"

"Yeah, I guess."

"So somebody planted the ID on the dead guy, maybe to mislead the cops, maybe for some other reason. Who knows? But the dead guy had no business being found, I can tell you that. The car, if it's the right car, shouldn't have been found either. I don't know who the dead guy is, the one in the car. Right now we don't even know whether the car is the target's car or some other car. Give me another one of those donuts, Ralphie, I'm starving."

"I follow you, Millie, but this thing ain't adding up."

"You know the drill, Ralphie. You do the guy, but you don't touch his ID. That's the proof that we paid off the right guy. Usually it's the proof. Not this time, though, because someone decided to get cute. It's gotta be the driver, Ralph. He's the only one it could be."

"You didn't whack the driver?"

"No, Ralphie, I asked you, 'Am I supposed to whack the driver?' and you said no, OK? 'Don't ice the driver.' Remember? Maybe you cleared it with the client, maybe not, but we already had a contract, and I wouldn't have done it anyway, a contract is a contract, and the driver didn't figure in it. But you said no, not the driver."

"OK, I remember, but who is this driver? Why would he get back into the picture?"

"You never want to know the operational details, Ralphie, that's why I didn't mention him. Also, it would have taken a year to explain how this guy's mind works because he lives on some other planet, so it's just as well, but he's the only one it could be."

"But where would he get another body? And why would he want to switch IDs?"

"Hell, I don't know, Ralphie. That's the money question. But he's the only link between the guy we did and the other guy." She took another donut, this time a glazed. Took a bite. Licked her fingers. "You know, I'd really like it if you could brew some more coffee, Ralph. If it's not too much trouble. Got a little headache this morning."

"I need some too. Somebody took mine. Don't eat all of those glazed while I'm in the kitchen, OK? Try one of the crullers, you like those."

A few minutes later he returned carrying two steaming mugs of coffee. They had the Patriots' logo stenciled on the side. "Good stuff, Ralphie. You could open up a franchise."

"Maybe I ought to. At least nobody comes in here saying, 'Where's the fucking body?'"

"No, but you gotta put in a lot of hours, day and night, and you're on your feet all the time, Ralphie. That's no kind of life. Look, maybe I can get back to the driver, ask him what the fuck, if you and our guy in Philly can't get the client to back off. I don't want anything to come back and bite us in the ass."

"This client, Millie, he ain't going to change his mind. I already told Philly, 'Tell the client, say to him, "Their mechanic does not do guesswork. There's no mistake here. This baby is wrapped up in a blue ribbon."' And you know what he said? He said, 'Look, I believe you. Your firm is A-1. Primo. Everybody in the business knows that. You don't hire fuckups. Well, except for your school teacher there, that ended up in the dumpster, which the client doesn't know about that.' He said, 'But the client, Ralph, he's not going to buy it. And I'll tell you why. He's a head case. A psychopath, I think you call 'em, where they all the time, they're ready to come uncorked and whack somebody. Anything sets 'em off. You can't talk to 'em. So I don't know what to do.' So what do you think, Millie?"

"I'll have to track down the goddamn driver, that's what I think."

"You figure he did the guy in the car, the wrong one, then planted our guy's ID on him?"

"Not a chance. What I think is, if he's at the bottom of this mess, he had a bright idea of some kind that went off the tracks. He pulled the pin to see what would happen. This is not a guy who thinks things through."

She arched her back. Stretched. "Another cup of coffee, Ralphie, and one of those chocolate-covered donuts, then I'll call Mr. Moustakas. I want some Epipens for this trip. Maybe the special sunglasses, plenty of ammo. You want to tell Mary Michael to book tickets for Kansas City? I'll use the Japonica Lake ID."

"Japonica Lake. You got it. How's the headache?"

"Oh, it's fine. All I need is a little coffee in the morning."

Chapter 8

Earle

Japonica Lake stepped out of KCI into a hot, humid Kansas day, sky the color of skimmed milk. She was wearing blue jeans, gray Nikes, and a long-sleeve, loose-fitting t-shirt. The t-shirt had white and blue stripes. A pale blue bandana circled her head. Outside the terminal she put on her Jackie O's, got on the bus to the car rental, and picked up the Honda Accord reserved in her name. Thirty minutes later she checked into a hotel in downtown Kansas City.

First thing, she built a double Seagram's Seven and rocks from the mini-fridge. Downed half of it. Then called Jauncey Chambers, hoping to unlock a few doors. He answered his phone with "What! That you, Lionel? Shut the damn door, Sharilla, I'm on the phone with Lionel! OK, I'm back, Lionel. Can't hear a damn thing in this house, that boy of Sharilla's playing Kanye and Future all day long. Lionel? Go ahead, man."

"Jauncey, this isn't Lionel. It's your fairy godmother. Remember?"

"What? Whoa, Jesus! Goddamn! Where you at, girl? You know I'm in big trouble after you do Mr. Kukich?

Where you get my number, anyway? You still have that phone you took from me?"

"That's not important, Jauncey. I need to talk to you."

"We talkin', ain't we? Damn! Why you wantin' to call me? Nothin' but bad luck since you do the man in my car. Don't need no more, case you wonderin'. You like, I give you some of mine."

"Jauncey, shut the hell up and listen, OK? I figured you were in trouble, that's why I'm calling."

"How you know that? Who told you about me?"

Millie considered how to keep the conversation moving in the right direction. She looked out the hotel window. Everything normal-looking in Kansas City. Yet here we are, Jauncey at the other end of the line, a speeding car without a driver.

"Let's just say you're a famous guy, Jauncey. I need you to answer some questions. So listen up, it might do you some good. First of all, what did you do with Sheldon? And don't lie to me, I'll know if you do."

"Sheldon? I did like you told me, I got rid of him."

"How?"

"Give him to my cousin Earle, used to work for him in his yard."

"You didn't take care of Sheldon yourself?"

"Give him to Earle, told him, 'Earle, put this man in the ground, I pay you five hundred dollars.' No problem for Earle, he do this couple times before."

"I don't like the sound of this, Jauncey. You were supposed to handle Sheldon yourself, make sure nothing went wrong. What did Earle think about you having a body in your car? Is this an everyday thing with you guys?"

"Nah, listen. Earle, he understand about Mr. Kukich and all. I told him a accident happen in my car, now I got to hide Mr. Kukich body."

Millie said, "You're giving me a headache, Jauncey. Jesus. Tell me the details, how your cousin buried Sheldon. Start by telling me where. Can you do that?"

"Where? Where you think? In the cemetery, where he belong."

"What, your cousin just goes to the cemetery and buries someone? Is that what you do here in Kansas City, show up with a corpse and shovel, bury a guy yourself? That doesn't happen, Jauncey." Millie had been walking around her room. Now she sat down on the bed and looked out the window again. The world still looked fairly sane, but she could feel it tipping out of control. Well, she thought, you knew this guy wouldn't stay tied to the ground.

"Nah, see, Earle, he work there. He dig the holes where they put people in. That's his job. He operate one them back-hoes, understand?"

"What did he do, bury Sheldon on top of somebody else? That could work."

"Uh-uh, not this time. He put Mr. Kukich out at the fence line, where they planting a row of trees. They told him, 'Earle, level this ground here, then dig down a ways for the trees.' So Earle, he just put the body under the hole for a tree. Nobody ever find it, less they dig up the tree."

"Jauncey—"

"Ain't nobody goin' to look for a murdered man in the graveyard."

He's jerking me around. This flaky son-of-a bitch is pulling my chain.

"Don't fuck with me, Jauncey. How could he do this in broad daylight? He doesn't dig holes in the dark, does he?"

"He dig holes every day. Nobody pay attention. Shoot, he want to bury a elephant, nobody see it. What you think, girl? You think it's hard to put a man in the ground? No way. You aks me can I get rid of a body that time, I say yes. Now it's done just like you want, and you still ain't satisfied?"

Jerry Masinton

"OK, never mind. Hang on a second, will you?"

Millie set the phone on her bed, reached into the fridge for another Seagram's, and poured it into her glass. She swirled the liquid around. Took most of it down. Keep him on track, she reminded herself. "Jauncey, what happened to your car? Who was the dead man the cops found in it?"

"That's somethin' else, see. I don't know what-all Earle done. Told him, 'Earle, bring me back my car soon as you unload Mr. Kukich here.' Said to him, 'I got to clean it up, give it back to my friend that lent it to me.'"

"I thought you said it was your car, Jauncey. You stole it, didn't you?"

"I borry it from a friend, he ain't usin' it."

"You're lying. You've done time for grand-theft auto. You see the Lincoln and it's too good to pass up. You couldn't resist. OK, let's get back to Sheldon. You needed to dump the car after I fixed him. But you didn't get it back from Earle. Did he put the other body in it? One more thing, Jauncey: don't fucking lie to me again. Unless you want way more trouble than you got now."

"I ain't lyin', I seen what you can do. Here's what happened. I take Mr. Kukich wallet and shit out his pockets, see what-all I can find. A few dollars, that's all. Them rolled-up hundreds you found on him must've been all he had. Wrist watch with fake diamonds not worth a damn neither."

"So who planted Sheldon's ID on the other dead guy—Earle?"

"Him and Lionel. Earle, he say to me, 'Jauncey, give me that wallet, I need it.' I aks him, 'Why you want a dead man's wallet? That's evidence they can use against you, man. Let me throw it away.' He say, 'I have another man could use it. Lionel need it for a dead man he know. We goin' give it to him.'"

Millie thought: It used to be simple. I'd accept a contract, pay the guy off, and then go home. Now this—down the rabbit hole.

She said, "Let me get this straight, Jauncey. You ask your cousin Earle, the grave-digger, to get rid of Sheldon. Earle says, 'No problem, I'll plant him under the trees in the cemetery. And oh, by the way, give me Sheldon's wallet with his driver's license and credit cards because I have a dead man of my own that happens to need some ID.' Have I got that more or less right, Jauncey?"

"Mmh-hmmm, yeah."

"Did you guys think that the cops wouldn't figure out that Lionel's dead guy really wasn't Sheldon? Did you doctor Sheldon's driver's license with a photo of the second guy?" She thought a second. "Never mind, that would be too complicated. Who was the second guy, and why wasn't he carrying his own ID?"

"Nobody told me 'bout all that. Lionel told Earle the man's fingertips been sanded off, so Earle and him figure Mr. Kukich ID good enough for the man."

"Makes no sense if the guy's face was untouched. Or was it?"

"Don't know. Don't think so, otherwise Earle say something. Po-lice right away say Mr. Kukich ain't the dead guy. Now they looking for Mr. Kukich. Figure he dead too, but then maybe not."

"How do you know all this?"

"Newspaper, right on the front page."

"So where does this leave you?"

"Cops goin' to be looking for me too."

"Why? Have they tied you to Sheldon?"

"Nah, Earle the only one know I drove the man to the airport."

"OK, so what then?"

"Cops trace the car, that's what."

"It's a stolen car. You should be in the clear."

"Nah, like I said, I borry it from a friend. Name Dwayne. Was like a long-term loan, know what I mean? Cops trace the car, find out Dwayne's been gone for two years, so now they looking for his wife, Sharilla. They find her, I'm next in line."

"Gone? What do you mean 'gone'?" Then the nickel dropped. "He's in jail, isn't he, Jauncey? Your pal Dwayne's in prison. And Sharilla—that's the name you used when you answered the phone. You're living with Sharilla."

"She divorcing Dwayne. He ain't goin' be around for a while. Me and her old friends. See her one time in St. Louis, where she used to live with Dwayne. I go down there to see Dwayne, see Sharilla instead 'cause he in Leavenworth. I aks her, 'What's he in for', she tell me 'In for anything you can smoke, swallow, or stick in your arm. This his third time, meaning he gone take out the old-age pension in prison. Wants me to wait for him. You believe that, Jauncey? Man so dumb he was driving around drunk with half a million dollars coke in the trunk. Gets stopped, tells the police he don't know nothin' about it. They get a good laugh at that one. Soon as I sell this house, me and my boy Trevor moving somewhere with no forwarding address. Let Dwayne think about that.'"

"So you and Sharilla got together. You brought her back to Kansas City. The Lincoln was part of her dowry."

"What you mean 'dowry'?

"Skip it. Is the car registered in her name?"

"No, still belong to Dwayne. I told her, the cops come around, tell 'em the car been stolen, you just goin' to call it in, been a little busy."

"They'll believe that like they believed Dwayne's story about accidentally having a trunk full of cocaine."

"Yeah, you right. This-all kinda funny, ain't it? If you think about it."

"How do you mean?"

"You shoot Mr. Kukich in my car, now the cops goin' be looking at me for it."

"Jauncey, I told you to get rid of the car. Torch it, I said, sell it to a chop-shop. Why didn't you do that? I told you they'd trace it. Even if it isn't your car, you should have done it right away. Sheldon's blood is in that car. If the cops tie his death to you, you're in the shit. Now you up the ante. It really didn't occur to me that you'd fuck up by putting an unidentified body in it."

"To confuse the po-lice, that's what Earle say."

"And how did that work out?"

"I see what you mean, yeah, but at the time I say to myself, 'Jauncey, get this man Kukich under the ground first, then take care of the car.' Didn't say to Earle I was going to light a match under it, just give it back so I can clean it up. See, I was still thinking 'bout which way to get rid of it.

"Then Earle call, say Lionel need to use my car that night. I say to him, 'What the hell you saying, man? Why's he got to use my car?' He say, 'Lionel's dead man—you know, the one needs that identification?— Lionel got to drive him somewhere after dark.' 'Christ Almighty!' I say, 'Car ain't a hearse. I got to get it back right away. Let Lionel use his own damned car.' He say to me, 'Lionel don't want to bloody up his new car. Yours already got blood in it, little more won't hurt. He gonna put the man in the back seat where your man was, so now they only one place you got to hose out.' 'Earle, Jesus Christ,' I say, 'we all goin' be in bad trouble if Lionel get caught.' I aks him, 'Who this dead man, anyway, Lionel got to make disappear? Why don't you plant him under the trees like you done mine?'

"He say, 'Slow down, Jauncey, ain't enough time to do that, I don't work at the cemetery tomorrow. What Lionel told me, he say, "Earle, I take this boy to North Kansas City, put him in the river there with rocks in his pocket. Nobody ever find him. But if they do, nobody ever reckonize the man 'cause he's been in the water a long time. And we got insurance with Jauncey's man's ID on him. So it's a mystery who's even dead, see? It'll be a unsolved crime," he say. 'Lionel figure the cops goin' close the file then 'cause they won't worry 'bout another black man found dead in the river.'"

"Black man, Jauncey? Your cousin Earle let this lunatic Lionel plant Sheldon's ID on a black man? Sheldon's white. *Was* white. You think the cops won't see that? And what about the medical examiner? You know they do autopsies on crime victims, don't you? The medical examiner's going to tell the cops what he found, and the cops are going to add that to what they've put together, and they're going to say, 'My my my, what have we here?' And you know what, Jauncey? They're going to follow up a case that they never would have given a shit about if Sheldon's ID hadn't been found on the body."

Millie walked to the fridge. Took out another Seagram's Seven. Didn't bother with the glass this time. She didn't look out the window at the normal world, either. Asking herself: what are the angles here?

"Earle never thought about it that way, I guess. Nor neither Lionel. Them two, they don't look down the road the way you and me do."

"You're a work of art, Jauncey, you know that? There's no you and me here. There's only you. Tell me the rest of the bad news. Where did the cops find the car?"

"Find it where Lionel left it, on the levee. Bust a wheel tryin' to drive over them big rocks that lead down to the river. Car won't run now, so Lionel get his head in a juncture thinking 'bout what to do. Finally decides, wipe down the car, get rid of the fingerprints, leave the dead man to explain the situation."

"You better to hope to God that Lionel wiped it clean. And that they can't tie the dead guy to Lionel."

"That's why I'm worried. Too many loose ends here."

"Probably more than you know. By now I'm sure the cops have searched Sheldon's house and car. We don't know what the hell they've come up with." After a pause: "You might catch a break here: they probably won't find anything that leads back to you. But I have some advice for you: when the cops find Sharilla—and they will, you can plan on that—you'd better be living a thousand miles away in a place that she's never heard of. That's the best I can do for now."

"I thought you goin' help me. Run away? You figure I couldn't get to that idea on my own?"

"That's all I have right now, Jauncey. I don't see a lot of options. Do you still have any of Sheldon's money?"

"Got about half."

"How much was in that roll?"

"Five thousand, all new hundreds."

"Where's the wrist watch?"

"Give it to Sharilla's boy, Trevor. He like it. Show all his friends."

"That's terrific, Jauncey. Shows it to all of his friends. Listen to me: get the damned thing back and toss it. Lose anything that can link you to Sheldon. By the way, Sheldon wouldn't have been wearing a watch with fake diamonds. That's all the more reason to get rid of it. It'll be insured. That information will reach the cops. If Trevor decides to show the detectives how pretty his new wrist watch is when they visit Sharilla, you're history, Jauncey. Do you follow?"

"Real diamonds? Man, that motherfuckin' Sheldon. Shoulda done him myself, sold his car and watch."

"We're going to end this conversation in one minute, Jauncey, but I want to know something first. What did you do with his suitcase?"

"What? Which?"

"Jauncey, I can find you anytime, anywhere, and you won't ever see me. Do you really want to keep jerking me around?"

"Oh, yeah, the suitcase. Well, I take it home with me, look through it. Some clothes and shit—shirts, underwear, pants, you know. Pair of good shoes, but they too small for me."

"Any papers, news items, photos, notebooks, address books?"

"I disremember exactly, but yeah, some shit like that."

"What did you do with it? Did you throw that stuff away?"

"I been meanin' to, can't get around to it."

"You figured it might be valuable, that's what you thought. So where is it?"

"Bottom of Sharilla's big sewing basket."

"And the suitcase itself?"

"City dump. I throw it in the trash."

"Good. Now listen up, Jauncey. You and I are going to have a little meeting tomorrow. I'll let you know where. Bring the papers with you. All of them."

"Hold on, girl, I'm spose to stay with Trevor tomorrow while Sharilla go to work. He got a touch of flu. What am I goin' tell her? Say, 'I'm meeting up with the lady shoot Mr. Kukich'?"

"Tell her you're going to sewing class."

Chapter 9

"The fuck's going on?"

Millie glanced out the window at the skyline and then flopped on the bed. The lyrics from a Broadway show tune popped into her mind: "Everything's up to date in Kansas City. They've gone about as fer as they can go." What the hell, Millie thought. Where did that come from? That's what a phone call to Jauncey will do to your head. You need a good workout.

Downstairs, in the hotel gym, she stretched, rode the bike for an hour, did lunges, then lifted. Topped it all off with a long shower and a massage. The masseuse had good hands and praised Millie's abs and thighs. Made it clear that certain delicate pleasures were available that evening. Tempting, Millie thought, very tempting, but no. She would never deceive Mandy.

Back in her room, she called Ralph to give him a run-down of current events.

"So, you say this guy, the driver, gave our friend to someone else to bury? And the other guy, his cousin, stuck him in the back of a graveyard? Isn't that illegal?"

"It's illegal to take out a contract on someone too, Ralphie."

"Yeah, but isn't this a little, you know, taking a chance? What if someone was looking?"

"No one was looking, Ralph. And anyway, the cousin was just going about his business digging big holes for the trees. He works part-time for the cemetery. Who would have noticed a body slipping into place in one of the holes?"

Ralph said, "I've heard of people switching coffins, putting empty ones into the ground, sure, even putting two in the same box, I been in the business a long time, but the way the guy's cousin did it, under a tree? Huh-uh, that's a new one to me."

"Well, they didn't have time for a regular burial with a funeral service, Ralphie, if that's what you mean. There's all kinds of ways, you said so yourself. The way they did it probably wasn't a bad idea. This guy, the cousin, has put bodies in unusual places before, I gather. The driver was just turning to someone with experience to help him out. Paid him for the service, too. That wasn't the problem."

"No," Ralph said, "the problem was, a second dead guy shows up, but the driver has already lent his car to the cousin—with our dead guy in it—and then somebody has the bright idea of giving up our dead guy's ID to the second dead guy, who for some unknown reason does not have any ID of his own. Am I close?"

"On the money, Ralph. But the driver wasn't there to cast his vote when the ID was lifted from Sheldon. He'd let his cousin Earle use his car, but he wasn't on hand when Earle worked out the arrangement with the third guy—the guy with the mystery corpse—to put Sheldon's ID into the guy's pocket. In other words, the driver said OK because he was at a slight disadvantage: he wasn't on the scene.

"But later he could see the advantage of confusing the police if they ended up finding a dead black guy with a dead white guy's ID on him. The advantage being, they all figured, that the cops wouldn't devote much manpower to the case because it only involved another dead black guy. I'm just telling you how they looked at the deal."

"And what did you think of all this?"

"I wasn't consulted, Ralphie, I was in Boston with you and Mary Mike."

"No, but I mean what did you think later, when this guy told you about these crazy fucking things?"

"What did I think? There was nothing left to think about, Ralphie, if you mean making sense of it all. I was a little surprised—more than a little, if you want the truth—to hear how many things had got twisted together. I'm used to seeing how fuck-ups operate. I saw plenty of 'em in the Army. But these three guys—boy, they take it to a whole new level. So, yeah, it was something to think about, but only to stay on top of, to get an angle on how to fix it, not to see if it made sense. Who cares, anyway? But listen: I have an idea."

"Wait a minute, OK? So now the cops in Kansas City are going to keep this case open because of the phony ID business, that's what you're saying? And these fucking guys are going to get caught because they got too fancy. Not to mention dumb, with our guy's ID planted on the black guy. They should have just put him in a dumpster. Or do they have regular pick-ups in Kansas City?"

"Yeah, the police will keep the case open for a while. They'll want to know why the second dead guy was carrying our dead guy's ID. That's a legitimate question. If the driver's cousin and the other guy hadn't come up with their brilliant idea, the cops would've given the case minimum attention and then turned the dead guy over to his family to bury. Case closed."

"That's what I mean: now these three geniuses are going to get nailed. Or two of them will, if the driver takes your advice and moves to fucking Pocatello or someplace."

"No, they're going to get away with it, Ralphie. The police will try for a week or so to find out who the un-identified guy was, and who did him. Then they'll close the file on him. They'll feel like they did their job."

"Just like that? How long do they keep a murder in-vestigation open out there?" Ralph seemed a little agi-tated, Millie thought. She wasn't sure why.

"How would I know, Ralph? Probably as long as they do in Boston. What I'm saying is, there's only so much effort the cops will give a low-priority case. The way I see it, unidentified corpses aren't that important, some of them anyway, it all depends. They don't get five-star treatment. Our three guys are home free."

"I don't see it. How can that happen?"

"You're not listening, Ralphie. They're going to get away with it for the reason the third guy, Lionel, came up with. Another black guy found dead in the river. Near the river. Whatever. Is he a murder victim? No question. Is he worth a lot of police time? Probably not. Sheldon's ID will make them wonder what happened, keep the thing alive a little while, but not very long."

"So these guys, they planned it all out the right way. Is that what you're telling me?"

"No, Ralphie, they fucked up every step of the way, except for the driver and his cousin putting Sheldon in the graveyard. That was OK. So you and I are OK too. But the other stuff? It didn't matter what their plan was: the third guy figured how it would all turn out. The cops will try to find out who the mystery guy was. But they'll have a hard time because his fingertips have been sand-ed off. Eventually they'll chalk up the murder to a bar fight, or to the drug business, something like that."

"Did I hear you, Millie? Removed the guy's finger-tips?" Definitely some agitation there. "The fuck's going on out there? Why would they do that?"

"No idea, Ralphie, but it doesn't change anything for us. I'm just telling you the story. You keep asking for details. That's not why I called you, remember? I've got a plan."

"Yeah, OK, what do I need all this for, anyway? My mom, Millie, you know, she used to tell me, 'Ralph, just shut up sometimes, will you? You don't need to know everything. What you don't know,' she used to say to me, 'what you don't know won't hurt you.'"

Millie pressed the bridge of her nose with her thumb and forefinger. "Ralphie," she said, "no disrespect, OK? But do you know how many times you've told me what your mother told you? I have absolutely and totally memorized what she said. And I know that she loved you. So why don't you just take her fucking advice and listen to me? No disrespect intended."

"No, no, Millie, you're right. But now I'm curious: help me to understand this thing. Let's get back to the dead guy, OK? Won't the cops wonder why he's in some guy's car instead of the river?"

"Sure. Why he's in the car, who he is, who iced him, whether he was shot in the car or somewhere else, what his connection with Sheldon is—there's a lot to think about. At first they'll figure the guy did Sheldon, but then why is he dead? So they'll ditch that theory. They'll see the ID as a plant. Why is he in a car that's registered to a guy who's been in prison for two years? Easy: the car's stolen, that's why. Who put him there, right where he'd be found? No way to tell, but the damaged car means somebody left in a hurry."

"So now what do the cops do?" Ralph said. "Now they have to follow up on Sheldon, right?" Again, the tension in his voice.

"Yeah, probably, but there's nowhere for them to go. They've got his ID, so a couple of detectives will talk to his neighbors, and they'll try to find out who he was. But I don' think they'll come up with much. And if they do, it won't matter. Who the hell was Sheldon Kukich, anyway? A hitter out of Toronto. If they can find this out, they'll be glad somebody put him away. They'll chalk it up to 'gang-related killing' and drop it. But you know what, Ralphie, I don't even think they'll get that far. They won't have any leads, and they'll give up."

"How do you know all this, Millie?"

"Guesswork, Ralphie, some of it. Some of it's just common sense. You've been around, you know what cops do."

"That's what I'm worried about, sometimes they get it right."

"Sure, that's what I'm banking on."

"What . . .?"

"Just listen. Tomorrow I'm going to meet with the driver. Dumb shit found some papers in Sheldon's suitcase and decided to hang on to them. Thought they'd lead to money, but really they're a hand grenade with the pin pulled if he's caught with them. They're probably not important, but you never know, they might tell us more about Sheldon."

"What do we care about him now? Forget about the damned papers."

"The point, Ralphie, is maybe we'll find something to get the client off our backs."

"Millie, just as long as the cops don't get too close to this thing. Wrap it up quick, OK?"

"No, Ralphie, we want the cops to stay on the case, that's what I'm getting at."

"What are you saying, Millie? Jesus, you're making me nervous. Our fucking client, Millie, remember that guy? Guy who wants his money back? He's off his chain with this one. So just, you know, keep the cops out of it, OK? Just find something to convince our client that Sheldon's past history."

"We could send him a fish wrapped in newspaper."

"C'mon, Millie, don't screw around."

"I'll find something, Ralphie. Quit worrying. You and

I are in the clear, remember. There's no trail leading back to us. Sheldon was the right guy, and I iced him, no matter what the client thinks. In fact, fuck the client. We honored our part of the contract. Also keep in mind the driver has no idea who I am or what I look like. And he's not going to know after tomorrow either. So relax."

"Relax? I'm completely relaxed, Millie, just like always. Cool as ice. But I still think it's a bad idea to encourage the cops. Fuck's sake, what am I saying? Of course it's a bad idea!" His voice now bouncing on a high wire. "I never heard anything like this before, Millie. The cops are not our business partners, you know, they don't buy shares and have stock in the firm."

"No, but they have resources that we don't. They can do stuff that we can't that will help us. Here's how we're going to handle it, Ralph. We're going to keep the cops in the game long enough to let them do our work for us."

"OK, Millie, I give up. You handle it. I just hope you know what you're doing."

"Don't I always? Listen, Ralphie, solving problems is the fun part of the job, you know that. Otherwise, where would we be? Now sit back and listen."

Chapter 10

Famous Gangster Comedian

H er idea was simple, she explained to Ralph. Get somebody to contact the cops, tell them there were two guys who got taken for a ride in the murder car, not just one. Tell them to check the blood samples for two sets of DNA. One profile will come from the black guy with the white guy's ID, the other from the white guy himself. Also remind the cops—just in case they don't think of it themselves—to look for powder residue in the back seat and on the black guy's clothing. The techs will figure out that there were two different shooters.

In other words, she said, give these guys a helping hand, show them how things played out: OK, first of all, Sheldon takes a bullet in the back seat of the car, buys the farm, but the body disappears. No one knows where. Second: person or persons unknown toss the other dead guy, the one with Sheldon's ID, into the back seat of the same car (reasons unclear), which they abandon after it breaks down. So, you end up with two different blood samples, powder residue in the car that doesn't square with the burn marks on the second dead guy, and who knows what other interesting evidence if you run some more tests? Don't forget that both guys checked out under circumstances that some would call murky. There's other stuff you could mention to the cops too, but why make things more complicated than they already are?

And finally, Millie added, explaining the fine points to Ralph, the newspapers would jump all over themselves to publish the story. Not to mention that the client's stooge in the Kansas City PD would pass along the interesting news to the client. Bottom line: the bozo client gets off their back.

Millie was in her room, early evening, snacking on the complimentary candy bars the hotel gave out (Snickers and Kit Kat, her favorites). Tiny bags of Doritos, stuff she adored.

"You don't think they'll figure all this out on their own, Millie?" Ralph said. "This is ABC police work. The forensics guys will analyze the blood samples, spatter patterns, gunshot residue. Check for prints. Vacuum for trace evidence—you know, hair, fibers, dirt. Give these guys some credit, Mil. They learn this stuff at the police academy. I know a guy who told me this."

"You're right, Ralphie," she said, "it's a no-brainer, if they decide to develop the evidence, follow it up. What I'm saying is, they might close the file early, maybe put other cases ahead of it. What if they have a busy week, a couple of high-end homicides, an arson case, maybe a hit-and-run, a bank robbery, a debutante gets kidnapped? Or, the mayor's wife loses her necklace at the country club, and the police chief has to send out a couple of guys to find an undocumented worker who put the thing in his pocket. Get it, Ralph? Contingencies, that's what I'm planning for. Why take chances when we can give the cops a little push?"

"I get you," he said. "But what'll they think about the guy that calls 'em? Just some citizen doing his civic duty? Him and his kids bring the cops donuts every Monday morning? I don't think so. Huh-uh. The cops, they'll want to find him, see how he connects to the dead guys, what angles he's playing. They'll see that this is another actor. And don't forget that we're in the middle of all this. Mil, you're the best I ever seen, no comparison, but this idea of yours, you know? I just don't know. We got a quiet little business to run. Our clients don't like publicity."

"You don't like publicity, Raphie. But we've never had any, except when it got out that your schoolteacher-guy ended up plugged in a dumpster. But that was a while before I joined the firm. You don't have to tell me, 'let's not bring attention to ourselves, it's bad for business, it could be dangerous.' But that won't happen. We're invisible, totally off the map. We're helping the cops connect the dots, that's all."

"You ever think you should of iced the driver, Mil? That would of simplified a lot of things, wouldn't it? You could be home right now watching *Monday Night Football*. No, today's Tuesday, but, what the hell, you know what I mean."

"Ralphie, let's be serious, OK? We don't do civilians, you know that. Only the guys named in the contract. We never involve civilians, period. No innocent bystanders, even if they deserve it. We follow professional standards. You shouldn't need me to tell you this stuff."

"I didn't mean it, Mil. Just thinking, that's all."

She fluffed a pillow against the headboard, relaxed into her bed.

"As far as what if's are concerned, the job would have been quick and clean if we hadn't let the bat-shit client interfere. That's where we fucked up. We should have shut down the operation the second we learned Sheldon wouldn't be driving himself home from the airport. But no, this guy muscled you a little, put some pressure on you. 'Repeat customer,' you said, 'he'll pay us double,' and then the corker: 'a guy you don't want to cross,' all that baloney. OK, we're here now, Ralphie, there's no going back."

"Christ, I know, Mil, I caved to that guy."

"Ralphie, here's the deal: you can't think about 'wouldn't it be nice if this or that happened.' You can't go back to square one. It's the first rule of this business. I learned it in the Army. What you have to do is, you look at things as they are, locate the push points, study the players on the board. Facts, Ralph—that's what I'm saying. We deal with the here and now. That's all we've got."

"Yeah, I know, only thing that makes sense."

"Your mother probably told you this when you were a kid, Ralph, gave you lots of useful advice, since you'd take over the business someday. Didn't she tell you, 'Ralphie, listen to me, keep your eye on the ball, you can't get distracted by the'—I don't know—'the butter-flies'—something like that? Didn't she want you to be a tough guy?"

"Butterflies? No, Millie, I guarantee you she never told me anything about butterflies. Only thing I remember is, you know, once in a while, it was an expression of hers, you might say, she'd say, 'Ralphie . . .'"

"Don't go there, Ralph . . ."

". . . she'd say, 'listen to me, Ralphie,' she'd tell me, 'what you don't know won't hurt you.' I don't know why, maybe I asked too many questions. She was probably just being protective."

"What? Can you rewind that for me, Ralphie? She was being protective? She's running a removals firm, bringing you up in the business of hiring professional killers, and she wants to protect you? From what? From the Cookie Monster? I'm missing a piece of the puzzle here, Ralph, can you help me out?"

"I don't know, Mil, could be she was just old-fashioned, you think?"

"You know what I think? I think I shouldn't have brought up the subject, that's what I think. Now where were we?"

But the subject of his mom seemed to encourage Ralph. He said, "You were telling me, we invite the police into the game. You gave me the big picture, but I'm still a little behind on the details. For instance: I don't get how we're going to contact the cops. You gonna call 'em on the phone? Say, 'Listen, umm, I want to report a crime, a murder. Who should I talk to?'

"Let me think about this, Millie," Ralph said, "how you'd do it. All right, you make the call, ask for one of the detectives, you wait a few minutes, then some guy comes on the phone, you can tell he's bored shitless, he's only taking the call because the other dicks are out riding around in their cruisers or buying dope from teenagers, and you say, you say, what. OK I got it," Ralph said. "You tell him, 'I have reliable information about a murder, you want it?' And the cop, the guy, says, 'Who is this?' And you tell him, 'Listen, you know that dead black guy you found with a white guy's ID on him, well, the white guy's dead too.' And the cop says, 'Congratulations, ma'am, but we already figured that out. There's no reward. But, hey, I'd like to know, how do you know this? And what did you say your name was?'

"He's not bored now, you can tell, he's trying to be cool. And then you say . . . let me think here, Millie," Ralph said. "Here's what you say: 'I'm in a hurry, officer, so clam up and listen. I got something important for you. The white guy? He died in the back seat of the car. His blood's all over the place.' 'Yeah?' the cop says. 'That's inneresting. Can you slow up a little, ma'am, so I can make some notes here?' But you just say, quick now, 'The black guy was shot, I don't know where, but some guys put him in the car that they took the other

74

guy out of and then dumped that other guy somewhere else, don't ask me why. Some of the second guy's blood's in the car too. You guys can figure out the rest.'"

"That's good, Ralphie, real good. Can I write that down, use it later?"

"Yeah, sure. Now, Millie, at this point, the cop will try to keep you on the line, track your signal, but you're way ahead of him, so fuck him, you end the call. I'm just going through this thing in my mind, Mil, I'm not completely sure of every little detail, you unnerstand, but what the hell else can you tell this guy, you follow me? You gonna tell him, 'How I know, dickhead, is I pulled the trigger on the fucking white guy'?" Ralphie, famous gangster comedian, now laughing at his own joke. Ha ha ha.

"You finished?"

"Yeah. Yeah, I'm finished."

"You enjoying yourself?"

"C'mon, Mil, lighten up. I'm just playing around. So, OK, what are you going to tell him? Are you going to disguise your voice, or what?"

She fluffed a pillow against the headboard, relaxed into the bed. No lights on in the room.

"I'm not going to make the call, Ralphie."

"Then who's the lucky guy gets to phone the police?"

"That's where you come in."

"Me? Jesus Christ, Millie, I don't know how to do this stuff. You're the one in the field. You're the expert. I've never even been to Kansas City."

"Last I heard, you can call anywhere from anywhere else. You don't have to be the guy in the field. It's the miracle of the telephone, Ralphie."

"Let's think about this, Millie. I am strictly the office guy. I take the calls from Philly, as you know. I OK the contracts. Have a meeting with the field agent—that's you. And pay the bills. That's it. I don't even know how to shoot a gun."

"You don't have to shoot the phone, Ralphie, you just talk into it, like you're doing now."

A couple of beats. "You're jerking me off, aren't you, Millie? Your crazy sense of humor. For a minute there, I thought, 'What the fuck is she doing, is she serious? What's going on here?' You were just getting back at me, right, for fucking with you?"

"I can't fool you, Ralph, can I? No, I don't want you to call the Kansas City PD. Somebody outside the firm has to, that's the beauty of the plan. We just set things in motion."

"Yeah, that's good, somebody outside the business. How do we do it?"

"One possibility: you're friends with a reporter from the *Globe*, right?

"You want him to make the call?"

"Ralphie, can you just listen for a minute or two? No, I do not—emphatically do not—want the fucking reporter to call the Kansas City PD for us. I'm not nuts. Though the two phone calls I've had today, I'm not so sure anymore. Give me a second here." Then: "OK. You know this guy, this reporter, he's pals with a detective on the Boston police force, correct?"

"Correct."

"The cop sometimes tells the reporter stories about the department. The reporter, who you went to high school with, you were sweethearts and so on, once in a while tells the cop some stories too, also correct?"

"We weren't sweethearts, for Christ's sake, Millie, we were just good friends. Buddies. I don't think you have to, you know, try and incriminate, is that the word . . . no . . . insituate . . . I can't think of it . . . ."

"Insinuate."

"Yeah, whatever . . . that me and this guy . . . ."

By this time it was dark. Millie, still lying on the bed, was now looking at the thick oblong of pale moonlight angling in through her window. She had stopped listening to Ralph. She was tired. "Ralphie, it's late, and I'm starving. I'm going to call room service and then get some sleep. I've got a big day ahead of me. Let's finish this tomorrow, OK? We're just going around in circles anyway."

"Just like that, you're done? What about my guy at the *Globe*? What's he's supposed to tell the cop? How does the cop fit in? You know, Mil, I'm not gonna be able to sleep if you leave this thing up in the air."

"I was thinking a minute ago, Ralph: maybe it's not such a hot idea, starting from your end. It'd probably be better to have somebody here call the cops. Same game, different players."

"You thinking of using those clowns that put Sheldon in the ground? Millie, those guys are out of control, you said so yourself. They're criminals. You can't trust 'em."

"I don't know who I'm going to use, Ralphie. Let me sleep on it. I'll let you know as soon as I work it out. Tomorrow I meet with the driver. Maybe he'll have something for me."

"So this's going to be a different story, then, right?"

"You could say that, yeah. Don't worry, though, I'll let you know how it ends."

Chapter 11

BIZARRE MURDER CASE CONTINUES TO BAFFLE POLICE

By Sherman Williams, Special To *The Star*

Kansas City police are still trying to develop leads in the murder of an un-identified man whose body was found aban-doned in a car last Friday night in North Kansas City.

The dead man, an African-American, was carrying a driver's license issued to a Caucasian man, now also believed to be dead. The police have offered no explana-tion for what appears to be a double ho-micide.

The car, a late-model Lincoln, had been driven over large rocks on a levee above the Missouri River. It was then apparently abandoned when a wheel rod snapped. The body lay crumpled in the back seat.

Police Chief Roy Weed said, "Whoever did all this was in a hurry. Looks like the suspect had planned to throw the body into the river, but his vehicle broke down. At that point he absconded."

Asked why the driver didn't use the access road to the river about fifty feet ahead, Chief Weed said, "It's pretty hard to think straight in a situation like that."

He was also asked whether he had further information on the car, which is registered to Reginald ("Sugar") Mott, 44, who has been in a Federal prison in Forrest, Arkansas, for two years. "Well, we figure someone stole it," the Police Chief said. "We're going to go from there."

The police are withholding the identity of the owner of the driver's license pending further investigation.

Chapter 12

Keep Ahead of the Carom

Millie, enjoying coffee and a Danish the next morning in the hotel restaurant, read *The Kansas City Star* article twice. She was wearing a navy pants suit with thin red stripes, a beige silk blouse, and black Stuart Weitzman brogans, a birthday gift from Mandy.

In her studded crossbody bag (Linea Pella) were the Epipens, a can of pepper spray, and spare IDs, along with several burners and her Jackie O's. Plus a few strategic make-up items: Blow Torch Red lipstick (a new product), kohl eye liner, and a knock-out mixed-color bob wig (brown and blonde) that almost reached her shoulders. Not that she gave a damn about all this femme get-up, but disguise is the better part of valor, isn't it?

And why not give the Blow Torch a shot, see what happens? The salesgirl had said to her, "Honey, if you want to marry poor, wear Revlon. If you want to marry rich, use this. And try to leave a few bite marks."

The cops don't know much, she thought. Unless they're holding something back. But does this Chief Roy

Weed sound like he has an ace up his sleeve? Huh-uh. Sounds like he's saying the well done run dry.

And this business of not releasing Sheldon's name: By now they've probably found out that he has no next of kin. They've also had time to search his house, pound on his neighbors' doors, ask the routine bonehead questions: "How well do you know Mr. Kukich?" Not real well. "Did he have any enemies?" Couldn't say. "Have you seen any unusual activity at his house?" I try to mind my own business. "Looks like he's been gone for some time. Does he travel a lot?" You got me.

And so on.

Now what? Millie turned the matter over in her mind. The cops figure Sheldon's dead, odds are good it's a murder case. That's something the public has a right to know about, isn't it? But the cops aren't giving it up—not yet, anyway. So, yeah, she thought, there's a possibility they've found a thread.

But if they tug it, where will the thread lead? In the case of Sheldon Kukich, exactly nowhere, was her guess. Gangsters don't leave a trail of bread crumbs. Write it down.

And the shenanigans engineered by Earle and Lionel? Forget it: draw the cops a map and they still wouldn't believe it.

The waitress walked over to Millie's table, topped up the coffee, looked down at the Stuart Weitzmans. "God, those boots," she said, then bent close to Millie's ear and growled. Winked back at Millie as she moved to another table, waving her nice ass. Millie smiled. Is this a great country, or what? I'll leave her a big tip.

But there's still something I'd like to know. Why was Sheldon living out here to begin with? He sure didn't move here for the climate. Mid-nineties forecast for today, humidity off the charts. So what then? Just why would he move to the capital of cow country? Peace and quiet? Clear blue skies? C'mon, Millie, think. Don't just run through the rural clichés.

All right, then, Millie, put yourself in his place. Hit man: OK, I can relate to that. Gang member, semi-big time for awhile: I've seen *The Godfather* two or three times, that's the best I can do. Remember Sal, when he says to Tom, "Tell Mikey it was just business"? Poor guy, he knew he was already a dead man. Maybe I should have said that to Sheldon, she thought. "It's just business, Shel." Made him feel better. I couldn't have kept a straight face.

But here's something to think about: this kind of guy doesn't move from bright lights and big city to the Midwest without a good reason. And that reason? Her thoughts traced a straight line: Sheldon had probably been hiding from someone. A guy in his line of work makes enemies. Enemies with long memories and savage ways of getting even.

Time to call Jauncey, maybe find out who that someone was.

OK, she thought, but: you know that a conversation with Jauncey is a ride on the loop de loop, don't you? Oh yeah, I know. You buckled in? Yup.

And at that precise moment a memory from her high-school years popped up. Instead of doing her math homework, as she damned well should have been, she was playing the pinball machine in a joint near her mom's house, guzzling Sam Adams.

That's it, she thought: keep ahead of the carom.

Chapter 13

T-Bone Charlie's

It was 10:30 when she phoned Jauncey. A woman answered the phone. "Hellooo."

Damn it, Millie thought, I told him I'd call. Where is he? Well, you knew there'd be ruts in the road with this guy. "Good morning," she said, "this is Justina Waters? I'm with the, um, Parks and Recreation, and I'm doing a survey? I'd like to speak with Mr. Jarnsey—have I got that right?—Jarsley Chalmers? We have a free gift certificate waiting for him. Please is Mr. Shalmers there?"

"Bitch, I know who you are! You ain't with Parks and Rec. You the woman tried to get close to Jauncey when we went to the Blue Room. No way you gonna talk to him. I know you and him talking secrets behind my back yesterday while I'm off at work. Don't call again, hear, or I phone the police." She ended the call.

Jauncey, two-timing this lady? I can't believe it. Why would he, if he's using her house as a hide-out? He's not that dumb, is he?

That's not it, Millie suddenly realized. Sharilla thinks I'm his girlfriend. That phone call yesterday: Jauncey walking into a quiet room alone so he could hear me.

And Sharilla's the jealous type. On top of everything else, I'm now in the middle of a soap opera. Well, fine, just another day at the office, but where is that fucking Jauncey?

Millie waited five minutes. Tried again.

"I'm calling the police this time, bitch! Be a warrant out on you by noon!" Sharilla hung up again, hard. The landline as weapon. She had a commanding voice, Millie noticed. Nobody to fuck with. No doubt the boss in that family. She checked her watch: almost 10:45. Jesus, I hate to depend on someone else to get things done.

She thought: I could drive to KCI, return my rental, and be back home for supper with Mandy. I could ask Mary Mike to make the call to the Kansas City PD, let her give them the story. She can pretend to be Greta Van Susteren, following a hot news item.

Now that I think about it, though, Mary Mike probably knows some guy who can do it on the Internet without leaving a trail. The guy could route the email through Kazakstan, the Kremlin, wherever. Better yet, through Toronto, she thought, Sheldon's old bailiwick. A little twist in the case to amuse the cops. Put it on the back burner, Millie. It's a possibility, a definite maybe.

But right now you've got one or two other things in play.

She called again. Jauncey picked up. "What! Lionel, how you doin', man? Where you at? Been waitin' for you. When you goin' give me that ride you promise me, that brand-new car you don't want to dirty up?"

"Jauncey, my goodness, how good of you to answer the phone. I hate to interrupt your morning tea, I'm sure you know that, but do you think I could have a moment of your precious fucking time?" A pause. "Where have you been?"

"Girl, it's hard around here, I got no privacy, that's why. Whoa, she comin' back in the room, so I'm talkin' to Lionel again, you follow?"

"I'm a patient woman, Jauncey. I think before I act. Normally I take a guy out only after long consideration, or for money. But in your case, I might have to relax my standards."

"Man, Lionel, you like the man on TV, can't think of his name, makes a speech every time he shoot somebody. White guy wears a cowboy hat? Scary dude." Jauncey having his fun, poking the tiger with a stick. "Only look, it's hard to hear you, man, your voice far away, like you holding the phone in the wind." Probably putting on an act for Sharilla, who wasn't likely to buy it.

"Jauncey, I'm going to say this once, and once only. Meet me in one hour—not two hours, Jauncey, one hour—at the Kansas City Airport Marriott. I'll be in T-Bone Charlie's Bar. You know the place?"

"Me? Yeah, Lionel, OK, I wait for you."

"And bring every scrap of paper you found in that suitcase. While you're at it, bring the diamond watch too, unless cute little Trevor has donated it to the policeman's retirement fund. We might be able to use it."

"You say 'we,' Lionel? Still can't hear a damn thing. Charge up your phone, man, I call you back later."

An hour and a half later Millie was still waiting in T-Bone Charlie's, nursing her second Seven and Seven, feeling loose and easy yet still pumped up with that feeling she loved at game time. On contract work she didn't drink. But today? Today she figured as simple recon, though with Jauncey you could never tell, could you? So she ordered coffee and a grilled cheese sandwich to offset the drinks.

She was sitting at the L-end of the bar, where she could see everyone who entered and left the place. A couple of college boys sat at a table near the entrance, lost in their iPhones. Three business types occupied a table to her right.

Ten more minutes passed. Millie went to the window facing the parking lot. She glanced out and—hmmm—

85

saw four men walking her way, slow-striding like the pack from *Reservoir Dogs*. Only these guys didn't strike her as thugs. They had the look of cops. Short hair, beefy bodies, too-tight shirts, those bulky black shoes policeman favor. And, wouldn't you know it, one of them with a badge clipped to his belt. Two of them had duffle bags. One had luggage on wheels.

Well, well, she thought. This could be interesting. Jauncey and I talking about poor dead Sheldon, the cops a few feet away sucking down beer. Perfect. On the other hand, what could be better cover? Doing business with the police standing guard? Maybe they'd like to join us, have a few laughs while we explain things.

A few steps behind the cops, right on cue, came Jauncey, slightly levitating in the heat waves that rolled off the blacktop. He wasn't alone. A man the size of an NFL linebacker was with him, the guy's shaved head a massive ebony sculpture. He was wearing Ray-Ban aviators and an oversize shirt hanging down over his waist. He seemed to be guiding Jauncey, like one of those ventriloquists working his dummy.

You wanted interesting, Millie? Here it is.

The four cops took seats close to her. They were loud, laughing, joking with each other. Two of them ordered beer. One guy asked for a double Jim Beam rocks. Ginger ale for the man with the badge. Must be on duty, she thought, maybe the welcome committee for the others. Or maybe seeing them off after some kind of convention. No way to tell.

The guy closest to her, the Jim Beam, swiveled around. Smiled at her. Tipped his glass. She looked right through him to the North Pole. He wasn't discouraged. "Buy you a drink?"

She shook her head. "Not during work." Millie dug into her purse, put on a pair of black horn-rims. A tiny bit of camouflage.

"Oh, yeah?" the guy said. "What do you do?"

"I'm an assassin."

"Business any good?" He signaled for another double Beam.

Well, she thought, I may as well string him along, find out what I can about these guys.

"A little slow. It's the off-season. What do you guys do?"

"Sam and Mike are with Witness Protection. Jimmy's local. I'm an Air Marshal. Top-secret stuff, you understand. Name's Ralph. What's yours?"

"Ralph? I can't believe it."

"It happens."

"No, that's not what I mean."

"What's yours?"

"Buffy."

"And you kill vampires, right? C'mon, what is it?"

"Ursula. I changed it."

"I bet you had good reasons, too."

"Why are you drinking, Ralph? Aren't you supposed to be sober when you get on a plane?"

"Afraid of flying," he said. "Classic example of poor career choice. But today I'm just another passenger."

"Remind me to take another airline when you're on duty."

"Not a chance. Then I wouldn't get to save you from the bad guys, would I." Sam," he said to the guy next to him, "Buffy here says she's a man-killer. What do you think?"

That brought the others into the game. Sam had to blink a moment to focus. "Good-looking woman like that, I'm not surprised. Be a nice way to go out."

"Hell, yes," said the guy next to him. Mike. "Sign me up, Buffy. You're just my type."

"Jesus Christ," said the one with the badge. Jimmy. He got off his stool. Turned to Millie. "Don't pay attention to these gorillas, they're not house-broke. They've been drinking since last Thanksgiving." The others laughed, slapped the bar. Ordered fresh drinks.

Meanwhile, Jauncey and Big Boy had come in. They were looking around, a little unsure. Not the scene they'd expected. Is this the woman we're supposed to meet? Are these four guys her protection? Jauncey was carrying a manila envelope.

Millie looked at them. Tipped her head to one side. Walked to a corner booth. They followed, but kept glancing at the cops. Jauncey sat on one side, knees bouncing up and down. Why is he doing that? she thought. She slid in the other side. Big Boy stared at her through his shades. Pushed in right next to her. See what a tough dude I am. Oh, boy, thought Millie, more shit to shovel.

"Hummmh, mmmh." Jauncey, clearing his throat. "This here Lionel. He give me a ride in his car. Where's that pillow you had that time, girl? Man, Lionel, this one, she know the moves."

"Why aren't you alone?" Millie said.

"Like I say, he drive me. I told you I don't have no car. Lionel here . . . hummmh, mmmh, he use it for some business he had." Jauncey a little nervous today. Well, Lionel had killed a man, stuffed him into the back seat of Jauncey's car. No doubt capable of further mayhem.

The waiter came to their table. Lionel ordered a double vodka rocks. Jauncey asked for a Boulevard beer. Nothing for Millie.

The waiter went for the drinks.

"So, Lionel," she said, "you're Jauncey's driver."

"Ain't his driver," Lionel said. "His business partner. You don't look like somebody could shoot down a man." He turned to Jauncey. "You sure this the right one?"

"Yeah, I think so, man. Never got a good look at her. But she here. Gotta be the right one." He said to Millie: "Girl, I don't know your name, you know? How we supposed to do business?"

"Did you bring the stuff I asked for?" she said.

"Yeah, she the one. See, she don't like to answer," he told Lionel. "Don't like to show her cards. Sure, I brought it."

He handed her the envelope. There was a lump at the bottom of it. Lionel snatched it away from her. "Listen to me, lady, 'fore we get down to it. You with the big boys now. Whatever scam you got goin' with Jauncey here, half of it's mine. Understand? Jauncey and me partners, like I said." He looked into the mailer. Brought out a diamond watch and some keys on a chain. "Damn, Jauncey, where you get all this? I keep it for you." He slipped the watch on his wrist. Put the keys on the table.

The waiter brought the drinks.

"Waiter," Millie said, "could you ask the man at the bar drinking ginger ale to step over here, please?"

"Yes, ma'am."

"Go sit with Jauncey," Millie said to Lionel, "so I can see who I'm dealing with."

"You talkin' to me, sister? I ain't movin'."

"See what I say, Lionel, girl's got style. Cold as ice. Get on over here, man, see how she operate." Jauncey enjoying the action.

Lionel didn't move. He put his hand on Millie's thigh. Squeezed hard. In a low voice he said, "Don't fuck with me, girl. Whoever's coming from the bar better not fuck with me either. Give Jauncey the money for the envelope, and we be out of here. Otherwise you gon get hurt."

Millie flexed her thigh muscle, raised her leg, and brought down one of her Stuart Weitzmans across his shin. He lifted his hand. She grabbed his index finger and bent it back sharply. It broke with a soft crack. Elapsed time for this maneuver—1.5 seconds.

Lionel gasped. He lifted his good hand, but couldn't decide what to do with it. Millie slapped him. His shades fell off. "Lionel, you piece of shit, listen up. If you scream, I'll break another one. Give me the fucking envelope." She took it from him. Grabbed the keys from the table.

"Jesus, oh man, Jesus!" Jauncey said. "Goddamn! I told you, Lionel. Whoa, damn! She too much for us." His knees moving like pistons.

"Help you with anything?" It was Jimmy, the ginger ale guy. He stared at Lionel's hand. "Somebody hurt here?"

"He's OK," Millie said, "he just sprained his finger. Have a seat."

"What happened?" Looking back and forth, first at Millie, then at Jauncey. Then down at Lionel's hand: "Jesus, look at that finger. It looks awful. I think you broke it, mister. Let me look at it."

Lionel was breathing hard, tears squeezing out of his eyes. "Bitch, I won' forget this." His good hand was supporting his injured hand. The broken finger was still bent back, swelling rapidly. He was starting to shake.

"What the hell's going on here?"

"I think he's going into shock," Millie said. "Call an ambulance."

"Jesus. Did you do something to him?"

"We were arm-wrestling. His elbow slipped. Isn't that right, Bo?" She was looking at Jauncey, who was glancing around the room.

Jauncey said, "Yeah, that's right, what she say. It all happen so fast, you know, seem like a accident. Lionel, he grab her, next thing I know he be holding up his hand like a dead bird. Lionel, talk to me, man. Didn't I tell you be careful?"

"You better call 911, Jimmy," Millie said. "Get up, Bo," she said to Jauncey, "it's getting crowded in here. Jauncey slid out of the booth, Millie right behind him. She reached back for her bag and Jauncey's beer bottle.

"Ralph," Jimmy called, "I need you to come over here." Then to Millie: "Did this man assault you?" Then to Lionel: "Or did she assault you? This is crazy." He punched the numbers into his phone. "Send an ambulance and back-up," he said. Described the situation. Gave the location.

"Gimme outta here," Lionel said. "Nothin' happen. I'm leavin.'" But Lionel was too dizzy to stand on his own. Jauncey reached over, pushed Lionel's vodka toward him. "Drink it down, man. Make you feel better." Lionel swaying, Jimmy trying to support him. Everything happening at once. Millie took a step back from the group. Jauncey followed her.

Ralph, Sam, and Mike were now standing near the booth.

Ralph: "Wow! Did you tangle with the little lady, bud? I could have told you she's a killer." Laughter from his pals.

Jimmy: "Get me a towel so I can wrap this guy's hand." The waiter was already there with towels and ice. He made a wrapping for Lionel's hand.

Sam: "I watched the whole thing, and I still can't believe it. Happened too fast to see."

Mike: "That's because you're blind drunk, big fella."

Jimmy: "We'll get you taken care of, then you can press charges if you want. First we gotta fix that finger."

"No one gon press charges," Lionel said. "I take care of it myself."

Mike: "Bend it back in place. It'll be OK. I did that once in football. Gotta play with pain."

Jimmy: "Will you just shut the fuck up, Mike, and get out of the way? Where's the woman? I want to talk with her. Goddammit, find her."

They looked around. No sign of her. Jauncey was gone too. Someone asked the bartender if he'd seen them. Yeah, he said, they were going out to the guy's car to get his asthma medication. Didn't want him to seize up. Woman said they'd be right back. Ordered drinks all around to help everyone stay calm. She said that the injured guy offered to pay. He'd just made a killing and had plenty of money.

Chapter 14

Lionel

Now what we goin' do?" Jauncey asked. He and Millie were driving away from T-Bone Charlie's in her rental car. She was wearing her Jackie O's again. "Man, Lionel goin' to kill me now, running outta there with you. Maybe I tell him you kidnap me, ain't my fault. You think he believe me?"

"Don't worry about Lionel."

"You plan to shoot him? Only thing goin' stop him, you know. We get Earle to put him under a tree, what you think? Earle goin' have to start chargin' to bury people. Me and you could go into business with him."

Millie took one of the prepaid phones out of her bag. Handed it to Jauncey. "Here, I want you to make a call."

"Me? What for? Who'm I suppose to call? I got enough problems already, you understand? Don't need any more. Tell you, girl, that day you do Mr. Kukich, all my troubles start. One headache after another. Now what you doin'?"

"Here's the number." She read it from her iPhone as she drove: T-Bone Charlie's.

Jerry Masinton

"What'm I suppose to say to the dude? 'How you doin'? What them cops doin' with my man? Treatin' him good?'"

"Just give me the phone," Millie said. It was ringing as she put it to her ear. She said to the bartender, "I need to speak to Ralph. He's one of the cops with the injured black guy. It's important."

"Who shall I say is calling?"

"Lieutenant Buffy. Official police business."

"Hardly hear you, Ma'am. You say 'Buffy' or 'Puffy'?"

Noise in the background: men's voices, thudding sounds, someone yelling "Fuck no!" Another voice: "Grab him!" and "I need help!"

"Get him, goddamn it. You're delaying an investigation."

Traffic back into Kansas City was light. Most of the other drivers were passing her, observing the unspoken law that says you can exceed the limit by 5 miles per hour. The sun was directly overhead, baking the highway. The car's AC was at full tilt.

She heard more shouting on the phone, the sound of glass breaking. Then what sounded like several gunshots, followed by more shouting.

Millie waited, 99 percent sure that the gunshots had something to do with Lionel. Make that a hundred percent. Finally Ralph got on the line: "Jesus Christ, Buffy—Ursula—what the hell have you done? Do you know what's happening here?"

"How would I know? You tell me."

"All hell broke loose, that's what happened. Where are you? People here want to talk to you. And where's that other guy who was in the booth with you?"

"I have something to tell you, Ralph. Are you sober enough to remember?"

"Sober? I've been jumped-up ever since the big guy started to shoot at us. Good thing you broke his hand."

"He had a gun? Good. Anybody injured?"

"He threw Sam over the bar and broke about a million glasses, plus Sam's arm. Then he pulled out a pistol and started shooting. Jimmy fired back, put him down with the first round. I wouldn't bet on his chances." He took a breath. "You said, 'good' when I told you he had a gun. What do you mean?"

"What set him off?"

"Beats me. Something Sam said to him."

"Ralph, how would you like to be a hero?"

"Not if it involves flying. Now tell me what's up."

"Listen hard, Ralph. I'm in a hurry."

Just then three police cruisers, sirens wailing and lights flashing, blew by, followed by an ambulance. Millie and the other drivers going south barely had time to pull over. Jauncey said, "Damn, looks like Lionel in bad shape."

"Police sirens," Ralph said. "You're on the highway. Who's with you? The other guy?"

"Here's what I have for you, Sherlock. Once only, so pay attention. The guy that Jimmy shot—see if his gun was used in the shooting of a black guy in North Kansas City last week. Black guy was carrying a white guy's ID. Both guys are dead."

"Shot?" Jauncey said. "They shoot Lionel?" His knees bouncing up and down again.

"How the hell do you know all this?" Ralph said.

"It's in the papers, Ralph. I read about it with my morning coffee. You can forget about this phone call, by the way."

"Then how do I explain this conversation?" His voice now at a higher pitch, trying to stay in the game.

"Just make sure the local cops follow up on the gun. They'll probably do it anyway, standard procedure, see if it's been used in some other crime. But make certain. You can take the credit. Forget that I called."

"Thanks, but I don't want the credit."

"You're aces, Ralph. See you around."

"Hey, when can I buy you a drink?"

"Next time I'm in town."

"I don't live in Kansas City. I don't even know your real name."

Millie ended the call. She looked over at Jauncey: "Ease up, Jauncey, your troubles are over. Stop that damned jiggling, you'll cause an accident."

"Lionel got shot? He dead? I told you, girl, you bring a storm with you. People end up dead when they around you. I wonder why I ain't dead too. If you shoot me that time you do Mr. Kukich, none of these aggravations come my way. Same for you too. You ever think of that?"

"Is that what you'd like?"

"Whoa, Jesus. Hell, no. We just makin' conversation here, you know? Thinkin' 'bout things."

"He must have had a gun under his shirt," she said. "Did you know that?"

"Lionel like to carry that thing under his belt. Give him some swag. Told me it was for important occasions, know what I mean? He wasn't expectin' no cops, though, just you and me today. I told him, 'Lionel, you goin' get yourself shot if you show that thing, hear? Somebody see you playing with it, they take you down. Or either you shoot the wrong man, like you done before.' Damned fool won't listen. Got to have it with him everywhere he go."

"You're telling me the dead guy they found in your car was an accident?" She looked across at Jauncey. "Lionel killed him accidentally?"

"Woulda been a accident if Lionel didn't decide to do it."

Millie turned a sharp right, took an off-ramp, tires squealing. Turned in at a gas station and convenience store. Hit the brakes hard. Jauncey was jolted forward. "Damn! You goin' get us killed, girl. Who chasin' us?" She cut the engine. They'd do without the AC. "Jauncey, what the hell do you mean? Did he want to shoot him or not?"

"Nah, he want to shoot another guy, but this one get in his way. They was all drunk in a bar downtown somewhere. Lionel and this light boy get in a fight over a woman. Light dude say she's his woman, been lovin' him all along. Lionel tell this boy, 'You stay the fuck away from her, motherfucker, or I cap you!' That's what I hear, anyway, people talkin' about it later. Then Lionel, he pull out that gun and point it at this kid. Kid throws his drink in Lionel's face and runs. Man standing next to Lionel steps between 'em—try to stop the fight, understand?—tells Lionel put that thing away, somebody goin' get hurt. Lionel say, 'Get out the way, monkey, or I shoot you too.' Man say, 'Ain't goin' to move,' so Lionel shoot him, and then Lionel look surprise when the man fall on the ground. Light dude gone by this time. What I heard from a neighbor of Sharilla's."

"That pistol is going to put you in the clear, Jauncey."

"How you mean, 'in the clear'? 'Cause he use it on the man that end up in my car? That just mean Lionel get conducted with the man's murder," he said. "I got nothing to do with it. I see that Lionel in the shit the minute you talk to that dude on the phone, but what he done ain't my worry. Or you mean somethin' else gone off the track that I don't know about?"

"Like what?"

"Like, OK, why'm I in the clear if I ain't in trouble in the first place?" Jauncey rubbed his head with both hands. "You know, girl, I figure something out since you put the gun in my face that day. I see they some things in life I'm goin' to know, and they's other things never goin' open up to me. Like, how I'm in the clear when Lionel shoot one man and you shoot Mr. Kukich? I'm the only one didn't shoot nobody. So I don't see how you mean I'm in the clear when none of this is my business."

"It's your car, Jauncey. Lionel tossed a body into it. Only now the cops aren't going to bother finding out who used it. They're not going to follow the string back to Sharilla. And that means they won't ever end up questioning you."

"You lost me, girl, I thought we talkin' 'bout the gun. You say the pistol save my ass. Then this stuff 'bout my car."

"Think about it, Jauncey. You got lucky. You should have torched the car before Lionel could get hold of it. But you didn't, and he used it in a capital crime. But he also left a lot of questions. Who is the dead man? Who is the shooter? Why did he abandon the corpse on the levee? Whose car did he use? Are you following me, Jauncey?"

"I'm gettin' a headache, that's what. I know all this stuff, what'm I suppose to do 'bout it now?"

"You figured that sooner or later the cops would end up talking to Sharilla about the car. It's in her husband's name. And if the police questioned her, they'd question you too since you'd been using it."

"But you say I'm safe now, the car don't matter. I see what you mean—too many other things in the way. They goin' blame it all on Lionel, ain't they?"

"That's the way I see it. Nothing else makes sense. Lionel's gun was used on the dead guy he put into your car, same gun he was waving around today. That's first- or second-degree murder. It won't matter which, if Lionel dies. And it looks like he will. The police will also blame him for Sheldon's death because they'll figure he planted Sheldon's ID on the dead black guy. Though they'll never come up with a reason why he did it."

"That don't mean nothin', anybody could put that in his pocket."

"Yeah, but Lionel is the only guy wearing Sheldon's watch. So it might all be circumstantial, but they'll make the case for it. And Lionel, or an attorney appointed by the court for him, won't be on hand to tell a different story. They'll claim that they've found both men's killer. They'll be happy to close the files on them."

"They goin' think Lionel stole my Lincoln, you figure?"

"They already know it's stolen. Why not blame that on Lionel too? He's turning out to be pretty convenient, isn't he? Dead men often are. So you caught a break with the car, Jauncey. No one will ever connect you to Sheldon." Millie thought a minute and then said, "Sharilla hasn't reported it to the police, has she?"

"Uh-huh, no way. She got more sense than that. Anyway, she got her own car, almost done payin' it off. What I like to know now, what's goin' happen to that new Cadillac of Lionel's? Be a shame if he die and can't drive it. No good to nobody then."

"Forget about his car." Millie looked at her watch. I could still make an early-evening flight, she thought.

"New Caddy, just sittin' there? That's honey to a bear, girl. Lionel, he owe me a car, you remember? Just makes good sense to use his, now that he's passed. Won't matter none to him."

"The cops will probably impound it, Jauncey. You won't be able to touch it." She turned toward him: "Those keys that Lionel took—what do you know about them? The big one looked like a house key. I'm guessing Sheldon's house."

"Mmm, yeah, you probly right." She caught the evasive tone in his voice.

"You've been in his house, haven't you, Jauncey? Why didn't I see that right away? You went there in the dark, poked around, and picked up a few things. Sheldon's not around to object, you thought, so it's all free. What did you find?"

"Man had nothin' to steal. Big house with stuff I can't use—some chairs and sofas, shit like that, clothes that don't fit me. Big TV that I can't get out by myself."

99

"I didn't see a car key with the others," Millie said. "There should have been. One of those black key fobs. You have it, don't you?"

"Damn, you too fast for me, girl." A little jokiness returning to him. "When I visit Mr. Kukich house, I check out his garage, you know? Nice big car there, like new. Only 15,000 miles. Not even broke in good. Car has my name on it, know what I mean?"

"An SUV. Black."

"See? I knew it! You way out ahead of me. I like to know how you do it." Millie glanced at her watch again.

"You figure to drive that car away one of these days, don't you? You're just waiting till you think it's safe. Don't do it, Jauncey. You'll be back in Joliet for seven to ten this time. You're not the only one who's been to Sheldon's house. The cops know about this car too. Or they soon will if they don't already. If it's missing, every black and white in the city and every cruiser on the highway will be looking for it. Wipe the key clean and throw it away."

"You makin' it so I can't see around this problem. Dead men with two new cars, and you say don't touch 'em. I see it's for my own good, but damned if it don't go against my personality."

Millie reached into her bag. Brought out the Boulevard beer bottle from T-Bone Charlie's, holding it with a napkin. "Here, Jauncey, you forgot something." She started up the engine. "I've got to go. You'll have to call someone for a ride."

"You bring me that bottle from the bar? What for?"

"Think about it. Don't be so careless next time. Get out, Jauncey."

"Who am I goin' call, this time of day?"

"Call Sharilla."

"What you sayin'? I rather walk down the highway backward than call that woman. She be all over me. Why can't you give me a ride home?"

"Out, Jauncey."

Before his door had completely swung shut, her car was flinging gravel.

Chapter 15

SHOOTOUT AT KCI RESTAURANT

By Sherman Williams
Special to *The Star*

Shortly after 1:00 p.m. yesterday, a gunfight took place at T-Bone Charlie's Bar and Restaurant at Kansas City International Airport.

A Kansas City policeman, Detective Jameson Twist, shot and killed Lionel Weathers, an African-American man, who reportedly fired a pistol at him and three off-duty Federal officers after a violent altercation with them.

Witness accounts vary as to what triggered the fight. One of the Federal officers claimed that the others were assisting Mr. Weathers after he had broken a finger. Another witness said that the officers were trying to take the man into custody.

A waiter at the restaurant, Sol Steep, said that he had seen the broken finger and had attempted to aid Mr. Weathers with ice cubes wrapped in a bar towel.

Mr. Steep also said that the victim had been drinking with a blonde woman and another African-American man shortly before the incident. Ralph Raven, one of the Federal officers, confirmed this account.

Mr. Raven also claimed that he had been drinking and talking with the woman, whom he called "Buffy," about twenty minutes before Mr. Weathers and his companion arrived at the bar.

When the two men arrived, he said, "Buffy" abruptly left the bar area, sat in a booth with them, and ordered drinks. She and the second man left the premises a few minutes later, before the fatal quarrel erupted. The whereabouts of the couple are unknown.

Mr. Raven, an Air Marshal, arrived in Kansas City several days ago to assist the other two Federal officers, who were on assignment for the Witness Protection Program.

During a debriefing session, Mr. Raven stated that the woman had brown, not blonde, hair. He then claimed that she had phoned him at T-Bone Charlie's after she had left the scene. According to Mr. Raven, she told him that the gun used by Mr. Weathers yesterday was probably the same weapon used in the killing of an unidentified black man in North Kansas City more than a week earlier.

The bartender, Hollis Dodd, confirmed that a woman identifying herself as a police officer had called the bar, asking for Mr. Raven on urgent official business. Mr.

Dodd, however, said that the woman had identified herself as Lieutenant Bundy or Purdy. Authorities say that no one with either name is listed as a police officer in Missouri, Nebraska, or Kansas.

At a press conference this morning, Kansas City Police Chief Roy Weed read this brief statement: "At approximately 1:30 yesterday, Detective Jameson L. Twist of the Kansas City Police Department and three visiting Federal officers were fired upon by a then-unknown assailant at T-Bone Charlie's Restaurant and Bar, near the airport. Detective Twist returned fire and killed the man, since identified as Lionel Barber Weathers. It is not clear why Mr. Weathers started shooting. At this point in time, we are looking at every angle to get to the bottom of this incident. According to several eye-witnesses, the detective fired his weapon in a situation of self-defense. We will keep the media apprised as new evidence is developed in this case."

A news reporter asked whether the man and woman who had been seen with Mr. Weathers were connected to the shooting. "We're looking into it," Chief Weed said.

A second reporter asked why an unidentified woman would call an Air Marshal based in New York to discuss yesterday's incident and an earlier murder in Kansas City. "Well, could be we might ask Mr. Ravine that question," Chief Weed replied. "He has been cooperating fully."

The chief then terminated the press conference.

Chapter 16

Ray Roth

It was going to take awhile before Millie could talk to Ralph about the papers Jauncey had taken from Sheldon's suitcase. Of course they might not make a difference to anyone now, she thought. If the cops in Kansas City follow up on my phone call, it'll be clear to everyone that Sheldon's dead. "Everyone" meaning the fucking client. Ralph won't have to worry about the bozo anymore.

Meanwhile she had to take out a guy in Des Moines, a compulsive gambler, who, according to Philly, had skipped out on his payments to a shylock in Brooklyn. The shy had lent him 10 large with a 50 percent weekly vig. For quite a while, the guy, a compulsive gambler, was able to meet the vig. He was on a roll. So then he decided to borrow another 10. That was OK with the loan shark. Just keep up with the weekly interest.

Two, three weeks later the guy falls behind on the vig, which was now 10 thousand a week on the 20-thousand loan. He had hit a bad losing streak: the Giants, the Steelers, even the fucking Patriots, who were having a good year, couldn't cover the point spread. So he decided to take the 5 or 6 G's he had left and multiply it in a New Orleans casino where he'd once won a few bucks at blackjack. This plan, to no one's surprise, fell through. Then he decided to stiff the shy and just disappear. It took the shy maybe a week to locate him. Now he wanted the guy dead as a warning to other business associates not to fuck with him.

In other words, Millie figured, this was a routine case with typical sordid details. Sheldon's case had had a lot of interesting angles. But this job? On a scale of 1 to 10 on the Interesting Scale, Millie put it on the 2, right above target practice in the rain.

So from the get-go Millie was a little bored with the career trajectory of the gambler. The whole thing a big come-down after the past few days in Kansas City with Lionel, Jauncey, and the Feds. But it was Ralph's job to give her the details on this contract, and it was her job to listen.

They were having coffee and donuts in his office. Ralph had a new plant near the front window, something with fat green leaves sitting in a bright red pot. Ficus, she thought. "Ralphie, why did you only buy glazed this time?" Millie asked, walking her fingers through the Dunkin' Donuts box. "I thought you liked a variety. You couldn't get enough of the old-fashioned the other day, or was it the crullers?"

"Funny thing, Millie. Today—this morning—Stuart, my friend on Washington Street there, he just gave me a dozen. Free. He came up to me, 'Ralph, you're here every day of the week, same time on the dot. Wish to hell I could get my employees to do that,' he said. 'Sometimes you buy three or four crullers, chocolate, whatever, sometimes a mixed dozen, but you always buy my donuts. For years now. Plus the coffee, of course. You're my best customer, hands down.' So I said, 'Stuart, you and I know each other now for what? Twenny-four, twenny-five years? At least. I like to come here, see you in the morning, pick up some fresh donuts. Gets my day going.'

"And Stuart, he says, 'Me too, Ralph, makes my day.' Stuart, you gotta understand, Millie, never talks. Just nods and shakes his head. So the little speech he comes up with, it surprised me. 'Tell you what,' he says. 'This batch here is right out of the oven. I'm gonna give you a dozen. No charge. Plus, here's a dozen donut holes, put 'em in a little sack for you. Also fresh from the oven. And here's a gift card here, it's good for a month. All you can eat, on the house. To show my appreciation.' I never heard him say that much in all the time I know him.

"'What can I say, Stuart?' I said. 'Is this your birthday? You have a new girl friend?' 'No, no, nothing like that,' he said. 'I won a thousand bucks on one of those scratch cards you buy when you get gas. So I thought, Give something back to the community. That's you, Ralph, and Mrs. Lemon that's the secretary for the car lot down the street. She buys donuts for the salesmen.' Then I ask him, 'Stuart, how many donuts do you think, how many donuts, crullers, chocolate, Bavarian, strawberry—all of 'em—how many of 'em do you think I must of eaten all this time? Jesus, Stu, I should weigh a ton, but I don't.'

"'Ralph, listen, you have to eat breakfast, OK? You come in for my donuts and coffee. So what're you sayin'? Think of it this way: If you ate Cheerios and a banana every day, would you count up all the little O's?'

"Christ, Millie, I broke up at that. You get it, what he meant?"

"I'm right there with you, Ralph. Very funny guy." She finished one of the donuts, licked her fingers, and reached into her bag. "I brought you something from Kansas City, Ralphie." She handed him a white plastic sack. "Bought 'em at the airport." Ralph pulled out two pairs of Kansas City Royals socks. They had alternating dark blue, light blue, and gray diamonds. At the top: KC

Royals printed horizontally at the calf. "Ah, Millie, you shouldn't of. I don't have any of these, so, you know, thanks."

"Sure. Hope you enjoy them. That dark blue there, they call it Royal Blue. They'll go with your jammies, the navy flannels. You can get comfy with those and your fur-lined L. L. Bean slippers."

"No, first I'm gonna wear 'em to show Stuart," he said. "You know, he likes team socks and stuff too, only mostly the Red Sox and Celtics. Nothing wrong with that, but, you know, life is short." He picked up a donut. Put it back. "That reminds me, Millie," he said. "I was telling you about this guy who got into the loan shark. Where was I?"

"You gave me the essentials, Ralphie. Looks like a slam-dunk. Not that I won't be prepared."

"You don't want to hear more about the shy?"

"No reason to. I'm not going after him. Sometimes we don't know the first thing about the client. Usually we don't. All I need is the name of his guy and where he's staying. Then I tail him, check out his routine, and take him off the board. Quick and easy. A day, day and a half tops, he's gone, everyone's happy, including him, because now he doesn't have to worry all the time about being tailed."

"Yeah, very cute, but you figure it right," Ralph said. "You know," he said, "this is the first time we had to whack a guy in Des Moines? That's inneresting. How could he be that dumb, though, think he could hide out in a place like Des Moines?"

"Why not?" she said. "People try all kinds of places. What's wrong with Des Moines?"

She found out the next evening, after she had checked into her hotel. Nothing against Des Moines per se, you understand, but Jesus. What do people do in this town? Ten o'clock at night and everything's boarded up. Well, what do you do at night? Millie thought. When you're not working, you and Mandy stay at home and watch TV. On a really big night you call in an order for Chinese or Indian. Otherwise it's pizza from the joint across the street or raisin bran. You might as well live in Des Moines yourself, or up in Salem with the dead witches. Yeah, but still, she thought: The guy should have tried L.A. or New York, where he'd have a better chance of getting lost and wouldn't die of boredom in the meantime. If he's a gambler, he probably likes night life. The only night life I've seen here is the manager chasing a wino out of the lobby.

The following morning, Millie followed the guy from his motel room on the north side to a nearby diner. The diner was nice and clean, as featureless as the Iowa landscape. It was silver and looked like one of those travel trailers you see taking up too much space on the highways.

She sat a few stools away from him and watched in the mirror as he ate scrambled eggs and toast. She ordered oatmeal, bacon, and toast. The guy looked at the front page of his newspaper the whole time he was eating breakfast. Either a slow reader or he has something on his mind.

She tailed him back to the motel, which would have been up-to-date in the 1950s or 60s, maybe. It was a strip of twelve or fourteen units set perpendicular to the highway fifty yards away. She guessed it was a place where a lot of people rented rooms at hourly rates. Not a single car was in the parking lot.

At 1:30 the guy drove back to the diner. This time he sat at a table near the front window. He ordered a toasted cheese sandwich and a Coke. Millie went with the triple-decker sandwich. The day's special. She sat two tables behind him. While he ate, the guy stared out the window at the corn fields across the road. Three guesses what he's thinking about.

He wasn't too bad-looking. Think George Clooney with more gray hair, a hangover, and three days' growth. He was very pale. Well, what do you expect? He knows the long odds against him, and he's trying to figure a way to beat them. Trying to remember whether there's one last ace in the deck.

After lunch, the guy bought some apples from a mom-and-pop joint and a fifth of bourbon from the liquor store next door. Then he went back to the motel and stayed the night.

Milllie was in the diner a few minutes before him the next morning. It was raining. She had followed him from the motel for a few minutes and then moved into traffic ahead of him, keeping him in her rear-view mirror all the way to the diner. After breakfast she decided to do the guy when he got back from lunch. If she got home early, she could have supper with Mandy, maybe at a good restaurant downtown for a change. She drove to the motel and parked in the vacant lot behind the building.

The lock on his room was a joke. No electronic locks and plastic ID cards at this place. What you got instead were hollow wooden doors and dime-store locks. Practice for middle-schoolers learning the trade. Inside, Jesus H: dark as a cave, with the odor of stale butts and unwashed sheets. A reminder of human sorrow and failure. Don't get sentimental, she told herself. Just do the job and remember to wipe down the places you've touched.

The guy walked in at 3:00. Millie was sitting in a chair at the back, sitting in a shadow, her Glock across her lap. The black snout of the silencer doubled the length of the gun. The dark rain clouds helped to dim the place. He set down a brown plastic bag that had a loaf of bread sticking out of it. Shrugged out of his raincoat. Tossed it over the arm of a chair. Then froze. "Jesus Christ!" he said. He turned toward her. "You scared the living shit out of me! Who are you? Does this dump provide maid service?" He was breathing hard.

"Sit down," Millie said. "Over there." She gestured with her pistol. "That side of the room."

He looked at her. Sat down. "I didn't think they'd send a woman. That's progress, I guess. One small step for mankind. Womankind." He wiped his mouth with one hand and took another deep breath. "Mind if I have a cigarette first?"

"Go right ahead. Don't do anything dumb." She could hear semis rumbling and hissing down the highway.

"Don't worry, I won't. Want one?" He held out the pack. "You and the condemned man sharing a smoke? It'd make a touching scene."

She shook her head. "Bad for your health."

"I'll try to remember that," he said. He took a drag on the cigarette, pulling the smoke down deep into his lungs. "Isn't this the foulest place you've ever seen?" he said. "I once stayed at The Mark, on Madison Avenue, if you can believe it, one time when I was flush. I'd just won big at the Taj Mahal, in Atlantic City. I didn't stay the night because I was afraid of losing everything back to that pompous shit Trump."

"Gambling," she said. "I could never see the fun. I don't like leaving things to chance. I have a question: how much did you pay the shylock, overall, in just the vig? And what do you owe him now? I'm interested in how much it takes for a guy to offer a contract on you."

He didn't have to pause: "Forty-five thousand. I still owe twenty thousand principal from two separate loans and—let's see now—another thirty thousand vig this coming Friday."

"So from the 20 thousand you borrowed, you've already paid this guy 45 in interest, and now you owe him another 30 for a grand total of 50?"

"That's it. The wages of sin."

"I'm in the wrong business," she said.

"Believe me, you're not," he said. "It ruins your character."

"And after you couldn't pay, he was going to break your knees. That's what they do, isn't it?"

"That's only in cheap crime fiction, sweetheart, breaking your knees. This guy—Joey Angels, Joey D'Angeli—was going to set me on fire."

"Isn't that a little extreme?"

"I thought so, yeah."

"So you figured you'd lam out on him and—what?—start all over out here with the cows?"

"Listen: I didn't know what else to do, I was scared. I was one step past the end of my rope. Here's how bad it was: one day I went to see him at his social club. This is something a sane guy doesn't do—go into a Mafia social club. But I was desperate. I couldn't pay the vig, and I knew what was ahead of me. So I went in, walked up to him, sweating like hell, practically peeing my pants, and said, 'Joey, please, you know that I'll pay you, I've always paid, but now I need a little extra time. I'm begging you.' I even told him I'd sign over my car to him. He said, 'OK, sign over the car to me.' So the next day I went back to his club and signed the title over to him. The car was worth 10 thousand, easy, it's only three years old. I figured he'd deduct that amount and give me an extension on the vig. An extra week, at least, and then I'd figure something out.

"You can see how deluded I was. Now I had no car. How can you run around raising money without a car? But I also felt relief. An extra week was an eternity to me." He lit another cigarette. "Is this OK?" It was getting darker outside.

"It probably won't kill you," Millie said.

"I was in bad shape," he continued. "I'd signed away my car with no guarantee from Joey D that he'd credit it against my account. He told me, 'Roth, you lousy Jew, you still owe me. You have till Friday to come up with

20 large. Art and Jimmy will be around to see you. You got three days.' I almost fell down, I was so scared. I was crying. 'Joey, please, I don't know what to do,' I said. He was enjoying it. This was fun for him. At least we were alone in a back room where nobody could see me."

"You said he was going to set you on fire. Did he tell you that?" Millie asked.

"He told me, 'Find the fucking money one way or the other, Roth, or you'll end up a toasted marshmallow like that fucking Castro. Remember him?' 'No,' I said, 'I never heard of him.' 'Ask around,' said Joey. 'Ask people what happened to Roland Castro when he insulted Joey Angels.'

"That night I asked a guy in my neighborhood, a retired cop. I figured he'd know. I didn't tell him I was in trouble. I just asked the question. This retired police officer, Manny Padilla, nice guy, looked at me and said, 'Ray, you're drowning in fear. I can smell it. The case he mentioned, Roland Castro, he was a guy who got torched in his apartment a few years ago, him and his cat. Story is, he was into D'Angeli for quite a bit—thirty, forty grand—and either couldn't or wouldn't pay. One version of it has him saying, "Fuck you, Joey, I'm not gonna pay you," but I never believed it. That's just committing suicide. Anyway, what happened, day or two later, Castro and his apartment went up in smoke. We found plenty of evidence to prove arson, but nobody was ever charged. You know why? We couldn't find anybody who'd talk. No mystery who was behind it, but try to find a squealer.' Then Manny told me, 'Ray, the only advice I can give you is go to the cops. Joey is criminally insane. If you're into him and can't pay, just go to the cops. That's your best chance.'

"I didn't even plan the next move. I grabbed some clothes, emptied my ATM, and took the first plane out of LaGuardia to Chicago. Next day, I drove down here in a rental. And now here we are."

"End of story," Millie said. "End of the line."

"Yup, unless you let me go."

"Can't do that. I got a contract."

"Refund the money. Say you couldn't find me."

"I didn't find you in the first place. The shylock did. Or some hacker did it for him."

He pressed his lips together. Raised his eyebrows. "My credit card. Shit. I used it to fly and I used it to rent a car. Somebody traced it."

"That's the way it's done, yeah. Did you use the card here at the motel?"

"I paid cash," he said. "Used a fake name. Maybe that'll help."

"It might've bought you a little time. It won't change anything. I found you. They will too. Where's your car? I didn't hear you drive up."

"I parked it by the office. My space was a big rain puddle. Look, we could torch my car, put all my stuff in it, my clothes, my ID, make it look like I went with it."

"And where would we get a body? The cops are sticklers, you know, they'd need to see the bones."

"I give up. Just make it quick, OK, sweetheart? One more thing: there's a duffel bag in the closet. It has a lot of money in it. I never used it to gamble. It wasn't mine. Give it to the Carmelite Sisters of Baltimore. They're a good outfit. They do a lot of good. I promised my mom on her deathbed I'd give it to them."

Millie nodded. "That's beautiful, Ray. Just beautiful. I'm impressed."

"I was hoping you'd like it."

"There's no money, is there?"

"Huh-uh."

"And Joey D wasn't going to set you on fire."

"No, but the demented fuck incinerated Castro and he put out a contract on me. You're not here to give me a blow job."

"Shall we get it over with? One more smoke?"

"He's going to get away with it again, isn't he? God-damn it. I hate that. He's even been bragging lately how he contracted out a kill on a guy who used to be a friend. They were buddies in a Toronto gang, back in the day. In Joey's mind, the kill is good advertisement, I sup-pose, showing how much reach he has. How ruthless he can be." The rain was coming down harder now. It was getting darker in the room.

"Run that by me again," Millie said, "that business about Toronto. And no lies this time, or I'll empty the pistol into your chest. Who was this old friend?"

"How would I know? Jesus. Joey just let it out that he nailed a guy who was going to testify against him. I didn't pay much attention, I had my own problems. The guy, I don't know, was supposed to be untouchable, but Joey got to him."

"How? How did he get to him?" Millie's eyes were wide, surprised-looking.

"Hell, I . . . I think . . . look, give me a minute here." He looked down, nodded to himself. "OK, the story on the street was, Joey got in contact with some hot-shot firm with a triple-A rating or something, guaranteed quick and clean work. A hush-hush outfit somewhere on the East Coast, nobody knows exactly where. He paid them to kill the guy."

"I never heard of such a place, Ray. Sounds like an urban legend. Or you're lying again. Tell me the rest."

"I don't know the rest, and I'm not lying."

"There's more, and you know it. The victim—how could he be untouchable?"

"Oh. Well, the government was hiding him some-where. Witness Protection Bureau. Is that it?"

"Close enough. Witness Protection Program." God-dammit, she thought, it's all been right in front of me.

"How do you penetrate that kind of outfit?" he said. "That's like the FBI or the Secret Service, for Christ's sake. But Joey's a maniac. That's the only explanation.

Nothing stops him." Ray looked at Millie. "He hired you to take me out, didn't he?"

"I've never seen or talked to your boy D'Angeli in my life. What else do you know about him?"

"Nothing. A rumor. Take it for what it's worth. He claims that the hitter who got to the Federal witness cheated him somehow. He's insulted. And now he's going to track the guy down and take him out. It's all bullshit, of course. Joey's just talking big after he got to the guy who turned on him."

"That son-of-a-bitch."

"Who, Joey? Or do you mean the dead guy? Did you know him?"

"Ray, where was the man when he was iced? That's the last question. Take your time. Have another cigarette." It was late afternoon now. Almost full dark in the room. The rain had stopped.

"Before I die, I'd like to know your name. You know mine."

"Will you for Christ's sake just answer the fucking question? Think. Can you remember where?"

"Yeah. Yeah, I can. Kansas City. What difference does it make? What if I'd said Waco, or Denver, or Miami? It wouldn't mean anything to you." He was sweating now. The drops were draining off his brows. "Just pull the trigger, damn it, I can't stand this anymore. I'm tired. Fuck it. Fuck everything."

"I'm not going to shoot you." She picked up her bag and put the pistol in it.

"What? What the hell? Now you want to torture me with false hope? No way, honey. I'm getting up now, and I'm going to get a drink." He pointed to the bottle on the night stand. "Shoot me when you're ready."

"I'm not going to shoot you, Ray. You're off the hook. I'm going to whack somebody else. You're the wrong guy. Relax. Pour me an inch of that bourbon."

"For Christ's sake, what's going on here? I fucking don't get it." He was holding a glass, but his hands were shaking. Most of the bourbon was dribbling on to the rug. "I don't get any of this."

"Let's just say that you drew to an inside straight flush."

Chapter 17

Iowa Take-Out

Ray tossed back his drink. Poured another and took it down. Millie sipped hers, savoring the sweet, woody taste. Then breathed in the aroma. She sipped a little more, letting the heat slide down her throat. It helped her think. Ray was slumped in his chair, moaning or sighing, she couldn't tell which. The rain had let up, but it was drizzling. Only a few smears of light remained in the room.

So, she thought, Joey Angels wants to whack the shooter who took out Sheldon. The shooter who got paid for the kill, but didn't immediately produce a body. I told Ralph, Let's call it off, we'll reschedule, what's the difference? Well, Millie, he wouldn't reschedule, and now here we are. Deal with it. OK: how would this clown know where to look for me? There's no trail. The phone blinds and cutouts are foolproof. So just relax, the guy's blowing smoke.

OK, but let's just say you wanted to do it, she thought. How would you go about it, taking down the shooter you'd hired to ice somebody else, but you'd never met? Where would you start? First thing: who are the players on the board? Joey Angels, of course, he's number one. How does he get it going? Joey talks to people, finds out from a low-life pal in his social club, say, that you call such-and-such a phone number if you want to put out a contract. Guy who answers the phone has no name, says he'll make some calls and get back to you. Same guy calls another number, and so on through a couple more links. Finally they get through to Philly, who calls Ralph, and we're all set.

Not even the Feds could trace those connections, let alone this gangster with his hair on fire. No way to follow them. Some calls are re-routed, some are made on flip phones that you burn after one call. There's no trail to follow. Yeah, that's all true if you start on his end, Millie. What if you start at our end? Could you do it that way? Start with the hitter taking down the mark. Tell the shooter where the mark's going to be. Get there first. Then shoot the shooter.

It's possible, she thought, but you'd need a second shooter or be there to do the job yourself. You'd have to be pretty good to pull it off, too. The timing would have to be perfect. And you'd have to figure out what to do with the guy named on the original contract. Is he going to patiently wait to be whacked while you . . .?

"Christ," Ray said, "I should be happy I'm alive, but I'm depressed as hell. Can I get up now?"

"Sit down. I'm trying to think," Millie said. "See if there's anything left in that bottle. Maybe there's some you didn't pour on to the rug." She was back in the chair on the other side of the bed. "If there is, drink it. Get yourself together. It's time for the next move."

"I'm really, really tired," he said. "My god, I feel awful. Being dead would be easier."

"Raymond, stiffen up, for Christ's sake. Balls on the floor." She paused to let that sink in. All she could see of him was his hand holding the glass. "Try to pay attention." Her voice was now calm, a smooth black ribbon streaming out of the shadows. She heard far-off thunder. She started to listen for other sounds as well.

"Ray," she said, "I think we're going to have a little trouble here soon," Millie said. "Those guys who work for your banker—what were their names? Artie and Something. You remember."

"Those guys? Art and Jimmy. Why do you want to know?"

"They might be on their way to see us."

"Those assholes out here, in Iowa? Why would they be here? They've never been west of Jersey City. They'd get lost trying to find this place."

"Joke all you like, Ray, but it adds up."

"What adds up? To me, nothing's made sense since I walked in that door. I thought Joey hired you. Why else did you plan to shoot me? But then I'm not sure why you changed your mind, either. God, I'd like to have another bottle of Jim Beam."

"Here's how I figure it, Ray: you're the bait. They're going to use you to get to me. At first I wasn't sure about the timing. But now I am. It makes sense. Hire me to whack you, but send out a couple of bozos ahead of time to see what happens. After I do you, they get rid of me. Understand?"

"First me and then you," he said, "just like that. You know, sweetheart, I hear your words, and I know I should understand them. But I don't. My brain is flatlining." He was clicking his cigarette lighter on, closing the lid, clicking it on again. Then off.

As he was talking, Millie pulled out the Glock. The pistol had a full magazine, fifteen 9mm cartridges, ready to fire. She reached into her bag for another magazine. Put it into her left jacket pocket. What else now? Don't stand in the sight line of the door. Stay away from the window. Tell Ray. OK, that's it. Locked and loaded.

"Ray," Millie said, "quit playing with that damned cigarette lighter, you're making me nervous. Give it here.

Don't turn on the light. Just hand it to me." He stood up and handed her the Zippo across the bed. It was then that she heard the sound she'd been expecting—car tires grinding slowly over the gravel of the parking lot.

"I wish I hadn't said it might be better being dead. Please, God, that was somebody else named Ray. I take it back."

"Be quiet."

"You know, it's funny. I'm not even Jewish."

"D'Angeli will be relieved to know that. Now listen up," Millie said. "Quit babbling. If you play your cards right, you might walk out of here alive."

"Cards? I need a fucking gun."

"Well, you can't have mine. Here," she said, as she walked toward him. "Here's a can of Mace. Be careful to point it in the right direction."

"Jesus, why don't we just leave? You ever think of that?"

"We have visitors. A car just pulled in next door. No headlights, very quiet. I don't think it's the Welcome Wagon. There's one guy for sure, maybe two. They're not out of the car yet."

"Maybe they're tourists, just checking in after a Big Whopper and fries," he said."

"Don't talk," she said.

"All right, all right. What do you want me to do?" He seemed to be paying attention.

"I don't know yet." She was whispering. What are the possibilities? Millie thought. Straight in through the door, gun in hand? What if there are two? One stays with the car, acts as back-up. OK. What advantages does he have? Visualize. What would he do? Is he another shooter? Or: Christ, she thought: Molotov cocktails. Joey's goons burning up that guy Castro. Will it be the first guy who tosses the firebomb, or the second? Millie heard the muffled sound of car doors easing shut.

"Ray, peek out the window. What do you see?"

"Car. Maybe eight or ten feet back. One guy, standing on this side."

"What's in his hands?"

"Gun in his left hand. Can't see the other one."

"Ray, when I tell you, open the door fast and stand to the side, against the wall. I'll be over here. Keep away from the window."

"OK," he said. It came out as "Khhaay."

They waited. Three minutes. Four. Ray's breathing made a whistling sound. Five minutes. Take a deep breath. Hold it. Release. Six minutes. Somebody started to twist the doorknob slowly, quietly. Millie hoped that Ray could stay cool. "Now!" she whispered.

Ray jerked open the door. The guy stumbled forward, recovered his balance, wheeled to his right, spraying the room with bullets. Turned back the other way, toward Millie, who fired three quick rounds into his chest. She glanced out the door. The car looked empty. He's out there, though, she thought. Down on the seat or waiting on the other side. Only places he can be. She quickly looked again, shot two rounds through the windshield. That's five. "Ray," she said, "drag this guy out of the way. Close the door." She moved out, fast, diving to the ground, rolling forward, now up on one knee, firing a round through each of the car's side windows, another round through each door. Nine. Ran to the rear of the car, keeping back a few feet, in a crouch now, then standing. She put three shots diagonally through the back window, hoping the guy would eat it if he stood up. Three more into the trunk, hoping to hit the gas tank. No luck.

Down on her knee again, Millie ejected the empty magazine, slammed another into the grip, looking right and left. No one. In a crouch again, she moved quickly to her right, came up on the other side of the car firing straight ahead. The guy was waiting for her but startled by the real thing. She hit him in the thigh, shoulder, and chest. The wick had been lit, and the guy was now struggling to throw the firebomb at her. Millie fired steadily as he went down, the glass bottle detonating in his hand before he fell. For a second he was a human torch. Then he was nothing. Less than nothing.

The burning liquid streamed in front of him and flowed toward the car. Millie ran back to the motel. The door was still open. She shouted, "Ray! Let's go!" Nothing. "Ray! Goddammit, let's go!" The first guy was still in the doorway. There was no reply from Ray. Not a sound. The air was humid, heavy, smelling of burnt fuel.

Millie knew what she'd find even before she flipped on the light switch: Ray, fallen against the wall, a bullet hole in his chest, blood on his pale shirt. But Ray wasn't there. Not in the bedroom, and not in the bathroom.

She ran out, looked for his car. Gone. That's your last ace, Ray. You'd better hope it's the right card.

What now?

There was one last thing to do. She hurried to the riddled car, aimed the Glock, and made sure she ruptured the gas tank. Then flicked the wheel of Ray's Zippo and tossed the lighter underneath. As she quick-stepped back, the car exploded. A bloom of shimmering yellow lit up the parking lot and warmed her face. A second explosion and an arm of orange-red flame thrust itself into Ray's motel room. Somewhere in her mind she pictured the dazzling night colors of explosions at Fallujah and Mosul a few years back, at the far end of nowhere.

She heard police sirens and wailing firetrucks in the distance. The whole place will be cinders by the time they get here, she thought.

Chapter 18

Story Time

I don't get it," Ralph told Millie. "I just fuckin' don't get it."

Ralph, Millie, and Mary Michael were sitting around the antique oak table in Ralph's kitchen having coffee and donuts. In the next room, Millie remembered, he had an old oak rocking chair with curlicues carved into the back and a rounded-out bottom made of something that looked like cardboard. Both pieces of furniture had come down to him from his mother, Sheila. She had received them from her mother, Brid. Continental Removals, of course, was another bequest from Sheila to Ralph.

Mary Mike was wearing what Millie at first took for a tie-dyed bed sheet. It turned out to be a green muumuu with pink Hawaiian flowers. Her hair looked like a bird's nest, something that no doubt began life as a Gibson Girl do. Ralph had on a pair of dark blue ribbed socks with kidney-shaped light blue blobs. Millie wore her matching black Under Armor leggings and pullover.

"It's not very complicated, Ralph," Mary Mike said. "It was a double-cross. The client tried to take out Millie.

First, he hired her to kill the Jewish guy in Des Moines. Then he sent out two shooters to finish her off after she did the first guy. Only she figured it all out and iced the two shooters instead. Fortunately for the Jewish guy, he got away."

"He wasn't Jewish," Millie said. "Remember?"

"I guess that's right, sweetie, but my point is," Mary Mike said, "the two men who showed up, they were there to put you out of business. The gambler—this Ray person—wasn't their biggest worry."

"Think of it this way, M. Joey Angels, our pain-in-the-ass client for a long time now, did want Ray dead. But he wanted me dead too. He thought I'd take out Ray and then hang around until his goons showed up and whacked me. Or maybe he thought they'd do Ray first—I don't know—and then do me. But that'd never work because I don't enter a scene unless I know it's clean and has a clear way out."

"So what you're explaining," Ralph said, "is the set-up you figured these jokers had to have, because otherwise how would it work?"

"You might put it that way, Ralphie," she said. "You know, I had a bad feeling about this contract almost from the beginning."

"This feeling you had, this hunch," Mary Mike said. "Something seemed a little off, so you weren't comfortable with the deal, is that it?"

"Um-hmm," Millie said. "At the beginning, I thought this job would be a no-brainer. This guy's scared enough to run, but dumb enough to leave a trail through the woods? Should be easy work. But then I got to thinking, maybe too easy. I was starting to get suspicious before I got on the plane."

"You thought it was a slam-dunk, that's what you told me," he said. "I thought so too. Coulda sub-contracted this one out to the cleaning lady, I figured, save airfare."

"Good luck finding a cleaning lady at that place," Millie said.

"So what started you off? You had easy contracts before that turned around on you. Why lose sleep over this one?"

"Yeah, but those other jobs developed a hitch on the scene, little things that were easy to fix. They didn't look spooky at an early stage of the operation. Anyway, I always think through an assignment, that's just my nature," Millie said. "Don't trust appearances. If there's anything I learned in Iraq, that was it. But being in this business, of course, you develop that attitude too."

"I'm proud of you, Millie," Mary Mike said. "Remember that story I told you about Sister Immaculata? 'Don't trust appearances'—her very words."

"Yeah, I remember," Millie said.

"'Wheels within wheels,' Sister used to say to us girls. And you know what, honey? Those words of wisdom have served me to this very day. Millie, you're just like Sister Immaculata—a deep thinker. Did I ever tell you about the time I had to fix up a guy in Saratoga? This man, he trained horses for the races there, and he decided to set up a little business of his own on the side. He started doping some of the horses on the sly, in cahoots with a couple of gangsters. So what you had was one operation going on inside the other. The long-shots won, and the favorites . . . "

"Mary Mike, I gotta tell you," Ralph said, "I gotta ask you, let's just clear up this other thing first, OK? And you know, I already know that story. I know about Viggo Lapinski there in Saratoga already, how you took him out with some of the dope he was using on the ponies."

"Wolanski, Ralphie, it wasn't Lapinski," Mary Mike said.

"No, but what I'm saying here is let's run through Iowa first, that's all."

Millie stood up and stretched. She pointed to the box of donuts on the counter. "Ralphie, are you saving those donuts for supper, or do we get more than just one? I'm not trying to push you here, I'm just wondering."

"Oh, sure, sure, Mil, have all you want. Let's finish 'em. Don't let 'em get stale."

"You should try a few from Linda's Donuts sometime," Mary Mike said, "over to Belmont there. Hard to beat Dunkin' Donuts, I know that, but one day I went there with this woman Muriel I know from our investment club, and my god, Ralph, you wouldn't believe how good they were."

"Come on, Mary Mike, what are you talking about?" he said. "Everybody knows Dunkin' is the heavyweight champ of donuts. They're the fuckin' gold standard of New England. Am I right, Millie? Help me out here."

"I'm still waiting for another one, remember? Right now, Ralphie, I'd give an ovary for a chocolate frosted or a French cruller. You know how hungry I get after a workout."

"Where the hell's my head today? Here, Millie, take one. But so: what were you worried about, with this job?"

"I wasn't exactly worried, Ralphie, more like leery." She ate the old-fashioned in two bites. Pointed at the box for another. "I was just being cautious, I guess, pressing to see where it was soft. After all, what you don't know can get you killed out in the field." She looked into her cup. Empty. "Ralph," she said, "what's the chance of getting a little more coffee too? Or you gonna warm it up in the morning?"

"I'd like some too, Ralph," Mary Mike said, shoving her cup across the table. "And then I'll make a fresh pot. But I want to hear what Millie's saying before I get up."

"So after Ralph and I went over the details, I ordered my kit from Mr. Moustakas. Not the CR-2, just the Basic Disposal. Keep it simple, I figured. Then I went home and packed the minimum—jeans, Nikes, black leather jacket, black turtleneck, a couple of wigs, dark glasses, and a nifty fedora, in case I wanted to pass for a guy."

"Mil, wait a minute here, will ya?" Ralph said. "What difference does it make if you're a guy? You're just gonna pop some stranger in a motel room—*patta-pow*!—and you're outta there. He's not gonna care if you're a guy or Shirley Temple."

"I'm just giving you the background, Ralphie—how I started out thinking I could just mail this one in, it was so easy. OK?"

"Yeah, OK. I just got ahead of the story, that's all. I thought you were already on the plane there, and you were going to tell us what changed your mind."

Mary Mike held up her hand. "Ralph. Ralphie. Let the girl tell her story the way she wants to. I don't mean to be critical, hon', you know that. She's just trying to answer your question in a way that we can all understand."

"What, I can't talk now?" he said.

"Ralph, dear, you can talk all you want, just please shut up, is what I'm saying," she said.

Ralph closed his eyes and nodded his head, managing somehow to convey both patience and wisdom.

"But you're going to have to wait a minute, Millie," Mary Mike said. "I have to visit the little girls' room. It's all that coffee going through me. I'll brew a fresh pot when I get back."

Two minutes flat, Mary Mike's back and the coffee maker's gurgling.

Millie continued: "OK, so I got to thinking: why would the shylock pay us a lot of money to ice this guy, maybe more than the guy owes in the first place? Why not just write it off, I thought, price of doing business. Like the banks with their credit cards. Some people can't pay, but you still make money on the high interest you charge. Or the shy could've asked a dumb-ass cousin who spends all of his time in the pool hall. Or maybe a Made Guy he knows from grade school. What I'm saying is, he had cheaper ways."

"So the shark's going to be out another stack of bills, and what does he get out of it?" Ralph said. "And if it wasn't the money, you're asking, what was it?"

"That's what I thought, yeah. But I didn't have enough information then to make a guess. At the time I figured, OK, he's busy running some other game or he wouldn't have hired a professional. But that didn't feel right. And I kept chewing on this other thing too: he had to pay an expert to track Ray all the way to Des Moines."

"I didn't think of these angles, Millie," Mary Mike said. "It looked like a simple contract to me. But you read the fine print, and you saw the Devil himself in the details, didn't you?" she added. "Isn't that what they always say, the Devil's in the details? Well, now you know it's true. Mother of God, I need a real drink. Ralphie, do you have any whiskey I can put in this coffee?"

Ralph reached into a cabinet for the Wild Turkey. He poured a shot into her half-filled mug. "All the way up, Ralphie, I'm thirsty." When he was done, he pointed the bottle at Millie. She shook her head no.

"And that story the shy put out, that he wanted to whack the target as a warning to other guys. Was that just bullshit?" Ralph said.

"No, he was serious," Millie said. "That's the way he thinks. But it makes sense only in his looney-tunes world."

"How do you figure?" he said.

"OK, he decides to send a message: 'See what happens if you don't pay me? You're a dead man.' So, yeah, people get the message: 'He's a tough guy, but so what? It doesn't apply to me.' How many broke guys are going to think about that kind of fallout? If a guy's down enough to borrow from a loan shark in the first place, he's not thinking about the future. He needs the money today. He'll deal with tomorrow tomorrow."

"That's from Shakespeare, right?" Mary Mike said. "I remember it from Sister Costanza's senior English."

"If it is, M, I couldn't tell you. I didn't do the homework."

"Well, I just have a good memory, I guess. But to go back to what you were saying, did you figure out this stuff before you met the mark?" Mary Mike said.

"Not all of it, no. I'm just saying that when I started to look at the money angle, the deal didn't stand up. Who hires a trigger to kill a guy who's already given you thousands in vig? What's the motive?"

"So it didn't look solid," Ralph said, and you thought— what?—this fucking client has put us in the shit before, what's he up to now?"

"Yup," Millie said. "Now, of course, we know that D'Angeli's completely out of the box. He's off the reservation. Capable of any twisted thing at all. We had no way of knowing that beforehand."

She got up again, walked to the counter, and brought back the box of donuts. A Boston Kreme and a blueberry cake donut found their way to her plate. She dipped the cake donut into her coffee. "Mmm," she said, "the way to a woman's heart." Mary Mike, in the meantime, topped up with a couple of fat splashes of Turkey.

Ralph said, "I can't get over how that son-of-a-bitch hired us so he could take you out. Plus, he wanted you to whack the runner first so he could get his money's worth."

"He's a real cupcake, yeah. Here's what happened, I think. When Ray did a runner, D'Angeli took it as a slap in the face, so he had to kill Ray to save his reputation. Then he must have figured, hey, this is a good time to take the shooter off the board too. Make it a two-fer. Whack Ray and me together."

"OK, so you're in Iowa now," Ralph said. "What happens next?"

"I went to my hotel, picked up my kit at UPS, and started looking for the target. There were only three or four possible motels, so finding him was no problem."

"Millie, I have to ask this, because I'm still in the dark about something. Did you see anyone else following your guy?"

"C'mon, M, you think I wouldn't notice? That's the first thing I think about: is there anybody else on the set? Nobody even looked at Ray. Believe me: there was no one."

"No, I know, dear," said Mary Mike. "I just keep wondering how those two fellows showed up when they did. They didn't see you go into the motel room. If they had, they could have shot you when you left."

"Um-hmmm."

"And they weren't late, either, or you'd have been halfway back to Logan when they got there."

"Um-hmm."

"All right, then: they didn't know whether you'd done Ray, they didn't know whether they were early or late, and maybe they didn't even know for sure whether they had the right place."

"They knew they had the right place," Millie said.

"How? You said Ray's car was gone."

"Not then. It was in front of the manager's office when the goons got there. They spotted it and went in to ask the manager which room was Ray's. They couldn't tell because there were no other cars in front of the motel, and all the rooms were dark."

"You didn't tell us this part, Millie," said Ralph. "Ray was the only guy renting a room?"

"The one and only guest at the Ritz Iowa, yeah," she said. "Sheets changed monthly, free Wi-Fi, get away from it all. I knew his room number from the day before, but D'Angeli's guys had to ask."

Jerry Masinton

"And so what happened? The manager told 'em, right?"

"Ralphie," Mary Mike said, "Millie doesn't know what the manager said, do you, hon'?"

"He must have told them, yeah. That's the way I see it. He gave them Ray's room number, and they killed him so they wouldn't leave a witness. One shot in the forehead. They probably forced him to talk, but I'm just guessing. The cops found the body before the fire had been put out."

"OK," Ralph said, "but something's missing here. This is where I fuckin' don't get it, how it worked out the way it did."

"If you'll just listen, Ralphie, she'll tell us," Mary Mike said. "She's getting to it."

"OK, I'm listening. But how could those apes time it perfect, to show up when they did? Any moron knows that a good hitter's in and out of that motel room in thirty seconds. No way for them to know the moment she's there, unless they followed her."

"Which they didn't, Ralphie," Mary Mike said. "Otherwise they wouldn't have talked to the manager."

"The timing was pretty good," Millie said. "I can't explain it. Maybe they drove past the motel a few times, waiting to see who showed up. After a while, they get impatient and decide to check with the manager. Who knows? But the important thing is: they got there when they did. They didn't know it, but they were dead on arrival."

"How do you mean, Millie?" Mary Mike said.

"Because I was ready for them. 'Readiness is all,' you ever hear that saying, M?"

"No, dear, I don't think I have. That's from the Bible, isn't it?"

"No, Shakespeare. I saw the Mel Gibson movie."

"Hey, what're you guys, showing off? 'A rose is a rose is a rose,' that's fuckin' Shakespeare, too, OK? Now:

132

why didn't you just shoot this guy Ray right off the fuckin' bat and come home. Then who gives a shit if you're ready or not?"

"I wanted to know how much he owed the shylock, that's why," Millie said. "Like I said, the contract didn't sit right with me. So I asked him—I asked Ray—'How much did you pay this guy in interest?' And: 'How much do you still owe?'"

"And what was it?" Ralph asked.

"Forty-five in vig. Fifty outstanding. But the fifty was bogus. D'Angeli had already made a lot of money off him."

"So you realized what, that this fucking Joey was bananas, which you, you already had an idea he was, right? But where does that get you? I'd a popped him there, took off, and went home."

"You?" Mary Mike said. "You never popped anyone in your life, Ralphie! Mother of God, you're strictly an office guy. Nobody's criticizing you, of course, but you don't even know where the trigger is, let alone how to whack a guy." Her bird's nest was now sliding over her left eye and ear.

Ralph closed his eyes and shrugged. What're you gonna do?

"Maybe I should have taken him out then, yeah," said Millie, "but I thought, give him a few more minutes, he's not going anywhere. Let him enjoy his last cigarette. I wanted to hear his story."

"I don't see why you took the time to hear this guy's story, Mil, I really don't. Look, you gotta be nervous as hell, your date has just showed up. The guy, the guy's probably so scared he's eating his cigarettes by now, not smoking 'em. And you stop for what, a story?"

"I actually think he appreciated the extra time, Ralphie. And no, I wasn't nervous. I was trying to learn something. Don't forget what I told you: I wanted to know why the loan shark put out a contract on him in the first place—that's the first question I asked. So he told me, and that part of his story led to the part where D'Angeli set Roland Castro on fire, and so on. Good thing I was paying attention, too, because later on I knew what to expect when those two alligators showed up.

"But," she said, taking a cruller from Ralph's plate and taking a bite, "but the big payoff—which you ought to understand by now—if you've been paying attention, which sometimes I wonder whether you are, Ralphie. Paying attention. You should realize by now that I had put the bits and pieces of Ray's story together—including the freaky rumors he had heard about Joey—and figured out how that slime-ball had managed to put out a contract on me even without actually knowing who I was. And that's why I'm going to visit Joey of the Angels soon and renegotiate the contract." She turned both palms up. "*Capisce?*"

"Millie, oh my god, I'm going to wet my drawers!" Mary Mike said, appreciating Milllie's little performance.

"Awright, awright, I get it, you made your point," Ralph said. "But what're the odds? It wasn't like this fuckin' bozo picked us out of the Yellow Pages. He just got lucky, right?"

"I don't think he's feeling too lucky, Ralphie," Millie said. "He's probably shitting a major brick because by now he knows that he doesn't know who the contractor is. He knows that Art and Jimmy have been iced, but he doesn't know who did it."

"Oh, Millie," Mary Mike said. "This is beautiful! The guy doesn't know who you are, but he knows you're going to try to whack him."

"Um-hmmm."

"And he can't put out a contract on you because, even if he hires another hitter, who does he say you are?"

"Yeah."

"I'll bet there's still more to it, isn't there?" Mary Mike said.

"Um-hmm," Millie said. "D'Angeli doesn't know who to run from. And he doesn't know whether Ray is involved, or just got lucky and escaped. So he doesn't know how many to look for."

"And he's not going to be looking for a woman," Mary Mike said.

"Lucky for me."

"But I still don't get one thing," Ralph said. "Or maybe I do, but it bothers me. It was pure chance that D'Angeli's two goons showed up when they did. Right?"

"That's right, Ralphie," Millie said. "They just got lucky."

Chapter 19

I know what you do, *Tesora*

That evening Millie and Mandy ate at George's Passing, an upscale place where you typically paid more for a meal than for a vintage Ferrari. Millie preferred diners and pizza joints, but Des Moines had convinced her that life could be dull as well as nasty, brutish, and short and that she and Mandy needed to get out more often. The restaurant was a tribute to high-modern discomfort: all squares and oblongs, polished wood, and brushed-metal tubes, with globes of light hanging from the twenty-foot ceiling.

Mandy was wearing a dark wool Ann Taylor blazer, first-world ankle jeans with savagely shredded knees and thighs, and red platform dress sandals. Along with the blazer she wore a white georgette split-neck blouse with nothing under it. She was trying for the slightly slutty but wholesome look of the all-American girl. Malcolm, her stylist, had arranged her hair in a French twist with a few artfully disposed loose strands.

Millie's dark hair was cut in a side-swept bob. She had on True Religion low-rise jeans, a black Bailey boat-neck tee, and a Saint Laurent olive-green bomber jacket that had cost four times as much as her new Sig Sauer.

Mandy pointed her chin at the bar. "Hey, *Tes, guarda quei due uomini.*"

The couple Mandy pointed out were thirty-something men with long, swept-back blonde hair and matching pink shirts. The sleeves were rolled once and pulled back to the middle of their muscular forearms. Millie glanced at the men and said, "Italian, Priss? What's the occasion?"

"Just using my education, *Tes.* Don't you think Daddy would like that? He practically lapsed into cardiac arrest, you know, when I majored in languages instead of something useful quote unquote. I said to him, 'Daddy, if you wanted me to do something useful, why didn't you sign me up as a plumber's apprentice instead of sending me to Yale?' I shouldn't have pushed him that far, should I? I hope I'm still in his will. At least he doesn't know what I'm doing now. He thinks I'm a fashion designer."

"They're gayer than springtime, Priss. Is that what I'm supposed to see?"

"No, *Tes*, it's their killer shirts, they're Jared Langs. Don't you just love them? That shade of pink is so carnivorously tropical!" She wiggled her shoulders. "The criss-cross lining of the cuffs? Yummy. Shall we try to pick them up? We could ask them where they buy their shirts."

"And then talk about what—thongs versus briefs? Shaving and waxing?"

"Gay men are encyclopedias about such things, *Tes.* Papillon—you remember him—knows practically everything about stuff like removing hair. I think he has a Black Belt in waxing. I totally couldn't exist without him."

"*Poverina*! Poor girl. Or should I say, *Beata te*? That's all the Italian I know, except for *capisce*."

"Pooh. You know more than that. I wish I had your bouncy pronunciation." Mandy raised her arm and wiggled her fingers at a waiter. "I am absolutely parched. Aren't you?"

"Good evening," the waiter said. "My name is Eugene and I'll be your server this evening. Welcome back," he said to Mandy. "Shall we start with a drink?" He spread his arms, as if he were giving a benediction. Mandy smiled at him. Millie looked at the gold earring on his right ear. Just short of thirty, she figured, a grad student wishing at this point he'd gone for the MBA instead of Fine Arts.

Mandy said, "I'd like a glass of the best chardonnay in the cellar, Eugene, not the house brand that comes in a black box with a spigot, though I'm sure it's perfectly lovely. Tonight I'm looking for something special, something that'll give me a fabulicious tingle. Can you do that for me, please? Hmmm?"

He looked at Millie, then back to Mandy: "It will be my honor to try," he said, following her lead. "Do you want to consult with the sommelier?"

"No, no, I can't wait, Eugene."

He turned to Millie: "And you, ma'am, do you want the tingle as well?"

"I'm not in the mood tonight, Eugene," she said, taking it a step further. "I've had a hard week."

"Oh, dear, I hope I haven't offended you." he said. "I'm not always tactful. Sometimes I carry things too far. But please," he nodded to her.

"I'm not offended, Eugene. I'd like a double Buffalo Trace, neat, please. Water on the side. Nice earring, by the way."

He reached up and touched it. "Thank you so much. You have very good taste in bourbon as well. Coming right up, ladies."

"You and Eugene are old pals, Priss?" Millie said.

"Emerson from the studio, believe it or not, took a couple of us to lunch here after the micro-thong shoot. Ginger von Toon and me. He was trying to sell us on the fuck-me look of the Mr. Oscar project. There he sat, lecturing on the aesthetic appeal of the Full Spread. Well, he should know, I thought. Ginger looked at me and crossed her eyes while she sucked hard on a breadstick. She and I sampled everything on the menu just to annoy him. That's when I met Eugene."

He brought their drinks, left so they could study the menu, and returned after a few minutes. The restaurant was now about half full, voices angling off the walls, the sounds of money and entitlement.

"Now that we've all gotten off to such a splendid start," Eugene said, "allow me to mention today's specials." He lowered his voice: "The specials are fine, but I don't think they'll suit you. I shouldn't say that, but there you are."

"Well, what are these fine-but-not-good-enough specials?" Mandy said.

He clasped his hands together. "Mmm-kay. Island duck with mulberry mustard, which is too precious. Pasta with lamb ragu—a little too rich. Chicken alfredo, which you can get anywhere. What you really want, ladies, if I may say so, is the Brazilian-style grilled tenderloin with new potatoes prepared with herbes de Provence, garlic, and olive oil. In fact, I insist on it."

"Eugene," Millie said, "have you worked here long?"

"Oh, please, now we're being condescending. Look, you're paying a fortune to eat here, right? Why not order something that'll warm your memories? By the way, how is the wine?" he asked Mandy.

"Super," she said, "I'm tingling all over."

"And your bourbon?" he asked Millie.

"Just peachy. Another double, please."

Jerry Masinton

"A second round of drinks, coming up. This one's on the house, but don't tell the manager or I'll be washing dishes again. And in a little while I'll bring you a peppery little Malbec from Argentina to go with your steaks. You'll thank me."

"But we haven't even ordered yet," Mandy said. "Though what do you think, *Tes*, the steak does sound good."

"Do we have a choice?"

"That attitude again," Eugene said. "How do you put up with it?" he asked Mandy.

"Do you browbeat all of your customers," Millie said, "or just us?"

"Oh, you're joshing! How nice! I thought you were mad at me. Actually, I'm not interested in most of my customers. They're hopeless and dreary. You two, on the other hand, might be worth saving. I wouldn't dream of letting you order something humdrum."

"Just why are we worth saving?" Millie said.

"Because you walked in here with pizzazz, that's why. You took total possession of the place." He smiled and left them. They were having a good time.

"He's cute, isn't he, *Tes*? And funny. I'm glad we came to this place."

"Me too, though god the prices. How do the merely wealthy ever afford it?"

"They save their pennies, *Tes*, and they're grateful for each and every morsel they take from the poor." A pause. "I'm really glad you're back, *Tesora*, and not in some godforsaken place shooting people."

"It's mostly business travel and office work, Priss."

"Oh, right! That Rick Owens jacket of yours is beyond hope. Were you playing in the mud? And it smells like smoke. What goes on in that office? I'll have to visit someday."

"You're not missing much. Why do you say shooting people?"

"It's more romantic this way, isn't it? You're out there doing all that serious stuff, and I take off my clothes for men's magazines. But you don't act all grim and morose, *Tes*, you're always upbeat."

"Gloomy's not my style. Why do you say shooting people?"

"Because I know what you do, *Tesora*. I've known for a long time."

"Well, I won't lie: I'm in the secretarial pool."

Mandy didn't reply. Their eyes met and locked.

After a time Millie asked, "How did you find out?"

"Process of elimination. I started with kindergarten teacher and worked my way back. Your habit of buying handguns and silencers was also a hint. And don't even mention the clothes you destroy."

"I should have told you. I was being protective. That wasn't fair, was it?" She reached across the table for Mandy's hand. "Am I forgiven for keeping it from you?"

"That depends."

"On what?"

"On whether you pick up the tab tonight."

"I'm broke. I just bought a new Sig Sauer."

"Yes, I know. I'll lend you the money."

"I'll pay it back with interest."

"I won't need the money if Daddy keeps me in his will."

"We won't let him change it."

"Do you plan to shoot him?"

"Your call."

"Then everybody in the family would be mad at me. One more thing: no more secrets, OK?"

"No more secrets."

"And you've got to teach me how to shoot."

Jerry Masinton

"Learn to shoot? Why?"

"My office is dangerous too."

Their meal arrived. Eugene waited until they'd had their first bite. Mandy opened her eyes wide and said, "Mmmm!" Millie nodded to Eugene.

"I don't like to say I told you so," he said to them, "but I told you so. Enjoy."

And they did. The steak was the tenderest, tastiest they'd ever eaten. The potatoes were drenched in flavor. The arugula, pear, and blue cheese salad was heavenly. And the Malbec was perfection itself.

They gave Eugene an outrageous tip. On the way out Mandy kissed him on the cheek, pushed her breasts against his arm, and thanked him again for the tingle.

Chapter 20

Local Yokels

Next day, Millie, Mary Michael, and Ralph are back in Ralph's kitchen having lunch. Millie's telling them what happened after she left Ray's motel.

"Were you surprised to see Ray again?" Mary Mike asked. They were eating chicken salad sandwiches, a specialty of Mary Mike's, and potato chips. She always used Rainbo Bread for the sandwiches, she said, because it gave them an old-fashioned quality. Soft white bread to go with the crunchy celery, apples, and walnuts. She was wearing a 1940s-style shirtwaist dress, navy with miniature white polka dots. She called it her grocery store dress.

"I'd of been surprised," Ralph said. He was wearing brown Sansabelt corduroys and black socks with a sushi décor. The socks had been out of stock when he ordered them, and he'd had to wait. "I mean, what the hell, why didn't he keep on going? Why stick around?"

"He didn't know what to do, Ralphie," Millie said. She had on a long-sleeve t-shirt, mocha with narrow red, white, and brown stripes. "He was in shock when he ran out of the motel."

"Hard to believe he got away so fast," Ralph said. "Didn't you see or hear anything?"

"I told him to stay put, but he panicked and just took off. Probably followed me right out the door when I went after Joey's goons. Fifteen, twenty seconds later the shooting was all done. I go back to get him. He's not there. You ask did I hear anything. Yeah. I heard the Glock fire twenty rounds. Heard the slugs hit glass and metal. And I heard that squishy sound like a water balloon dropped from the roof when the fire bomb went off. That's it."

"Fast work, Millie," Ralph said.

"You can do a lot of damage in a few seconds."

"And then—what—you spot the guy out on the road?"

"Not at first. I was driving north on the highway and saw four or five cars pulled over to the side. They'd stopped because the cops and fire trucks—sirens going, lights flashing—were heading our way. I pulled over to the shoulder too, twenty yards behind the last car. That's when I noticed the make and license tag: black Camry with a Texas plate. Ray's car."

"So," Mary Mike said, "he couldn't've been very far ahead of you."

"Well, he was probably driving a lot slower than I was when I left the Iowa Hilton. I caught up right away."

Millie took a bite of her sandwich. "This is good, M. I haven't had a sandwich like this since I was a kid. Do you make tuna salad too?"

"Oh, sure, Millie, plus roast beef, anything you like. Put anything between two slices of bread, you've got a meal. I'll teach you how to make the chicken salad."

"I'm not the cook in the family, M, but thanks." She took another bite, swallowed. "There we were, a line of cars. Good citizens obeying the law. When the parade went by, Ray didn't get back on the highway. He took his foot off the brake and put the car in neutral. He lit a cigarette. Just sat there, smoke floating out his window.

The smoke was blue in the mist. Ten or twelve minutes pass, Ray's chain-smoking, spinning the butts away on to the gravel. Finally, he drives off, and I follow him. I'm thinking to myself: 'Remember when you thought this case would be boring?' Then I thought, 'You'd better be adding up all the things that can go wrong in this situation.'"

"He'd had a hard day, hon'," Mary Mike said. "That's why he just sat there smoking. He was pulling himself together. He was supposed to be dead twice, you know, and here he was driving down the highway. He had things to think about. Like you said, he was in shock."

"He's a civilian. Civilians think that life comes at you one catastrophe at a time. They're never ready for every damned thing at once. But Ray was beginning to learn."

"When you drove away from the motel, Mil, you figured that he'd, that you'd never see this guy again, right?" Ralphie said. "Because what're the odds?"

"Ralphie, Jesus, you and the odds. We talked about this yesterday, remember? Sometimes you hit the long odds, and sometimes you don't. And even if you hit them, they're not always winners. Think about it: D'Angeli's guys had a window of how many minutes— three or four at the most, before I left the motel—and yet that's when they paid us a visit. OK, you say, what are the odds? They'd been in Des Moines for two days, and they rolled the dice on those few minutes and hoped they'd get lucky. Which in a way they did. But they still came up losers, because at any other time they wouldn't have walked into a trap. So I'll be honest with you: no, I wasn't particularly surprised to see Ray again. It'd been that kind of day."

"You know, Mil, it's funny. All these years in the removals business and I never figured a fucking client would put out a contract on us. And then this Joey Angels did, but you figured out the set-up, and you turned it back on him. Beautiful. Yesterday after you left, me and Mary Mike had a good laugh about it. I said to her, I said, 'Mary Mike, Jesus Christ, can you believe how that happened? Who says there's no god?' I didn't mean to say it that way, but after I did we both broke up laughing, you know? And then I thought, I said to Mary Mike, 'somebody ought to write a book about this.' And she said, lemme see. . . how did you put it, Mary Mike?"

"I said, 'Nobody'd believe it, Ralph, it'd be a waste of time.'"

"Yeah, that's it. Because it sounds like something that'd never happen."

"I told Ralph, 'If you write a book, it's got to make sense. And even if you say on the cover "A True Story," nobody'd believe this one.' Otherwise I'd write it myself and make a million."

"Yeah, I know," Millie said, "but it happened. I was there. I agree with you about the book, though. It'd be a total waste of time."

"What happened then?" Mary Mike said. "Did he stop somewhere for the night?"

"He drove a couple of miles and pulled into an empty lot. It looked like it might have been a rest stop at one time. Now it was just a deserted city block with a few bushes along the edges and trees at the back. Most of the pole lights had been shot out. Somebody had bulldozed the rubble into a low wall on one side. The city should've set out some barricade lights or put up a big sign that said, 'MUNICIPAL CRIME CENTER.' You'd have to be crazy to stop there at night, but Ray did.

"I drove past to do recon, going about thirty-five, keeping track of him in my rear-view mirror. I think he got out to pee. Then he got back into his car. One or two cars passed me, but traffic was light. I decided to check on him. I wanted no surprises, so I popped a full magazine into the Glock and tucked it into my waistband."

"You were free and clear, Mil. Me, I'd of gone straight to the airport," Ralph said. "The guy was OK, he had a car, you didn't plan to ice him, so why not leave, is the way I'd see it."

"I hadn't finished the job, Ralphie. Joey Angels had opened a whole new game. Maybe Ray had more information on him. So I turned around and drove back. Ray's car was parked near the back of the lot. I rolled in. Pulled up about twenty yards behind him and studied the location. We were parallel to the highway, maybe seventy-five yards back. I slipped on my night glasses, got out, and walked ahead, letting him see me in his side mirror. The window slid down, and he said, 'Don't tell me—you've changed your mind again.'

"'You would've driven off if you believed that.'

"'Can I have my Zippo back?' he said.

"'I don't have it. I needed it to blow up a car.'

"'I've never tried that. I've only used it to light cigarettes. I'm trying to get used to these damned paper matches now,' he said. 'You want to tell me what happened back there?'

"'You should have stuck around to see.'

"'I saw quite a bit from the car,' Ray said. 'Looked like half the city was on fire.'

"'The guys who came after you had firebombs.'

"'I told you Joey Angels wanted to set me on fire,' he said. 'But you didn't want to believe me.' He got out of his car, reached into his pocket for cigarettes, and lit up. It took several matches before he got one going. 'Dumb question,' he said, 'but what are you doing here? Are both of Joey's guys dead?'

"'I think Joey's going to have to hire two new boys. That's two questions.'

"'You took 'em both out? Jesus, honey, I'm glad you decided not to shoot me. By the way, I still don't know your name. We ought to be on a first-name basis by now, don't you think, all we've been through? I'd even go for pen pals.' The air was heavy and dank. The rest stop smelled rancid.

Jerry Masinton

"'Not a good idea, Ray,' I told him.
"'Fine, just give me your business card then.'
"'Why are you still hanging around here?'
"'Why are you following me?'
"'What are you going to do?'
"'Is Joey going to come after me again?'
"'How would I know?'
"'Aren't you an expert on criminals?'
"'Whatever gave you that idea?'
"'What do you think I should do?'
"'How much money do you have?'
"'How much do I need?'
"'Do you plan to keep running or go back?'
"'What if I went back to Brooklyn?'
"'What have you got to lose?'
"'Are you kidding?'
"'Would you like to get back at Joey?'
"'Do I look like the heroic type?'
"'Don't you think he'll be too afraid to do anything?'
"'Why didn't I think of that?'
"'Shall we stop playing Twenty Questions?'
"'You've been counting?'

"'OK' I said, 'here's the deal. I don't think Joey will come after you again, at least not now. By tomorrow, he'll realize that he's the one with the target on his back. He'll know that someone's going to come after him, and he has no idea who. He'll hire some new muscle and stay off the streets. In the meantime, you could go back, rent a new apartment, and stay away from his neighborhood. Or move to Queens, anywhere you like. He'll think that you're still on the run.'

"'What'll I do then?'

"'Jesus Christ, Ray, do I have to hold your hand? Read the newspapers, go to the movies. What do you usually do?'

"'When I'm not playing cards? Read the papers, see some movies. You know—pass the time.'

148

"'Well, what do you know? I got it in one. Another thing: sit tight and expect a phone call.'

"'Just a minute here, honeybunch, this is starting to sound serious. I barely survived the festivities this afternoon. A phone call? You want my help to take down Joey? Huh-uh. I have a college degree in cowardice.' He lit another cigarette, drew the smoke way down. 'I'm out of my depth. You know I am.'

"'All right, you could try this, then. Turn in your car at the airport. If you're afraid that Joey's still got someone checking on you, book a flight for next week to Miami or Caracas. Doesn't matter where. You're not going to use it anyway. Use your credit card. If Joey's got someone still checking, that'll throw them off. Ride the Greyhound bus home or go to Vegas and play the slots. But I see him pissing his pants, that's all. You're not at the top of his to-do list right now, believe me.'

"'That's why you asked if I had any money, isn't it? Stay out of sight for a while. Buy meals. Rent a new place. That could be expensive.'

"'How much do you have?'

"'Five or six hundred in cash, a few grand left on my Visa.'

"'You'll manage. Give me your phone number and let me see your driver's license.'

"'Does this mean we're going steady? I don't normally give out personal details.'

"He handed me his wallet. I took a photo of his driver's ID. Then he gave me his phone number. 'When do I get to know what you're planning?' he said.

"Just then a big pickup rumbled into the lot—Dodge Ram with a quad cab. The driver trained his high beams and the double overhead light bar on us. He drove until he was about fifteen yards away. I didn't figure this was a neighborly Midwestern house call, but I didn't say anything to Ray. We stood there blinking into the lights

Jerry Masinton

for a second. I said to Ray, 'Look my way. Don't let those high beams blind you.' I had my hand on the Glock.

"A minute later, two beefy guys got out and walked toward us in the light. They were wearing work boots and shirts with the sleeves cut off at the shoulder. Big arms, thick necks, short-cropped hair. I couldn't make out their faces in the glare. The passenger carried a pump-action shotgun pointed down. How many shells in the chamber? I couldn't remember. Plan on five, I decided.

"They came a few feet and stopped. Were these guys killers or drunk local farm boys out for a night of fun and mayhem? Ray said, 'Son of a bitch. Is this a typical day for you?'

"'You got a nice ass there, little lady,' the driver said. 'Is that gentleman tryin' to put his hand on it?' I didn't answer. My eyes were on the one with the shotgun.

"'Butch,' the driver said, 'I b'lieve we got us a situation here. Poor little lady can't talk. Prolly needs rescuin'. You reckon?'

"'Kinda looks that way, bud. Which one of them cars is yours, Mister?' Ray was quiet. 'I said, goddammit, which fuckin' car is yours, asshole? That one there?' He pointed the gun at Ray's Camry. Ray shrugged his shoulders. I knew what was coming.

"The guy raised his shotgun, used both hands to aim from the waist, and sent a blast through the Camry's passenger window. At the same instant, I pulled the Glock, fired two rounds at his gun hand, missed, and hit him in the thigh. 'Ah, Jesus fuckin' Christ, Arlen, she shot me!' He was on the ground, the shotgun flung out away from him. I wheeled around to the driver and shouted, 'On the ground, on the ground!' He didn't seem to hear me. I fired a round into the gravel in front of him. He got down on all fours. 'All the way down, Arlen, or I put the next one in your gut.' He heard fine this time.

"I went over, picked up the shotgun, chambered a round, and blew out the pickup's windshield. Put the next one into the light bar. That killed it. I blew out both of the headlights and then ran out of shells. I used the Glock to shoot out the front tires. The engine was still running. Butch lay with his arms curled over his head, whimpering. Arlen hadn't moved.

"No one on the highway slowed down or stopped to watch.

"Ray had instinctively ducked and stumbled back when the shooting began, but now he was standing near me. I gave him a little credit. He was on full alert now and didn't seem too jumpy for a change.

"He said, 'What do you want me to do?'

"'Wipe the prints from that shotgun with your hand-kerchief,' I said. 'Use your shirt if you have to. Then toss the gun into the bushes. Not too far—I want the cops to find it.'

"Butch started moaning and crying again. 'Arlen, man, what're we goin' to do? I'm hurt bad.' Arlen looked up. I walked the few steps and kicked him in the ribs. 'Shut up,' I said. He hadn't said anything. It occurred to me I was being aggressive because my period had just begun. I wondered how much blood Butch was losing.

"'Arlen,' I said, 'do you want to live?'

"'I sure god do, ma'am. Please don't shoot me. We were just having a little fun.'

"'Take off your pants and boots.'

"'What? Hey, please, honest to god, just let me go home.'

"I shot another round into the ground by his head. Arlen did what I told him.

"'Now help your friend to that low wall over there so I can keep an eye on him.' He half-carried, half-dragged Eustis to the wall. Butch moaned all the way. Arlen said, 'He's blood all over, ma'am. He's gonna bleed out on us. Let me go get some help.'

"'No.'

"'Aaaah, god, Arlen! Jesus!' Butch said. 'Stay with me. Don't leave me here.'

"'I ain't leavin' you, Butch. I'll figure out something. Just goddammit let me think.'

"'Arlen,' I said, 'you are now going to drive that truck forward a few yards. You're going to smash hard into that Camry. Then you're going to get out and take care of your pal. Don't close the door. I'll have my pistol trained on you. Turn off the engine when you're done.'

"He was confused. 'Whut? Why do I need to do that? The air bag will explode on me. Christ, what's happenin'?'

"'Your choice—the air bag or this pistol, Arlen. Three seconds. . .two . . .' Even in the near-dark, I could see his pale legs shaking as he walked to the cab. He opened the door, got in, and drove on those flat front tires right into the Camry. The air bag deployed. Arlen was pinned to the seat. I put a round into the bag and he stumbled out. I pointed to Butch. Arlen was wobbly but made the distance to him.

"Drivers glancing over from the highway wouldn't have seen much. A pickup truck in a dark lot by the roadside. Two other vehicles parked farther back. Nothing moving. Nothing to claim people's attention. The whole scene was a low-visibility nighttime combat operation."

Mary Mike and Ralph had been listening in silence. Mary Mike had her hands pressed to her cheeks, her mouth open. Ralph was a Sansabelt still life. His face was in a half-grin, his eyes squinted almost closed.

"Jesus, Mary, and Joseph, Millie," Mary Mike said. "That was scary! Did you hear that, Ralphie?"

Ralph didn't answer. He was thinking. Mary Mike bent over the table and looked at him: "Ralphie, can't you say anything?"

"Say?" he said. "It's unfucking believable, that's what it is. It's better than the movies. Who coulda figured it?

What're the . . . ?"

"Don't, Ralphie," Millie said. "No more about the odds, OK? Things just happened, that's all. Another day at camp. Those two hicks were nitwits. They were pre-tend-outlaws. Scare the shit out of the man and woman in the rest area, shoot up their cars, who knows what else? Rape? Maybe. With Ray looking at a shotgun bar-rel while it happened? Who knows? I think they were just a couple of sadist yokels playing it by ear."

"Did you shoot them, hon'?" Mary Mike said. "It would have been self-defense." She had no doubt about it.

"'Are you going to shoot them now?' Ray said. 'It'd be self-defense.' He didn't sound too sure.

"'No.'

"Butch had gone silent, but I could see he was still alive. Arlen was jabbering something to him that I couldn't hear. Big-time escape plans, maybe. I said to Ray, 'Take the gas cap off your car and stuff your hand-kerchief and anything else that's dry into the opening.' He lifted his eyebrows but didn't say anything. He could see what was coming. While he did the Camry, I re-moved the gas cap from the pickup, never losing sight of the two guys on the ground.

"I twisted one cuff of Arlen's jeans into the opening of his gas tank. The other cuff hung to the ground. We doused the jeans from a five-gallon can of gas in the back of the pickup. Then we poured a line of gasoline from the jeans to the Camry and doused the handker-chief and a wad of paper napkins Ray had found in the car. We emptied the can running another line of gaso-line out toward the middle of the lot.

"'You're not going to shoot them,' Ray said, 'you're going to blow them up with the truck.' He was having trouble framing the thought.

"'They're well away from the truck,' I said. 'They're OK. Somebody'll pick them up soon.'

"'You're not afraid they'll ID us?'

"What'll they say, she said—'We tried to scare the bejesus out of some tourists, only they took our shotgun away, and the woman made me take off my jeans, and then shot up my pickup with the shotgun, but first she shot Butch with her pistol, and the guy with her didn't say shit'?"

"'OK, OK, I get it.'"

"Butch started up again and I fired a couple his way to shut him up. 'Butch,' I said, 'I'm trying hard not to kill you. But another sound out of you and I will.' I turned to Ray: 'It's starting to drizzle again, let's get the hell out of this place before somebody tries to mug us.'

"We walked to my car. Ray tried to light up again, but the matches kept flickering out. He rested both hands on the hood, head down.

"'Too dangerous here, Ray. You really should break that habit,' I told him.

"'Another day like this one, and I'm going to stroke out, princess. Cigarettes are the least of my worries.'

"We got in the car and drove to where the trail of gasoline ended.

"'Want to do something useful?'" I said to him. I nodded at the blue-black line of gas on the ground. Ray drew a deep breath. He got out. Struck a match. His hands were shaking, but the match caught the first time. He let it fall on the gasoline. Got back in, fast, breathing hard. He put his head back and closed his eyes. I drove away as the orange and yellow flame raced toward the wreckage. The truck sent up a whitish-gold fireball a few seconds later. The Camry blew next, flaring out red in the shape of a donut. That was three cars I'd torched in a little over an hour. But this time I didn't leave any dead guys behind."

Chapter 21

TRIPLE HOMICIDE LIKELY CONNECTED TO ARSON NORTH OF CITY

COUNTY SHERIFF SUSPECTS TERRORIST CELL

By Lily White, Special to
The Des Moines Register

State and local police are investigating three murders and two major fires that took place yesterday evening north of the city. Authorities believe that the crimes are connected.

Shortly after 7:00 p.m. firemen and police responded to a 911 call from motorists reporting a large fire at the Bide-A-While Motel on North 6th Avenue. When firefighters arrived, the entire structure and a car parked in front were in flames.

Jerry Masinton

The bodies of the manager of the motel, Gabor al-Sisi, and two other men were found at the scene. Al-Sisi had been shot dead before the fire started, according to Polk County Sheriff Billy Withers. His body was saved from the flames by firefighters.

The two other victims were consumed by fire and could not be identified. One of them lay alongside the burning car, which had been riddled with bullet holes. The other man died in one of the rooms. Sheriff Withers says that autopsies would be performed on the bodies and the car would be examined by forensic experts.

The second fire occurred at about 8:45, two miles north of the motel in the disused old rest area nicknamed "Cocaine Junction" for the drug deals that allegedly take place there. A pickup truck and a car, both damaged by shotgun blasts, had been set afire. Two men, one of them seriously wounded by gunfire, were found in the lot about thirty yards from the flames.

One of the men, Eustis ("Butch") Bragg, had two bullets in his right thigh and was bleeding profusely. He was unconscious at the time and was rushed to Mercy Medical Center. His condition is listed as critical.

The second man, Arlen Budworth Munford, wore no pants or shoes. He could not give a coherent account of what had happened. Mr. Munford was also taken to Mercy Medical Center and is being treated for shock.

Both men have criminal records for assault and destruction of public property.

There are at present no suspects in either the arson or the murder cases. Sheriff Withers, reading from a statement, said, "We are at a preliminary stage of our investigation, but in my mind everything points to these crimes being the work of foreign-inspired terrorists. The scale of destruction tells me we most probably have a terrorist cell attacking our way of life. These men were well organized and efficient. Rest assured, however, we will apprehend the evildoers and bring them to justice."

Sheriff Withers has requested assistance from the Iowa Division of Criminal Investigation, which specializes in arson probes. He has also called on Governor Lacey de Vere to provide National Guard troops. According to a spokesman, however, the governor will likely dismiss the request, as these crimes do not in her opinion fit the categories of national defense or threats to homeland security required to bring out the Guard.

Chapter 22

Unknown Unknowns

"I'm trying to picture it, Millie," Ralph said. "You and Ray get the hell away just as the two cars explode. You're in a big hurry. The two hicks are in bad shape, but they're safe from the fire. Then what—you jump the median to go the opposite way from the cops?"

"Uh-uh. This wasn't an outlaw movie, Ralphie. There was no lunatic getaway. I didn't want to draw any attention. I got onto the southbound highway legally."

"Yeah, OK, but it wasn't a drive through the country-side either," Ralph said. "It had to be dangerous. Stressful. Maybe you should take a little vacation, rest up before the next job."

"I'm not much on vacations, Ralphie, you know that. Anyway, I relaxed last evening with Mandy. We went out for supper at George's Passing."

"Never heard of it," he said.

"Very tony place, Ralphie. Not your style. Arty types, big-time jocks dating celebrities, rich people trying to act cool."

"You don't think I got class?" he said. He thought a moment. "Well, you're right, I'm more of a pizza and burger guy. I don't see you with the hoity-toity either, Mil, tell you the truth. You're not that type. Course, the ritzy clothes you and Mandy wear, plus the fancy manners when you need 'em, you guys can turn the temperature way up."

"Well, I don't usually put my napkin in my shirt collar, if that's what you mean. It was a night out for Mandy, a little present to make up for my being away. She knows what I do, by the way. What we do."

Ralph had to think a moment or two. "She told you this? You mean she knows about the removals business? You're jerking my chain," he said.

Millie shook her head. "Huh-uh."

"The fuck we do now? She won't say anything, right?"

"Mandy? C'mon, Ralphie. Get serious. She was amused, that's all. She's known for quite a while, it turns out. Maybe I shouldn't have kept it secret. But I thought, why broadcast what the firm does, why tangle Mandy up in stuff that wouldn't do her any good? But last night I realized she's probably safer knowing than not knowing."

"Millie, hon', you're absolutely right," Mary Mike said. "You can't have secrets from your partner. I didn't know she didn't know in the first place. I thought she knew. Did you know, Ralphie?"

"I just told you I didn't know, didn't I? Makes me nervous, Mil, somebody outside the firm knows."

"You know a guy who works for the *Globe*, right? You two get together sometimes, have coffee, play footsies, tell each other stories. Can you trust *him*?"

"Jesus, Millie, this guy. I never told this guy. I told you. I said to you, 'I told him we're moving and storage.' Remember?"

"Sure, but he's a reporter, and you've known him since—what—high school? He knows where our office is, it's practically in you guys' old high-school parking lot. Do we look like a trucking firm? This is a—what do you call it?—gentrified old house in Newton. It's strictly *Better Homes and Gardens,* Ralphie, not *The Van and Storage Bulletin.* Around back there's only that little white panel truck that Mr. Moustakas drives. And don't forget, your pal is good friends with a local cop, too."

"You know, Mil, if he did know, he'd keep his mouth shut. I mean, what could he say? He could say, he could tell Kagan, the cop, 'Kagan, I know this guy, buddy of mine from high school, he accepts contracts on guys. Has this little office, they run a front that they claim they're moving furniture, but they only have this one clapped-out old panel truck. Their real business is icing guys and sometimes cleaning up after, make everything disappear, see? So listen,' he says to Kagan, 'this's a big-time story—unnerstand?—and now I'm gonna publish it in the *Globe.* And then you can go arrest him, and then we'll both be famous.'

"And the cop, he'll say, he's gonna say, 'Jeez, O'Bannon, thanks, I was just wonderin', how I can increase my case load—you know?—with about three homicides a month downtown, and the dispatcher running my ass off with domestic calls every fuckin' day, and whatnot with minor things like rapes and break-ins, so maybe I got, my unit and I got, twelve-fifteen active cases day in, day out, not to mention the fuckin' phone . . . '

"Ralph . . . ," Mary Mike said. Tried to say.

"'. . . never stops ringing when you're at the station, people pissin' and moanin' about this and that, stuff that nobody gives a shit about, and so now, now you wanna give me somethin' else to investigate and write up and put on the pile, is that right? My wife, she's gonna like that too, 'cause, you know, I don't spend enough time at home as it is, she says.'

"Ralphie . . ." Millie this time.

"'What she says,' Kagan said, "Kagan, I think you should see your fuckin' son once or twice more before he graduates high school, because now, you know, he thinks you're just a boarder with bad manners, which he's right about your fuckin' manners when you do bother to show up," she says. "Not to mention our sex life. I don't know about you, mister, but I haven't had sex in six months, not that I'm complaining, because I get home from my shift at the hospital too tired to give a shit one way or the other, but I thought maybe you ought to know in case you don't remember the last time you asked me to play with Mr. Popeye."

"'Well, O'Bannon,' Kagan says. He says, 'tell you what I'm gonna do, just because me and you are old pals and I appreciate what a big deal you have for me here. Me and my boys, we'll look into it first chance we get, OK? Next Thanksgiving, Christmas for sure, we pull out that file and we knock this guy over. And, by the way, pal, it's your turn to buy the coffee.' Never happen, Millie."

"Bravo, Ralphie," she said. "Terrific performance. I believe you. And it won't happen with Mandy, either. I was just letting you know she knows. End of discussion, OK?"

"Yeah. Who cares, anyway, right?"

"Ralphie, you're taking an attitude here," Mary Mike said. "Millie just said her girlfriend knows what she does and she doesn't care. If you can't trust her, who can you trust?"

"Trust who?"

"Millie. She always knows what she's talking about. Which is more than I can say about some other people, dear. If Millie says she's not going to say anything, then she won't."

"You mean Millie?"

"No, Mandy. Just trust her."

"Trust Millie."

"Yeah. Millie. And Mandy too, if Millie says so. Mandy's golden, you know that. Besides, who's she going to tell? Those guys who take pictures of her wearing nothing but a band-aid? Or that—what is it?—modeling agency or whatever it is that she works for? They're in another world, Ralphie. The world of high fashion. Right, Millie?"

"High fashion," Millie said. "Mandy will love that. They cut each other's throats there too, you know, only nobody gets buried."

"The world of glamour and style—it's dog-eat-dog, huh?"

"More like cats clawing each other's eyes out, but basically the same thing, yeah."

"Millie," Mary Mike said, 'let's get back to Ray. Is that OK with you, Ralphie, or do you need to know more about women's fashion?"

"I'm fine. Just keeping up my end, that's all. Yeah. So: what did you do with the guy? But also: why did you torch the truck and Ray's car, Millie?" Ralph said. "The car at the motel, OK, I see that, why you did it, because the goon had a lit gasoline bomb in his hands, which he was gonna burn things down anyway. So bingo! you make a statement to Joey Angels by setting fire to his stooges. Good, now he's gonna think, 'Jesus Christ, both of my guys wiped out like that? Maybe I'm next.' That's a smart move. But in that vacant lot, what's the point of blowing up more cars?"

"It was tactical, Ralph, a cover."

"A trick, that's what you're saying? To throw people off, fool 'em."

"Yeah."

"I don't see it."

"Ralphie, Ralphie," Mary Mike said. "Let her finish."

"Sure, all right. Go ahead on, finish."

Mary Mike shook her head. Oh, boy. "Who wants fresh coffee?" she said. "Or should we have a little drink? It's close to four." The others shook their heads. "OK, I'll wait a few minutes."

So Millie continued: "We drove south, toward the

airport. Doing fifty-five, sixty, flying under the radar, like I said. Traffic was picking up, and it'd begun to rain again. Ray's head was drooping. He was falling asleep. He'd lit another cigarette the second we pulled away, and I guess he'd forgotten about it. It was burning close to his fingers. Christ, I thought, this guy. I poked his arm and said, 'Wake the hell up, Ray, you're going to set us on fire.' His head jerked up. 'Wha? Wha?' he said. The cigarette fell on to his lap. 'Oh shit! Goddammit!' he said. He slapped at it, but it rolled between his legs. 'Ah! Jesus Christ! Ah! Ah! Stop the car! Where'd the damned thing go?' You see what I had to deal with.

"I kept driving. There was no place to pull over. 'I can't find it! Stop the fucking car!' He unhooked the safety belt, lifted himself, and swiped at the seat. The seatbelt chime started in. Ray looked like he was trying to breakdance. Finally, he found the cigarette and flicked it out the window. I could smell burnt fabric. Had to be his pants because the seats were leather. 'Goddammit, why didn't you stop?' he said. 'No one's chasing us, are they?' The air outside was humid, and the AC was working hard to keep the windows from fogging up.

"'How many times have I told you not to smoke, Ray?'

"'You're getting to be a nag, you know that?'

"'You fell asleep with a lit one in your hand. It burned your crotch, didn't it?'

"'You happy about that?'

"'Ray, give me a good reason why I didn't shoot you this afternoon.'

"'You couldn't resist me, that's why. Kill a beautiful guy like me? Not a chance.' He crossed his arms. 'I was scared shitless, you know that? Then I got to thinking, Well, if she's gonna do it, she's gonna do it. Have a drink and quit worrying about it. Except I was still worried. Sorry about the cigarette, by the way. At least your car didn't burn up. Jesus, that reminds me: What am I gonna tell the Hertz people?'

"'Tell them your car was stolen.'

"'You think they'll believe me?' He held his palms out. 'They'll say, "When was it stolen? Where?" What'll I tell them?'

"'Tell them anything you want. You went for a walk, came back to your room at the motel, and the car was gone. You were going to call the police, but then all hell broke loose. You heard shooting. It was coming from your room. Couple of seconds later, somebody else's car, the motel—everything—went up in flames. You went into shock, wandered around for a couple of hours, not knowing what was going on. Finally you remembered to call the police about the rental.'

"'They'll ask what was going on in my room. That'll implicate me.'

"'Leave that part out, then.'

"'It was raining. Why would I go for a walk in the rain?'

"'I have to tell you, Ray, you are one exasperating son-of-a-bitch. Can't you think of something? You're a gambler. Don't you ever bluff? Tell them you were depressed, you were out of work, you were in the middle of Iowa. That ought to convince them. Make something up. Can't you figure out a good story?'

"'I'm no good at making up stories,' Ray said. 'I'd just end up contradicting myself.'

"We were moving past the outskirts of Des Moines now," Millie told Ralph and Mary Mike. "There were bars, motels, fast-food joints along the road, a couple of car lots shut down for the night. The wipers were smearing the neon colors across the windshield. I was fed up with the whole damned day and was tired of talking with Ray. For a gambler, he didn't show much moxie. I started to look for a place to dump him. I'd started out the day planning to ice him, and now I was babysitting him."

"You know, Millie," Ralph said, "that's actually pretty funny."

"Yeah. 'OK,' I told Ray, 'tell them something you don't have to make up: you were on the run from a shylock who'd sent out a couple of hit men to kill you. Another person you met up with—a woman, by the way—took out the hit men and set everything on fire. And, oh, yeah, just to fill in the picture, remember to tell them that she was planning to shoot you before the killers arrived, but she changed her mind. You managed to get away from the motel during her shootout with the killers. You were scared and confused. You don't have to mention your car. How's that? You think they'll go for it?'

"Jesus, no, not a chance. They'd think I was crazy.'

"'I would too. You see the problem here, Ray? Who's going to believe something like that? That's why you have to invent a story. Hertz won't give a damn what you say. They just want to fill out some forms, send the information to the home office. If the cops question you, tell them what you say to the insurance company. They're not going to care either. They've got arsons and murders to worry about. They'll probably decide that the guys who pulled off the shootings at the motel stole your car, drove it to the empty lot, and torched it when they blew up the pickup. Nobody'll be able to figure out who these guys were, or why they did it.'

"'You think the cops will consider me a suspect?'

"'I don't think so. You don't fit the profile of a shooter, and you have no reason to destroy your car. You're just some down-and-out guy who got caught in the cross-fire.'

"'Thanks a lot. That's reassuring.'

"'Don't mention it. Just consider yourself lucky.'

"'Oh, I do, I do. People have been trying to kill me, I'm on the run, and I'm riding in a car with a woman who likes to blow things up. What else could I ask for?'

"'Tell me how you felt when you dropped the match on the gasoline. Tell me it wasn't a rush.'

"'Yeah, yeah, it was. It was like the feeling I get when I'm betting the farm with Aces full of Jacks. I liked it. But I don't want to do it again. How about you?'

"'Not unless I have to, no. But that pop of adrenaline you get—you don't forget it, do you?'

"'Let me ask you a question: I get why you set that truck on fire, but why my car? Why didn't we just leave? It would have been a lot simpler than what we ended up doing.'"

Ralph jumped in. "That's what I've been saying." He lifted both hands. "Why take all that time to blow up more cars? I know you're a pro, Mil, but you could of just gone home when those two guys were on the ground. I thought you didn't want to call attention to yourself. Christ—another big fire? You figured people wouldn't notice?"

It was now late afternoon in Newton.

"Think about it," she told Ralph.

"What do you mean?"

"I just told you it was cover. Remember?"

"Yeah, but what does that mean? Cover for what?"

"OK, I'll lay it out for you. Listen. It's what I told Ray. I told him, 'Torching both vehicles was cover, Ray, for both of us. You drive away in your shot-up car, somebody might eventually tie it—and you—to the two fires. The one at the motel and the one in the open lot. You're the common denominator. Of course you might come up with a good story in the meantime to explain why you were at both places, how the fires got started, and why your window was shot-gunned.'

"'But what if this story of yours has holes? Then what? Then you're a prime suspect. You're innocent, but who's going to care? You're driving the car that was at the scene of a crime. It's been shot-gunned, like the pickup, so it's probably a getaway car. Everything points to you. That's the way the cops will put it together. See?'

"'Jesus Christ, what a mess. What if they force me to give you up?'

"'You wouldn't. I saved your life. Besides, you'd be afraid I'd come after you. And if you did say anything, they'd think it was a fairy tale. Things like that just don't happen. Bottom line, Ray: you'd be the perfect patsy.'

"'How long did it take for you to figure all this out?'

"'I don't know. Not long. There are only so many moves on the board.'

"'I need a cigarette and about four drinks. How about you? We could stop somewhere along here and belt down a few.'

"'Uh-uh. We're getting close to the airport,' I told him. 'I'm not taking you with me. You're going to check into one of these motels along here. Get some sleep.'

"'Just like that—get out, it's been good to know you? You haven't even told me the rest of it, your angle in the explosions.'

"'You're a smart guy, you'll figure it out.' I pulled off the road at a Motel 6. 'This is clean and cheap, Ray. A big step up from the Bates Motel. Nobody's going to stab you or put a gun to your head. I'll be in touch.'

"'Hey, wait. Hold on a minute, will you? I told you already—I don't want to have anything more to do with Joey. I don't want to be involved. '

"'Don't you get it? You're already involved. You play the hand you got.'

"He cleared his throat a couple of times. Nodded. Opened his door and slid out. He leaned back in: 'Hey, I just thought: I'm alive thanks to you. Maybe you're my lucky charm. Think that's possible?'

"'Don't bet on it, Ray. Remember the last time you felt lucky?'

"I drove off, spent the night in an airport hotel, and caught an early flight back the next day," she said. "Let's order a pizza, OK? I'm starving. We've been here all afternoon."

Low-angle sunlight streamed through the windows.

"I could go for a pizza," Mary Mike said. "Let's have a drink or two while we wait. What do you think, Ralph? You hardly touched my sandwiches at lunch."

"OK by me, but I'm still curious about something, Mil. You fixed it so Ray's not in the picture. I see that. But the explosions—how did they give you cover?"

"Ralphie, the pizza?" Mary Mike said. She brought out the Wild Turkey and set three tumblers on the table. It was now 5:00. "Let's order first, then she can explain. Half-pepperoni, half-cheese. That's what we usually get, isn't it? What do you think, Millie?"

"Half-shoe leather would be fine, as long as we get it quick."

"Ralphie, order some salads too, will you? You never have vegetables in your fridge. I'm not complaining, dear, just reminding you. I know Sheila tried to get you to eat plenty of vegetables when you were a kid. It never took, did it?"

Ralph shrugged. He phoned in the order. When he sat down again, he lifted his eyebrows and opened his hands: well, I'm ready. They all took a drink of the Wild Turkey.

"It worked the same way for me, Ralphie. Like you said, it was cover. The fires were set to complicate things. To send the wrong signals."

"To the cops, you mean. OK, but how do all the pieces fit?"

"Simple. I blew up the first car as a ruse. To make the cops think there was more to the business than just the shootings. It was pure luck that the car took the whole motel with it. Then I saw that blowing up two more cars would confuse people even more about who set the fires at the motel," Millie said.

"Make 'em look like they're part of the same job, but they're not," Ralph said.

"Um-hmmm. You have two big fires a few miles apart within a couple of hours, maybe less. Incinerated cars in both of them. A lot of shooting. Major casualties. That makes a pattern. But the pattern is misleading," she said.

"OK, but what's it supposed to mean in the first place?"

"At first it looks like the same guys started both fires."

"Well," Mary Mike said, "that's true, sweetie. You did start 'em both."

"Sure, but who's going to see that? They'll think that several people had to be involved, considering all the damage. The motel play will look like gang activity—retribution for something, maybe. Or a robbery that got out of control. Not long after, the gang gives a second performance at the empty lot. Maybe drugs are involved, men's brains boiling over with meth. There's a lot of that stuff in the Midwest, I hear."

"I follow you," Ralph said. "But the guys you left alive will say they saw a man and a woman. They'll make up some story about a crazy dame that tried to kill 'em. She took one guy's pants off first, though. Nice touch there, Millie."

"A story that nobody's going to swallow, Ralphie—if those two actually get around to telling it. If they try to explain how a woman brought them down, they're going to be asked what they were doing with this lady to begin with. They'll also have to explain why they had a shotgun, why they killed two vehicles with it, and why they tried to hide it in the bushes. My guess is that they'll be happy to play dumb. It won't be too hard for them."

"Sure, but why couldn't the same woman—you—be the suspect for the motel crimes plus later ones?"

Jerry Masinton

"Too much of a stretch, Ralphie. One woman, acting alone? No way. That's why you hired me, remember? You wanted a woman. You said, 'No one's going to pay attention to a young woman who's just going about her business.' That's the deal here too: no one's going to guess a woman's the mechanic, let alone search for reliable witnesses and solid evidence."

"This story has more layers, too, doesn't it?" Mary Mike said. "There are more wrinkles."

"Yeah, a couple. How'd you know?"

"I know how you operate, so I figure you have more cards to deal."

"Well, just a couple of things to think about," she said. "Remember, there was no one left at the motel to tie me to the scene. Ray won't say anything about me. He just wants to disappear. But if somehow the cops did question him, he won't have anything that's believable, let alone useful. He doesn't know who I am. How to contact me. He doesn't even have a good idea of what I look like."

"Because everything happened in the dark, right?" Ralph, shaking his head in admiration.

"Dark or dusk, yeah," she said. "Then there's the second scene—the two guys in the pickup, the shooting, the shot-gunned vehicles, the fires. That's such a far-fetched connection to the first scene that nobody's ever going to understand it, assuming that anyone can even uncover the facts."

"So you're saying the cops will decide there really was no connection between the two incidents?" This was Ralph, doping it all out.

"No, you were right the first time, they'll think it was the same guys. The evidence will be incomplete, but that's what they'll conclude. Forensics will eventually ID the thugs at the motel. The cops will see that there's no tie-in between Joey's hoods and the rubes in the pickup. Two big-city hoods and two Iowa farmers? Huh-uh. But the police will decide that the fires at the motel were started to cover up the three killings there. And then they'll assume that the later fires were set to cover up the shooting spree that went on there, too."

"And so," Mary Mike said, "they decide that the shooters and arsonists at the motel are the same guys who shot up the cars in the lot and then set them afire."

"I think so, yeah. It's a story that fits what they'll find, which seems to be a lot but really isn't. The cops, the papers, TV—they'll all buy it. It leaves out the key players, but they won't know that. So they'll figure the story has to be the truth."

"In other words, the cops come to the right conclusion," Mary Mike said, "but they blame the wrong guys. They stick to a familiar but untrue story, and in the meantime you and Ray slip through the net."

"That's the way I see it."

"Just a sec', Mil," Ralph said. "I need you to go through that again, OK?"

"OK, look at it this way, Ralphie. The cops don't have a clue that Ray and I figure in this case. And they never will. We're invisible. Maybe they'll never connect Joey, either. But without us, all the rest is a guess. Pure fiction.

"See, there's stuff that they know—obvious stuff like the fires, the bodies, the deliberate explosions. Doesn't mean they understand these things, but they're facts. OK?"

"Yeah, OK."

"And finally," Millie said, "there's also stuff out there that they don't know they don't know. Unknown unknowns. Which is what'll keep them off our backs. See how that works?"

"I think so, sure."

"It's perfect," Mary Mike said. "You get it, Ralphie?"

Jerry Masinton

"Absolutely. I saw it all along. I just needed to have it explained. The cops will fool themselves. They'll figure they know what's what, but they won't because the important stuff is missing. And so our girl is free as a bird."

"That just about covers it," Mary Mike said. "Now get the door, Ralphie, I think the pizza's here. And give the boy a good tip."

Chapter 23

Caffe Angelina

A week later, Millie's thinking through the details of how to hit Joey. She's had a couple of sessions with Mr. Moustakas. The meetings were pretty pro forma, but Mr. M was the weapons guy of the outfit, after all, and if you want the truth, a noted craftsman of assassins' paraphernalia. So. For this job, he'd designed a sexy, unobtrusive little ankle holster for her right boot. (Her Max Mara black pants suit with the slight flair would easily cover either the Sig Sauer or the Glock when she used the holster.) For her left boot, Mr. M had come up with a neat, slim scabbard for her double-edged Troodon combat knife. He had shown real flair with these items, the genuine artist's touch. He was clearly entering his mature phase.

Millie had decided some time ago that she didn't want to work in off-the-rack clothes. She'd learned from Mandy that couture wasn't optional for the professional woman. Dressing for work was as important as reliable back-up weapons. Careful preparations are half the battle, as everyone knows. Style is substance. Well, maybe, she thought. And maybe I just like wearing knock-out clothes.

When Mandy saw what Mr. M had created, her inner fashionista bolted awake. "Ohmigod, *Tes*, how chic," she said, "you absolutely must ask Mr. M to make me a pair of ankle holsters!" She stroked the fine Spanish leather, quoted some snooty French philosopher or other on the virtues of stark, simple design. The look, the style, the whole sexy vibe—she had a deep affinity for the whole package. "God, the steamy photo shoots we could do for the magazine, *Tes*. Emerson might even perk up and stop pursing his lips all the time like what's-her-name, that actress. Maggie Smith. I keep telling him, 'Emerson, darling, Punt is so fucking flabby and quaggy these days. It needs pizzazz, dash, a little style.' He never listens, of course. But with smart accessories like ankle holsters, or who knows what, gun belts and assault rifles, chain mail, baldrics—just imagine: Supermodels in micro-thongs with semi-automatic pistols strapped to their legs. Battle-hardened blondes with body armor. What do you think, *Tes*? That'd be perfect for *Punt: The Man's Man's Magazine*. A full spread, every issue. No punt intended."

"Baldrics? My god, Priss. Come down from the ceiling, will you. Mr. Moustakas won't do it. He's strictly old-school. He doesn't do fashion accessories. This stuff's combat gear. And, by the way, the sex-and-guns thing has already been done to death."

"Tell me about it, *Tes*, I'm in the fucking industry. I just got carried away, that's all. You know how I adore cutting-edge style," she said. "I do think that Gucci or Coach ought to make designer holsters, though, don't you? Women buy a lot of guns these days. Just read the papers. Or Louis Vuitton, he has those darling little canvas pochettes. Maybe I could special-order something glam from Vuitton."

"Priss, you can borrow my stuff once in a while. I prefer the hip holster, anyway. It's faster. You can squeeze off a dozen rounds in the time it takes to bend down and pull your pistol from an ankle holster. I have too much gear already."

In her cross-body bag, Millie had : two Epipens, Oakley night glasses, a silencer for each pistol, pepper spray, four burners, a pair of sheer black lambskin gloves with wrist straps, and a couple of other brand-new things, also courtesy of Mr. M. In one of their meetings, she'd sort of hinted that pepper spray wasn't all that damned interesting. What she'd actually said was: "Pepper spray is for wusses. I like things that blow up." Mr. M thought for a minute. "Yah, OK, I make something special for you. But keep also the pepper. For me is no good." A few days later he showed her what he'd come up with— three C-4 explosive devices plus—she couldn't believe it—half-a-dozen packets of Alka-Seltzer. Inside each packet were two tablets of a sodium-potassium alloy: "Explodes when touches water. Also can explode in humid air sometimes. Don't forget and drink, OK?" He was perfectly serious.

The other thing: Millie was planning to drive from Boston to Brooklyn to do recon, a five-and-a-half-hour drive. She didn't figure this was an occasion for her killer wardrobe, so she wore fatigues and a pair of grunge biker boots she'd bought on Ebay. "*Tes*, sweetheart— Ebay?" Mandy'd said. "Just don't let anybody know that, all right? Though on you they look tres sexy."

And then, glancing up at the true-black t-shirt Millie was wearing: "My god, Tes, did you paint that on, or did it shrink in the wash? I can see the pores on your nipples."

"It didn't shrink. Sometimes I just like to show off the girls."

"Show them off in your pick-up? Who's going to see?"

Jerry Masinton

"You never know, Priss, I might get lucky."

"You bought it at Shirts and Destroy, right?"

"Huh-uh," Millie said, "Gap. $14. Perfect for a day on the road."

Millie's thought had been: why not give the Silverado a workout, enjoy the ramped-up horsepower of the new C10 Vortec under the hood? Combine work with pleasure. Right before the Iowa job, Mr. M had installed a little swing-down case on the driver's-side door panel that would hold a pistol and two extra magazines. He'd also rigged up a magnetic gun mount under the dash. He liked to keep busy.

She didn't need all this firepower, of course, but then where was the harm? And Mr. Moustakas liked to fiddle with the tools of the trade. Though god knows how I'm supposed to use those damned Alka-Seltzers, she thought. If I need to blow up something big, I'll use the C-4 blocks.

So the trip to Brooklyn amounted to routine surveillance, but this time around there was also the personal element. Joey Angels had put out a contract on her. Her job would be pay-back. She wondered: should I explain things to him before I wave goodbye, or just do the job and go home? She was tempted to tell him the whole twisted story, see how he'd react when he found out that the shooter and the intended target were the same person. But that wouldn't be entirely professional—would it?—though there's no hard-and-fast rule about it. Maybe I'll just kill him, go home, and get a good night's sleep.

Time to call Ray again. Millie needed more info on Joey's operation. She'd phoned Ray two days earlier, but the service was poor and there was noise in the background.

"Hey," he'd said. "I told you. I alway *groke kack fee.*"

"Can't hear you, Ray. You're breaking up."

"... *goo buck,* now ... *up ucking hay gann,* think of that?"

She couldn't make out what he'd said. "Where the hell are you? We have a lousy connection. Noise in the background too. Go someplace that has a decent signal. I don't need you to be fucking around. Can you hear me?"

". . . hear you fine."

"OK, good, then just shut up and listen. Does Joey have any businesses, besides loan-sharking?"

"Cocky slop. Gelato. *Gzzk. . .wiches.* Small time. *Fee,* four garbage . . . *nesses ooo* . . . Teamsters Union."

"Garbage and sandwiches, I got it. Where is the coffee shop?"

Suddenly his voice was crystal-clear. "I've been telling you, to hell with Joey Angels for a minute. I'm up eighty fucking thousand dollars here! You're my good-luck charm, remember, and now . . ."

"Where?" Deep breath. "Are?" Another breath. "You?" Why didn't I shoot him when I had the chance?

"Missouri. I'm at a casino. And listen, these guys, these dumb fucking . . . . Easy ten, fifteen grand every day."

"Listen up, soldier. Quit while you're ahead. You're playing against the house."

"I'm on a winning streak, Lucky, my gut tells me to ride it out."

"That's a lot of shit and you know it, Ray. You're drunk. Your head's floating. I'll call back in two days. One o'clock sharp, thirteen hundred hours, understand? It's getting close to game time, so don't fuck up. Get to a place with good phone service. That's possible in Missouri, isn't it? And Ray? I'm losing my patience."

I end up working with a compulsive gambler, she thought, how's that for irony? And now he's shit-faced. I should just dump him. Mary Mike can find out all there is to know about Joey D'Angeli. She's done homework on other targets. She could break into the Pentagon's security system if I asked her to. Time to tell Ray, "You're out, Flash, just like you wanted. You have my blessing to piss your life away."

Except that he might know a thing or two about this coffee shop that's useful. For instance, who goes in and out, who works there, does Joey have an office there? And the big one: does Joey usually hang out there, when he's not at his goombah social club? If he's often out on the sidewalk, strolling up and down in front of his place, I can ice him before he blinks twice. No one would know what happened, including him.

Two other things she'd like to know: first, what kind of car does he have? Easy to do him if he's driving along on the street, *pap pap pap*, he's gone. A routine hit. And the second item: where does he live? That's another area where Ray might help out. When Mary Mike tried to locate Joey's house or apartment, nothing popped up. No surprise for someone in Joey's line of work. Never know who's going to make a social call.

Two days later, she's in Brooklyn, checking things out for herself, driving the Silverado, which has fake New York tags, just in case. It's one o'clock straight up, Central Standard. She calls Ray. He picks up after one ring. "Hi. Sorry about Wednesday. I was riding high, you know? I didn't even need sleep. Did I tell you about my streak?"

"How much have you lost since then?"

"Lost? Whadda ya mean? I'm gonna call you Lady Luck. I'm up another twelve grand. Jesus, this feels good."

"OK, so what's my cut?"

"Your what? Oh, your cut, 'cause you're bringing me luck? That's funny."

"In a month you're going to be sleeping in doorways, Ray. You don't need me to tell you about house odds."

"Ain't gonna happen, Lucky. I'll get a feeling when the streak slows down. I have an infallible instinct for it. Then I'll pull the plug here and go back to sports betting."

"One month, tops, probably less."

"Not this time."

"Chit-chat's over, Ray. I need you to focus. Give me the address of Joey's coffee shop."

He did. She wasn't far from it. A tiny place near the corner of Bay Parkway and 85th. She'd already been circling the block for an hour. She'd become familiar with the shop-fronts. She'd also driven through the narrow alleyway behind the block, where the owners had their own parking slots. The alley was narrow and it was dark, even in daylight. Dumpsters here and there and litter pushing ahead of the wind.

"OK. Now then. What's it called?"

"Angelina's. For his mother, Angela D'Angeli."

"Of course. I should have guessed." She was looking for a parking space. "Just a sec', Ray, I'm trying to park." Then: "OK, I can see the place. Who works there? I assume he doesn't hire high-school kids." The day was sunshiny and clear.

"A woman on the weekends. Somebody's cousin, I think. Adelina. Otherwise, it's just two guys, that I know of. They're the only other ones I've ever seen behind the counter. Sometimes just one of them, but sometimes both."

"Names, Ray, c'mon."

"Yeah, let's see. Adelina I already mentioned. The guys are Vinnie Coccimiglio and Sal Luccio. You got a pencil? I'll spell 'em out for you."

"No thanks. I'm not writing their biographies. What do they look like?"

"Vinnie—well, he reminds me of that actor way back when, can't think of his name, guy that played a bad-ass in the movies sometimes. Kind of heavy-built. Had a mean-looking grin, gap-toothed. Italian name, I think."

"That narrows it down to how many, Ray—a hundred, hundred and fifty? How many Italians do you think played bad guys in the movies?"

"No, this guy, I remember, beat up Frank Sinatra in one of those old black-and-white Army pictures. I watched it a couple of times with my mom. She loved that movie. His name was Maggio. I still remember."

"Maggio was Frank Sinatra. The guy who busted him up was Fatso. Ernest Borgnine."

"You sure? I don't recognize the name. How do you know so much about movies?"

"So this Caravaggio looks like Borgnine. What about the other one?"

"No, it's Coccimiglio, not Caravaggio, OK? You sure you don't want me to spell it out?"

"It was a joke, Ray, forget it. What does Luccio look like? And don't say Frank Sinatra."

"Luccio. OK. You can't miss him. Short, built thick like a fucking fire hydrant. Curly hair. Strong as hell. Cocky son-of-a-bitch. Nobody ever beat him at arm-wrestling. Not known for his friendly disposition. Stay away from this guy."

"Thanks. I promise not to arm-wrestle him. How old are these beauties?"

"Hard to say. Fifty, maybe, I don't know. Only seen them a few of the times when I went there to borrow money from Joey."

"Do they have guns under the counter?" She was now parked across the street from Caffe Angelina. In the window hung a sign—"Fresh Cannoli." The place wasn't what you'd call upscale. She had a good angle on who went in or came out. Her Red Sox ball cap shadowed her face.

"Are you kidding? Is the Pope Jewish? They all have guns in that neighborhood. I figured you knew. It's the Wild West there. Guns in the shops, guns in the street. You know, tough black kids that deal, cops of course, a few wannabe hoods, nowadays the Russian and Albanian gangs that're moving in, trying to muscle out the other gangs. Lot of guys packing, but usually not the Italians, at least not on the street. They don't want to get picked up with a pistol under their arm, the cops discover they got a sheet going back ten years. Anyway, guys behind the counter want to protect themselves, you know?"

"Poor Joey, all those criminals on the street."

"I just meant that his guys have guns. You asked, remember? Don't be surprised to see Vinnie waving a 12-gauge by the gelato."

"Do they sell a lot of coffee and ice cream in this place, or is it just another goombah hangout?"

"The place is a laundromat, basically. Not many people go in there. Maybe once in a while a few college kids, or some lady ordering coffee to go. Sometimes one of his soldiers comes by with a bag of money or to get instructions. Joey's into a lot of other stuff besides loansharking."

"This whole set-up is like a cheap gangster movie, Ray. You know that? You're one of the stars."

"Uh-uh, I keep telling you. I'm not even in the actors' union, believe it or not. I'm one of the guys behind the camera. Best Boy, whatever that is. You can give me a quiet phone call or two—that's OK. But being in the middle of the action? Sorry, it is just not gonna happen. Do you want to know how many times I've fired a gun in my life?"

"How about Joey—did you ever see him with a gun?"

"No, you don't get it, Joey's a big-shot operator. It's beneath his dignity to carry. And anyway his thugs take care of business for him. Story is he shot plenty of guys in his time, but not recently. Now he just has to say, 'So-and-so's making trouble,' and the guy's body turns up full of holes in a car trunk at Newark Airport. Or he tells his boys to set fires—don't forget that."

"I won't. I have a good memory. They almost torched you in Iowa."

"I guess you're right about this being like the movies, Lucky. I never really thought of that. Jesus, why did I ever borrow money from that bozo?"

"Don't call me Lucky, OK?"

"Why not?" She didn't reply. "Never mind, I won't. I meant it as a good thing, though. I've gotta call you something."

"We don't have that kind of relationship, Ray."

"I'm beginning to get that impression," he said. "Listen, why don't you just shoot this son-of-a-bitch on the street? Or follow him home and pop him through the window. You've got a million ways to do it and never be noticed, right? I can give you a description."

"I already know what he looks like."

"No kidding. What did you do, find his yearbook?"

"Better than that. His mug shot. He's been booked quite a few times. He's also been in the papers. Very popular guy with the Feds." She rolled her window down and was immediately aware of the intermingling odors of the neighborhood. Everywhere you go in New York, she thought, that big-city smell. Diesel fumes and dust, the East River or the ocean, depending on the borough. Always something stale and overused. And the aroma of foods, every kind—Spanish, Italian, Chinese, you name it.

"Yeah, he was supposed to be on trial for murder not long ago, but the key witness disappeared. Supposed to be in Witness Protection, I heard, but somehow Joey got to him. I don't know how, but he did. Now the guy's probably at the bottom of Jamaica Bay."

"No, he's buried under a tree in Kansas City."

"What? C'mon, what're you saying? Nobody knows where the guy's buried. Kansas City? Not possible."

"Believe it."

"How the hell would you know something like that? Unless you iced him for Joey? No, that's impossible, because Joey's guys wanted to kill you too there in Iowa, didn't they? Am I wrong? Jesus, none of this makes sense. You see why I don't want to be involved?"

"Wouldn't you like to take him down?"

"What I'd like is to stay away from him. You do it, you're the pro. I just told you how. Wait till he's alone somewhere. Kapow! You don't have to go into Angelina's, order a double cappuccino, then take a chance he won't show."

"Thanks for the tip. I'd never have thought of that. How do you know so much about this place? I thought Joey was just your shylock."

"Where do you think I picked up the money? We didn't meet at the bank. I went to Angelina's. He has a big safe in the back room."

OK, she thought. If the safe's full of money, Joey's likely to stay close by.

"How did you contact him? You have him on speed-dial?"

"Ha ha. Listen, nobody contacts him directly. I did it through the two guys you shot in Iowa. Now that they're gone, I don't know how his loan business works. He's probably got two more apes."

"Did he let you go into the back room?"

"Sure. He'd pull the money right out of the safe. Then he'd tell me how many balls he'd cut off if I didn't keep up with the vig."

"But you weren't scared."

"Why should I be? I always won plenty."

"Until you didn't."

"Yeah, up until that time. But now my luck has changed, I just told you."

"Did your mother read you fairy tales when you were a kid, or did you just watch movies together?"

"Huh? You mean I'm a sucker, that it?"

Someone was knocking on the passenger-side window. A skinny black kid in his teens wearing a hoodie. Big Eddie Murphy smile. Lots of teeth. Motioning with his hand: roll down the window. Millie shook her head no. Waved at him to go away. The kid looked up and down the sidewalk and then tried the handle. No luck. Still smiling at her, he slipped out a slim-jim from his jeans and went to work on the door. Millie sat and watched this dumb kid operate. He popped the lock and opened the door. Slid in and swung a pistol in her direction in one fluid motion.

Not too bad, Millie thought. Her Sig was pointed at his midsection, two inches away. With the silencer screwed on, it looked like a cannon.

"Motherfuck! What you got there, lady?" he said. A couple of seconds passed. "A damn gun? That's serious-looking hardware." His eyebrows climbed his forehead. He started to breathe through his mouth. "Shit! Where you get that thing?"

Millie didn't say anything. She could see how nervous he was.

His knees started to bounce. He tried to smile. "Whoa! Goddamn! We just playin' here, lady, OK? Nothing serious goin' down. Just a little business we got to do."

He nodded at the Sig: "OK, then, OK, you better put it down," he said. Pause. "Give me your money, bitch, you won't get hurt," he said. His demand seemed rehearsed.

She just sat there, the Sig steady in one hand, phone in the other. The afternoon sun was disappearing behind the buildings on their side of the street.

"Ray, I have to call you back. Something's just come up."

"Who's there? What happened?"

"Nothing. Some kid wearing a hoodie is trying to rob me. He's got a gun."

"No shit? In broad daylight? I don't believe it. Let me talk to him."

Millie handed the phone to the kid. "It's for you," she said.

Chapter 24

Charlemagne Favors

The kid looked at the phone. "Whut?" He stared at it like someone inspecting a bomb. The fuck's this? What'm I supposed to do? Said, "I don't know nobody on that phone. You messin' with my head, ain't you?" Tried to smile. She studied his uncertainty.

"We'll have a three-way conversation," Millie said. She set the phone on the dash. "It's on speaker."

"Damn, lady, whyn't you just do what I tell you? Then I leave you alone. Why you makin' this hard for me?" Shadows from the awning over the sidewalk were moving across the pickup.

"You better lower your weapon before somebody sees it," she said. "If they do, I'll have to kill you." She was a couple of moves ahead of him.

He glanced out the windshield. Put the gun on his lap, still pointed in Millie's general direction, but without conviction. He was breathing hard, through his nose now. Probably trying to figure out what he'd gotten himself into.

"What the hell," said Ray. "Are you discussing the fine points of a hold-up with this guy? What's going on? How old is this guy?"

"I don't know—sixteen, seventeen. What do you want to tell him, Ray?" Millie said. "Say it quick, while he can still answer." She pushed the Sig against the kid's ribs— not too hard, though, because she didn't want his gun to fire accidentally. He stopped breathing. He glanced down at his lap. Shook his head: damn. The only sounds came from the street.

"Listen, kid," Ray said. "I'm gonna give you some good advice, OK? Put down your fucking gun before she shoots you. She'll do it too. She's probably pointing a pistol at you right now. Am I right?"

"How you know 'bout that?"

"I just know. I saw her take down four guys one day. Two of 'em were professional killers. You keeping up with me? Another guy had a shotgun pointed at her. She blew him away. Sucker never knew what happened. She didn't even blink. Just another day at the office. You think you're gonna scare her?"

"I don't know, man. Few minutes ago I did." He didn't know where to look—at Millie, at his gun, out the windshield at the pedestrians?

"Does she look scared?" Ray said.

He looked up, into Millie's steady gaze. "Nah-ah. Just kinda quiet." A pause. "That's bad, ain't it?" His voice started to tighten.

"What about you?" Ray said. "You afraid?"

"I'm getting' there, man. I'm close. She gonna kill me?" His voice was racing up the scale.

"Not if you put your gun down. Unless it's already too late."

"Look, here it is," he said to the phone. "See?" He placed it on the floor in front of him. "See that, lady? Now you don't have to shoot me." His speaking accelerated. "I didn't mean nothin', understand? Gun don't even have bullets in it. Or maybe one or two, I don' remember. Some guy I know gave it to me." His knees were pistons running too hot for the rings.

"Hand it to me," Millie said. "Use two fingers, or you're dead."

The kid reached down. Tried to pick it up. Dropped it. Tried again. Picked it up with thumb and forefinger, delicately, a guy holding a soiled diaper that he needed to get rid of. He handed it to Millie. His hand was shaking. The pistol was an old 7-shot Colt Auto. Black electrical tape wrapped around the grip, mob-style. Millie popped the magazine. It was full. She checked the chamber. Empty.

She slipped the empty Colt under her seat. Dropped the magazine into her bag.

"Full magazine. And you forgot to chamber the first round," she said to the kid. "Good thing you didn't try to fire the damned pistol, or you'd be dead."

"You mean, like, you shoot me first?"

"Um-hmm."

"I wasn't goin' to pull the trigger, see. Just wave the gun around to scare you a little. Lemme go, OK?"

"Hey," said Ray. "Is everything all right? Did he give you the gun? Did I talk him into it?"

"Yeah. My hero. I gotta go now." She ended the call and put the phone into her bag.

"You haven't done this before, have you?" she said to the kid.

"Me? Shit. Nah," he said. "Never used a gun before. Was too scared. What you gonna do with me now?" He folded his hands under his arms. Twisted around to face forward. The hoodie covered most of his face. Shadows now fully blanketed the pickup.

"Nothing. Get out."

"What about my gun?"

"You'll live longer without it. Now get out before I get tired of dealing with you." She rested the Sig on the console between them, her finger still on the trigger.

"Lemme aks you a question, all right?"

"Make it fast."

"That guy Ray, he say you shoot down four men. For true? Or he usin' some bullshit to scare me?"

Millie thought of something. "Why did you try to rob me? Who sent you?"

"Me? Why you aks me that? Nobody, that's who. Did it on my own. Stole my uncle's gun a week ago, one idea chase another, next thing you know I'm jimmying you truck with you watchin' me. I figured you too surprise to know what's happenin', know what I mean? Now I'm thinkin' maybe I made a mistake."

"Your uncle ever do jail time?"

"Mmm, yeah, he done time. He out now. Why you need to know?"

"What was he in for?"

"Shoot somebody by accident. Judge say three shots in the back ain't a accident."

"He was in for murder?"

"Man didn't die."

"What then—attempted murder? Manslaughter?"

"Don't know."

"How long was he in?"

"I disremember. Couple of years, could have been. Good behavior, he got out early."

"Ex-cons shouldn't own a pistol."

"I do him a favor, take his gun." The big Eddie Murphy grin returned.

"Are you still in high school?"

"Damn, you full of questions today. I thought you told me get out."

"You didn't graduate, did you?"

"Decided to graduate early, go into business for my-self, understand? Try some armed robbery. If that don't work, try somethin' else, work up the ladder."

"You chose the wrong job," Millie said. "You don't have the knack for it. Why would you rob anybody in a battered old pickup? Look at all the fancy cars around here."

"Reason why, you the only one sittin' in they car. Other ones all empty. Don't make sense tryin' to rob a empty car."

"Maybe not, but what made you think I had any money? What did you see?"

"Ahh, nothin', just you black shirt."

"My black shirt, through the windshield. What about it?"

"Oh, man," he said, "don't get mad, OK, but I notice it fit too tight and I get confused."

"Confused? Did you think I was hiding money in my t-shirt?"

"Huh-uh, no, I could see you wasn't hidin' nothin'."

"What's your name?"

"What's that got to do with anything? You gonna turn me in?"

"Just answer the damned question, OK?"

"Name Charlemagne Favors."

"'Charlemagne'? You're jerking me around."

"Uh-uh. What my mama name me. Cause me a lot of grief too, kids getting' on me at school, dudes at the bar-ber shop. Mama say, 'Boy, that name give you dignity. Be proud of it.' But man, I don't know. I just call myself Chuckie, let it go at that. Chuckie Favors. Other one's too much weight." He seemed to relax. "Can I go now, seein' as you don't plan to shoot me no more?"

Noises from the street drifted in through Millie's window. The aroma of Mexican food nearby. She imag-ined beef tacos, refried beans, rice, a sweating bottle of Sam Adams.

"Shut up. Let me think."

"Think 'bout what? Don't call the cops, OK? You done brought me to Jesus, I promise. I'll be good from now on." He turned toward her. Gave her the toothy smile again.

This fucking jokester, she thought, he's a con man. That's his true calling.

Then the penny dropped: "Chuckie," she said, "you've been lying to me."

Chapter 25

Chuckie's Lucky Day

"Y ou shouldn't have lied," Millie said. "That's not healthy."

He slowly reached for the door handle. "Don't do it, Chuckie." She waggled the Sig at him. "I have some questions for you. You'd better have some solid answers."

"Oh, man," he said softly, "like falling on ice today. Can't find no which-way to get up. Just lemme go, OK? I wasn't lyin' to you, like, per se." Speaking again in the upper registers, barely able to get the words out. Here was Chuckie Favors, curled around his thoughts in the dark cab of a pickup. How'd he get here? Street lights were blinking on.

"You kept saying things that didn't add up, Chuckie. That story about your uncle was paper-thin. He'd be in prison till you collected Social Security for that kind of shooting. A couple of years in prison? Out for good behavior? You gotta learn to tell a better story."

"I tole you I don't remember exactly. It was a long time ago. He don't live at my house."

"And the black tape wrapped around the grip—who the hell does that? People who see too many gangster movies, that's who. Your uncle got it from somebody else, didn't he? And then you stole it from him."

"Yeah, you right, he got it from somebody, that's what I think now. Borrow it to shoot squirryels in his yard. Lemme aks him, OK? We talkin', I say to him, 'Uncle Latrell, who give you that gun, huh?' Then he tell me and we clear all this up, that's all we have to do." He wasn't whispering, but he wasn't reaching the back of the theater, either.

"Who sent you to rob me? If you lie again, I'll squeeze the fucking trigger, even if it means getting blood all over my truck."

"OK, OK, just slow down, OK?" he said. Paused for a few seconds. He seemed to make up his mind about something. "Nobody send me. The man in Angelina's give me the gun. Name Coach Mayo. He hire me to make deliveries after two of his friends got killed. They go out of town someplace looking for this dude, goin' shoot him, but he shoot them instead. What I heard, anyway. Mr. Coach Mayo and his boss get scared after that."

"They're afraid of the shooter."

"Yeah, scared the man come after 'em now. Then they have another problem: after they friends go down, they don't have people to do work for 'em no more on the street. So Mr. Coach Mayo, he say, 'Charlie'—what he call me—'I want you to do the deliveries.'"

"So now you're an errand-boy for gangsters."

Chuckie drew in a long breath. Let it out. "Then he hand me the gun. 'Take this gun with you when you deliver a package or make a pick-up for me. Anybody gives you shit, show them you gun. Shoot 'em if you have to.' He say, 'But you prob'ly won't have to. Nobody goin' argue with you, anyway, 'cause you doin' jobs for the boss. Gun just make you feel better.'"

"How'd you get to know this guy in the first place?"

"Man's boss owns the coffee shop. Joey Angels. Use to get me and my friend Jameer to buy cigars from this store a few blocks from here. Little Cuba Cigars, what it's called."

"Kids buying cigars? Sure you're not lying?" But she had a feeling he wasn't. The whole story was just absurd enough to be true.

"Naah, huh-uh. They know we buyin' for Mr. Joey. You like, I show you the place. We tell 'em, 'Mr. Joey send us out for his cigars,' and they wrap 'em up for us. Didn't need money, just say who's it for and they do it. We do what we want, nobody say you can't do it. My man Jameer got killed in a drive-by few weeks ago. That only leaves me."

"How often do you see Joey?" She looked across the street at the coffee shop. No customers that she could see. It was 7:00. They might not be open too much longer, she thought.

"Don't see him these days. Mr. Mayo out front tell me what to do. Mr. Joey stay in back in his office all the time these days. Makin' plans or somethin'. People I deliver to say Joey goin' move far away. I believe it when I see it."

"What if I told you these guys were killers, Chuckie?"

"Wouldn't be news to me. Everybody already knows."

"Do the cops know too?"

"Nobody tell me 'bout that, but they on the street too. Gotta know."

"What do you think about that, being a bag-man for criminals?"

"Nothin' to think about. They tell you, Do this, you do it. They say, Do somethin' else, you do it. Otherwise you end up in bad trouble, understand?"

"So everybody's afraid of them. One of them gives you a gun and a dangerous job, and now you think you're a big-time guy too. Part of the Mob. Am I in the ballpark?"

"If you mean are you right, yeah, I get respect, but sometimes I'm scared too, know what I mean? Can't say no, whatever they tell me to do. Can't say I got to do homework no more."

"And now that you've fucked up your career in armed robbery, and you don't have the pistol that Vinnie Coccimiglio gave you, you don't know what your next career move is. Right?"

Chuckie was staring at her. "You know Mr. Coach Mayo? Goddamn! I don 't believe this." Chuckie bent over. For a full minute she thought that he had passed out. Even with her window open, it was hot and stuffy in the Silverado. It had the odor of stale breath, the smell of sweat. Maybe it had been too much for him, she thought. But I need information now, and he's all I've got.

"True that. I don't see what I'm goin' do," he finally said. "Don't know where I'm at. Can't figure out what-all's gone wrong. That dude on the phone—Ray: damn, felt like he reachin' right through that thing to squeeze me. And now you know Mr. Coach Mayo. Makes my stomach hurt. Can I aks you a question?"

"No."

"Did he tell you to shoot me?"

"He doesn't even know me, Chuckie."

"So how you know 'bout him?"

"Ray told me."

"Whoa! Damn!" he said. "I don't understand what you said, lady. You breakin' my head. How you friend Ray know 'bout all this? How do you and him know each other?" She couldn't tell from his tone of voice exactly how high he had floated.

Then something changed. He seemed to relax. "This some kind of game you playin', ain't it? You fuckin' with my head all day, I don't know why. But I see what you doin'."

"You're the one who broke in with a pistol, Chuckie, not me. I didn't have any plans for you."

"Yeah, maybe, but this shit ain't real, you know? It's pretend, like. You just been playin' aroun' with me." Even in the thickening dusk she could see that crazy smile returning. His confidence starting to return.

"What I told you is the truth."

"Tell me how you know all this stuff, then, OK? I keep it a secret."

"It's a long story. You'd never believe it."

"I don't believe what's goin' on now, you follow? Like, why you sittin' here all day with a gun? And tellin' me Mr. Joey and his friends are killers."

"What time does the place close?"

"Eight, eight-thirty. You goin' buy us some coffee? They got some they call flat white. You wan' try it?"

"Don't be cute, Chuckie. Are they both in there now?"

"Um-hmm, yeah. Mr. Joey like to close up himself, lock the doors."

Millie let out her breath. Unscrewed the silencer. Put the Sig in her bag. If Joey was planning to leave town right away, she realized, she'd have to move her time-table up. She couldn't take any chances. She'd have to kill Joey Angels tonight. "You got lucky today, Chuckie, you know that?"

"Man, I know it. Still can't believe you didn't shoot me. Was it somebody else you want to shoot?" A few beats. Then: "Whoa, I just see why you been waitin' here with that gun. You goin' shoot Mr. Joey, ain't you? And Mr. Coach Mayo. They do somethin' to you or Ray, you got to get 'em back?" His voice had changed again to a higher pitch. "Man, what's goin' on?"

Chuckie had figured it out. Except he didn't know that today was just supposed to be recon.

"Change of plans, Chuckie. I want you to do a job for me. I want you to buy a cup of coffee and then make a telephone call. I'll pay you."

"Telephone call? You don't need me for that, lady. You want me to talk to that man Ray again, tell 'im how we spend our afternoon? Tell 'im we all friends now?" Chuckie was smiling again. He shook his head. "Cain't figure you out. First you goin' shoot me, now you want to give me money for talkin' on the phone."

"I don't want you to talk to anybody. Just punch in a number when I give you the go-ahead. Think you can remember that?"

"Um-hmm, but sound like we go to jail, we get caught." He folded his arms, stuck his hands under his armpits. "Let me aks you somethin'. You do this all the time? You know, carry a gun, shoot down people want to kill you, shit like that? And now give me money to call somebody on the telephone? What you goin' do while I'm busy callin' folks?"

"You don't need to know."

"Why you want me to drink coffee first? Man on the other end of the phone goin' aks me do I use cream and sugar?"

"Chuckie, Jesus Christ, it won't be a conversation. I'm going to need a few minutes while you're in Angelina's with your coffee. I can't take you with me. I want you to sit there drinking coffee so the place doesn't close early. And maybe see how many people are in there, if it crosses your mind."

"Yeah, I got it. You want me to buy you some coffee too?" he asked. "You like it cream and sugar, or black?"

Chuckie's joke a sign of nerves. "Just do what I said, Chuckie. Here's a hundred dollars, plus coffee money. You'll get two hundred more when we've done."

"You goin' have to give me more money for coffee, lady. That high-class stuff cost five, six dollars a shot, you know that? They stealin' from you every time you walk in the door. That's why I never go in a fancy place like that. Eat a donut too, you out some serious money."

Jerry Masinton

"Talk about stealing, I already gave you twenty. Here's another twenty. Now listen up. Get out of the pickup. Wait here on the sidewalk exactly fifteen minutes. Then cross the street and do what I told you. One other thing, Chuckie: don't ever mistake Angelina's for a fancy place."

Chapter 26

The Readiness Is All

Millie looked at her watch again. It was 7:45. The kid had been gone nearly thirty minutes. It doesn't take half an hour to order a cup of coffee, she thought. She'd told Chuckie explicitly: sit down with your coffee at one of those tables in front of the big window, where I can see you. Just sit there and wait for me to call you on this phone. I'll be waiting outside with your money. I'll give you a number to call and a time to do it. Don't use the phone for anything else. Got it? When you've made the call, walk away, keep going, and never come back.

But now, thirty minutes later, where the hell was he?

She'd given him an old iPhone 6. It had only two numbers programmed into it. One number would receive calls from the iPhone 6 she was using. The second number was activated to ignite the charge in a C-4 bomb. She'd told Chuckie nothing about the phone, nothing about the bomb. Neither phone would ever be traced.

"All right, Chuckie," she'd said. "It's ten after seven—time to rock and roll. Are you ready to go?"

"You talk like this is somethin' dangerous, lady," he'd said. "If it's just buying coffee, like you say, I know how to do it."

At 7:15 she had watched Chuckie walk into the coffee shop. He'd looked at the cannoli in the display case and then had moved to the rear for his coffee.

Millie had then driven to the alleyway back of Angelina's where she'd done recon earlier in the day. She needed to double-check one or two things. Mainly: are there going to be a lot of cars and people back there? Driving through it this time, she concentrated on the middle of the block, where the coffee shop was located. A sign next to the individual parking spaces identified the name of the business in white lettering. On one side of Caffe Angelina was a flower shop. On the other side a baby and kids' clothing store. Both were closed. The parking slots were empty.

A car was parked behind the coffee shop. Had to be Joey's because Chuckie said the guy always closes up. It was a new black Lincoln Continental, pulled almost nose-up to a dumpster near the back door. The place had a heavy metal door—something she hadn't noticed before. Looked like the only one in the alley. Maybe Joey figuring to protect his safe full of money, she thought. The Lincoln sported a silver-rimmed vanity plate—CANNOLI. Guess who.

She parked the Silverado about fifteen yards away. Turned off her lights and got out. Looked both ways: no one else in the alley. It was dark—just the way she liked it.

She unlocked the metal toolbox behind the cab and removed two 1.25-pound C-4 explosive devices and four blasting caps. She inserted the blasting caps into the devices, as Mr. Moustakas had taught her, connected the batteries, and programmed the phone on each bomb to receive a cell-phone signal. The signal would set off the relay connected to the blasting caps, and the blasting caps would detonate the bombs.

Millie stuck one bomb to the frame of Joey's car under the driver's seat. She taped the other bomb to the back door of the coffee shop, snug-up to the middle hinge. She could have used two C-4 packs for each bomb, but one pack would be plenty. In Iraq she'd seen IED's this size upend armored vehicles.

Fifteen minutes later she was once more parked across the street from Angelina's. All three tables were visible through the large plate-glass window. It was 7:35. It's been twenty minutes. He should be in plain sight. All he had to do was walk in, order coffee, and sit down at a table. How hard is that? How long does it take?

From where she sat, the coffee shop looked deserted. She couldn't see all the way to the rear of the place, but no one seemed to be standing in front of the coffee bar. She couldn't make out anyone behind the counter, either. That was the blind spot, back and to the right, where the coffee maker had to be located.

She'd seen no one go in during the afternoon except for two women who were together and two overweight guys wearing sweats. Millie thought that the guys looked like extras for *The Sopranos*. The women had come out after a few minutes carrying cardboard containers of coffee, talking loudly to each other. The two men, who had arrived a few minutes apart from each other, didn't emerge for more than an hour. There was no reason to think there'd been a stampede of customers in the twenty minutes she'd been planting the explosives.

Millie looked at her watch again: 7:40

She waited until 7:45. No sign of Chuckie. He's not going to show.

She'd have to go in after him. If she did that, she'd be giving up the advantage of knowing the full layout of the coffee shop. And she wouldn't know how many men were in there waiting for her to show up. Because if they've made Chuckie as the dummy, she thought, they'll know someone else is going to follow. And they'll know it's going to be a woman. If they've roughed up Chuckie, she figured, they've made him talk.

OK, what do I need? Millie pulled on her new Army Surplus olive field jacket. Thinking, this was just supposed to be a recon day. No need to dress up. Just t-shirt, fatigues, and Ebay boots. Until that crazy Chuckie showed up. Then things started to slip sharply to the side. But then you ended up knowing that Joey's in the coffee shop.

Another thought: would Chuckie have tried to rob me if he hadn't been turned on by my tits? If he hadn't seen the girls, then jimmied the door lock, and told his cockeyed story, would I have ended up going after Joey Angels this evening? Nope. I know what Ralphie's going to say. He'll say that it was Fate—tight t-shirt, Chuckie out looking for trouble, me squeezing the truth out of him, and now Joey's big day. Ralphie will say that it was some kind of cosmic plan. She didn't buy it, but she didn't have time to think about it now.

What next? The Sig on my hip and the Glock in the right ankle holster. No, better to slip the Sig in the front waistband. Easier to use that way. Troodon in the left ankle holster.

She put the silencer for the Sig in the left-hand pocket of the field jacket, along with extra magazines. In the right-hand pocket, an extra mag for the Glock, plus two small smoke bombs that Mandy had given her after a photo shoot.

"Smoke bombs, Priss?" she had asked. "I thought those guys just pointed the camera at you while you took off your clothes."

"It's the big thing now, *Tes*. Red smoke. Blue. Whatever. You're supposed to look like you're emerging from this heavenly cloud and having an orgasm or something.

It's totally bat-shit. I told Emerson, never again, don't even think of booking me with creeps who need smoke in their fucking photos. I'll stick with motorcycles and leather."

"You're just an old-fashioned girl," Millie had said.

Now she thought, am I ready? Pepper spray? Epipens? God no, I don't plan to get that close. But on an impulse she did grab a handful of ball bearings, which she put into the left slash pocket of her pants.

Then she pulled on a black wig and smeared kohl under her eyes and on her eyelids, Goth-style. Stuck the Oakleys on top of her head.

OK, let's roll. Stride right on in to Caffe Angelina like you own the fucking place.

Chapter 27

Closing Time

Millie walked across the street. It was 7:55. She looked up and down the sidewalk. Nothing to worry about. Looked through the big plate glass window at the front of Angelina's. No one at the counter, nobody sitting at the four small tables to the left. The back of the place was too dim to make out anything.

She opened the door with her left hand and walked in, keeping her right free for the Sig. A little bell pinged. Who the hell walks into a coffee shop expecting to draw a gun? But then that's the kind of day it's been.

The lights were dim, but Millie could see all the way to the back of the shop. Nobody. She felt calm. A little excited, sure, but calm.

She turned the CLOSED sign on the door toward the street. Twisted the blinds shut. Walked to the back, past the pastry shelves, until she was in front of the coffee bar. Next to it was an open freezer with large metal tubs of gelato. Still no one in sight. The door to the back room was half open.

"Hello," she called. No answer. "Hello," she tried again. "Anyone here?" She was on full alert now. The emptiness and silence a warning.

Millie decided not to stand there wondering which flavor of gelato she'd like. She slipped quickly to the other side of the bar, looking for the shotgun that Ray had told her about. There were stacks of bar towels, a tiny sink, a rack of glasses. She couldn't see the sawed-off, but that didn't mean it wasn't within reach. Or maybe some guy's got it in his hands, waiting somewhere. I'm not going to stand here and find out.

She screwed the silencer on to the Sig. Stepped silently to the restrooms at back, pistol drawn. Slipped into the Ladies' room, swung the Sig right, left, the full 180 degrees. Up. Down. Nothing. The stall door was open. Empty.

The Men's room was a wash too. OK, either the place is deserted or they're planning a surprise party for someone. And still no sign of Chuckie. A lot of bingo balls in the air.

She held the pistol in front of her, pushed open the door to the back room, and scanned it. A cheap wooden desk with a chair behind it. A small metal cabinet. Nobody there, but she saw an open door to her right, a light bulb dangling above it, apparently leading down to a basement. She heard footsteps on the wooden stairs.

Millie returned to the coffee bar, fast. She kept the Sig against her leg, pointed down, where no one coming from the back could see it.

A heavy-set guy walked through the door from the back room. Closed it. Dropped the black gym bag he was carrying. It made a heavy sound. The man didn't look much like either of the guys Ray had described. Maybe looked like Ernest Borgnine a little, but with quite a few years and pounds added on.

"Sorry, we're closed," he said. "Coffee machine's turned off. Try the guy on the corner." He had a big gap between his front teeth. OK, yeah, Borgnine, definitely.

"Hey, that's OK," Millie said, deciding on the spot to give her best air-head impersonation, maybe keep the guy off-balance while she looked around. "I just want to buy some cannoli, actually. Otherwise you'll have to throw 'em out. You know, 'cause they're not fresh? And I promised a friend I'd buy a bunch for him. He's a real big fan. Is that OK? I'll take a dozen, and couldja put 'em in one of those white boxes like donut shops use, you know, so they don't get all smushed?"

"Too late, lady. They're arready stale. You wouldn't like 'em. We're closed. Matter of fact, we're going out of business after today. Sorry." Sorry? He seemed tired. He glanced at the bag on the floor to his right, then back up at her. Then he stared at her chest. Opened his eyes a little wider. My god. He kept staring. Big bags under his eyes. He seemed to be puzzling something out. "You know how it is," he said. Millie meanwhile turning this way and that, with plenty of time to take in the layout. Estimating distances and shooting angles.

"Oh, sure," she said. "but this friend, he was going to meet me here before closing time, you know? Maybe you know him? Tall black kid wearing a gray hoodie? Told me all about Angelina's. Hey, if you're closing for good, maybe I could grab some left-overs? What's in the back room there?"

"Don't go in there," he said. "It's private." Uh-oh, not a nice tone. The guy was getting frustrated. Unprepared for a dame like this. "I told you, we're selling out," he said, "it's nothing but an empty room now. Look, I'm busy, OK? We're closing up."

"OK, OK, it's just, I'm from out of town—upstate, you know? We don't get good cannoli up there. No Italians, I guess." Maybe she was pushing the air-head bit too far, she'd have to see. Keep him jumpy—that had been the plan—but still. "Kid's name is Charlemagne, by the way. Is that cool, or what?"

He gave her a hard, flat look. "I don't know what you're talking about," he said. "I don't know any kid like that, either. I'm gonna say this one last time, lady—g'wan outta here. Go away. I got a headache, and it's closing time, and I got a big hunch you're playing me. That's not a smart idea. Play dress-up soldier somewhere else."

"Sure, don't get mad, but first I have a message for Joey."

"You're telling me you have a message for Joey. How do you know Joey? I never seen you here before, and you got a message for Joey? I don't believe it." Then: "What is it?" He was sweating.

"It's not for you, Vinnie, it's for Joey. It's from Ray. Ray Roth."

"The fuck? What the hell're you saying? I warned you, lady, I said go home, I gave you plenty . . . ," he said, reaching his right hand under the counter.

"Don't move, Vinnie," Millie said. "Don't even think about it. Put your fucking hands on the counter." Her Sig was pointing at the bridge of his nose.

She counted one-Mississippi, two-Mississippi. "Now, Vinnie. I won't say it again." She steadied the Sig. Vinnie's eyes were cold and dead. The sweat beaded out on his forehead. She stared back at him, waiting for the next move. "OK," he said, nodding, breathing hard, a tight grin forming. "OK." He put his left hand up, palm out, but his right hand kept moving toward the shotgun that she knew was there. It must be attached to the underside of the counter, she figured.

She pivoted left, knowing how it would play out, fired a round into his left temple, then another into his neck as his head rocked back. The shotgun went off at the same time, blowing chocolate mousse and mint gelato all over the wall. Shotgun art.

Two seconds later the lights went out. Millie slipped the Oakleys down over her eyes, crouched low, reached for the iPhone 6, and pressed one of the keyed-in numbers. The back door of Caffe Angelina blew out violently, making a deep whooshing sound. The door to the back room exploded into the coffee shop. Smoke pushed toward her. Flames from the back alley reflected dully against the walls of the back room.

Any second now, she thought. Any second, and Joey Angels will make a run for it. And he'll come this way. He'll want to avoid the fire in the alley.

She waited. Relaxed herself with a few deep breaths. She heard a raspy voice, mumbling, shuffling feet, then saw him stumble his way from the back room. He was holding Chuckie in front of him as a shield. They'd come from the basement below the coffee shop. Joey D looked back and forth, back and forth, having trouble seeing through the smoke and shadows. Millie watched him through her Oakleys. She aimed the Sig at Joey's exposed right arm, the one with a revolver pressed against Chuckie's head. Possibly a Taurus 6-shot, she thought. In any case, no more than six shots. Joey a tall, wheezing bald guy with horn-rimmed glasses who might scare your dog if you had that kind of dog.

Millie dug into her pocket, pulled out a handful of ball bearings, and tossed them to her left. The ball bearings clattered and rolled, hit the opposite wall. Joey fired three Hail-Mary shots in the general direction. One of them shattered the large plate-glass window in the front of the shop. Somebody's going to call 911, she thought.

She didn't move. The smoke continued to rush in from the back room. She rolled a few more ball bearings toward Joey. He fired two more slugs into the floor in front of him. That's five, she thought. Only one shot left. She stood up, staying in the shadows against the coffee bar. "Let the kid go, Joey. I'm only going to ask once." The Sig was pointed at Joey's right shoulder.

He finally looked directly at her, a denser part of the shadows. "I'm gonna whack this fuckin' kid if you don't get outta my way," he said. He was swaying from side to side, an after-effect of the explosion, she figured, or from the effort of holding Chuckie up.

"Chuckie," Millie said, "what're you doing here?" An element of casualness in her voice, maybe confuse Joey, help keep Chuckie safe. She held the Sig steady. Can't miss from this distance, she thought.

"Oh, man, me?" Chuckie said. "I don't . . . Mr. Coach Mayo, he say, he say . . ." and Chuckie collapsed. Joey had now lost control of his hostage. Take him out, Millie, what are you waiting for? I've got to tell him, she thought, that's why. I have to let him know.

Joey pointed his pistol down at the kid. Looked over at Millie, saw the Sig in the dim light from the street, said, "Put down the fucking gun or the kid dies."

"You've got one shot left, Joey. Shoot him and you're mine."

Joey swung the pistol away from Chuckie, toward Millie, but she fired three quick rounds before he could squeeze off the shot. She hit the revolver—*pinggg*—the other two hitting his right arm and shoulder. The force of the slugs slammed him against the door frame behind him. "Ahhh! Fuck you! Ahhh!" He slid down to the floor, his feet straight out. The gym bag was in front of him. "Son-of-a-bitch! What the hell do you want?" He was breathing hard.

"Get over here, Chuckie," she said. He groaned but didn't move. She walked the few steps to where Joey's pistol lay and kicked it out of reach. "Joey, I have a message from Ray."

"Who the fuck are you?" He groaned. Tried to get up. Couldn't. "I knew he was alive. That deadbeat son-of-a-bitch Jew owes me money. I got a message for him, you hear me, you rancid bitch? Tell him. Tell him this time he's a fuckin' dead man." He made it up to one knee. Reached for the gym bag with his good hand.

Millie fired two rounds into the floor in front of it. "I don't think he's Jewish, Joey. Now back off. I'll take care of the bag for you."

"This is my fuckin' money, bitch. I'm not leaving here without it. You'll have to kill me. Who the fuck are you?"

"I'm the shooter you hired to whack Ray, Joey."

"Bullshit! Roth is alive—you said so yourself. Christ, my fuckin' arm! Help me." Then: "Look, I'll pay you." He was wheezing hard now.

"You already paid me, Joey. Sorry about Ray, but I whacked Art and Jimmy as a bonus. You got double your money."

"What the hell do you know about those dumb fucks? You're nuts! This is a set-up. Jesus, I don't know what you want."

"Remember Sheldon Kukich, the guy in Kansas City? You wanted him dead too."

"Shel? Christ Almighty! Look, I'll give you half of the money, OK? There's a million dollars in there. All stacked and banded for you. Jesus F. Christ, don't shoot me!"

Millie fired three rounds into the floor in front of him. "Get out. Now. Back away." She fired the remaining rounds into the floor, near his legs, and into the wall close to his head.

Joey, gasping with pain, slowly stood up. He made a weak try for the bag, but Millie fired two shots into it. Joey stumbled back, cursing, dragging himself to the back door.

"Don't you want Ray's message?"

He seemed to be gargling, "Ahhhhh, ahhhhh," from deep down in his chest. She heard him get into the Lincoln and shut the door. She was reasonably certain that the car would start. The dumpster in front of it was big enough to cushion the blast. She waited. Then she heard the car engine. She counted three, four, five, giving him time to back out of the parking slot, scrape a fender against the brick wall opposite, and punch the accelerator. Then she made the call. The explosion blasted against the alley walls like thunder, ricocheting in both directions. Fat flames funneled past the missing back door.

"That was the message."

She heard sirens in the distance, a little surprised that the cops weren't closer. But she'd have to hurry. It was 8:10.

She screwed the silencer off the Sig and holstered it. Pulled Chuckie to his feet. "What the hell are you doing here?" she said. "Didn't you get it, that these gorillas like to kill people?" She pulled the Glock from its ankle holster and chambered a round. Didn't bother with the silencer. No reason to use one now.

Chuckie was upright but wobbly. "Try to stay on your feet," Millie said.

The sound of voices came through the large shattered window in front. People in the street curious and maybe scared, waiting for the cops to arrive to see the show.

"Chuckie, party's over. Cops will be here any minute. Can you walk?" The sirens growing louder.

"Yeah. We get to the door, I'm goin' run. You never see me again."

"Not that way, Chuckie, we're going out the back."

At that moment the front door burst open and a squat, square shape peered into the dark, turning his head to listen. Sal Luccio, she thought. Fine with me. The Glock was still in her hand.

How well could he see? When would he make his play? She was on automatic now, all adrenaline, nerve-endings, instinct.

Sal must have sensed something ahead in the shadows. He ducked his shoulders and barreled toward them, a bull, his massive head down. She fired, put a round into his right side, belt-high. He slipped and fell, got up quick, and charged toward them again, lurching one way, then the other, trying to find his balance, a hard target to hit. Millie fired three more times, the Glock loud without a silencer. Every round hit him—right side again, right thigh, a gut shot on the left —but he didn't go down. She pushed Chuckie away from her and tried to side-step away, but Sal got his left shoulder into her and brought her to the floor.

The fall took her breath away, but she managed to fire a round into his left hip. He still wouldn't quit. Goddammit, I should have stuck with the Sig. He grabbed Millie's wrist and tried to shake the pistol loose. She held on, but now he was on top of her and the other hand was reaching for her throat. Her left hand was free, but she couldn't pull his hand away. She couldn't breathe.

Chuckie had hold of Sal's belt, trying to drag him off her. Couldn't do it. He tried kicking him, but Sal kept squeezing Millie's throat. She reached with her left thumb for his eye, but he twisted away. Then she slammed her fist into the side of his head. His grip on her throat loosened a little, enough for a quick intake of air. Then she brought her left knee up, pulled the knife from its scabbard, and plunged the blade into Sal's throat. The Troodon made the job easy, a Girl Scout's pocket knife slipping into a fat cantaloupe.

Millie pushed him away and got up, her field jacket and t-shirt covered in blood. She wiped the blade of her combat knife on Sal's jacket. "We're going out the back, Chuckie."

"I'm ready. I been ready. Figured I might be leavin' alone," he said.

The flashing blue and red lights were now in front of the shop, the wailing sirens turned off. Millie took one of the smoke bombs from her cargo pocket, pulled the string that ignited it, and tossed it toward the front door. A lovely bright blue color, a close match to the revolving blue light outside. As she and Chuckie ran out the back door, she turned and tossed the second smoke bomb, this one a deep crimson.

She was carrying the black gym bag. Her watch said 8:15.

Chapter 28

Million-Dollar Pizza

Millie and Chuckie ducked out of Angelina's with the bag of money. There were three businesses off the alley that hadn't yet closed—a pizza place, a tobacco shop that sold newspapers and magazines, and a Polish deli on the corner. She tried the door of the pizza place. No luck. But the door of the tobacco shop swung open when she pulled. Good, she thought. If anyone's looking through the magazines at this time of day, it'll be men with their noses buried in the pages of girlie mags. They won't pay much attention to Chuckie and me.

Millie pulled Chuckie into the shadows between the back doors of the tobacco shop and the pizza joint. She unzipped the gym bag and dumped the money into a dumpster half-full of pizza boxes. Uneaten slices of pizza lay on top of the boxes. "Jesus, lady, whut you doin' with that money?" Chuckie whispered. He sucked air through his teeth. "Whoa, don't do that." The air going into his lungs now a cross between a wheeze and a wail.

"Shut up," Millie said. She took off her field jacket and spread it on the ground. Placed the pistols, extra ammo, the knife—all the hardware, plus the holster and scabbard—on the outspread jacket and rolled every-thing into a tight bundle. "Chuckie, take off your hoodie, quick." Meanwhile stuffing the bundle into the gym bag, working fast but not getting ahead of herself. Then she reached into the garbage can for one of the greasy boxes, tossed a few scraps of pizza and bread sticks into it, and squeezed it into the gym bag. It covered the rolled-up field jacket. Millie zipped the bag closed.

Chuckie observing this scene without moving. "We've got about five more seconds before the cops find us, Chuckie. Give me the fucking hoodie." He just looked at her. She grabbed him by the wrist, twisted hard, and locked his elbow. "Don't make me do this, Chuckie." He nodded his head yes, OK.

She put on the hoodie. It was long enough to cover the blood stains on her pants. Chuckie was wearing a long-sleeve Under Armour tee. It was black. Perfect. Who was going to look twice at the tall gangly teen-ager wearing a UA tee and the girl with a gray hoodie cover-ing most of her face?

The magazine shop turned out to be empty. There was no one doing field studies of the cheap porn in-dustry. Nobody stood at the cash register. Everyone's outside on the sidewalk and street, watching the show in front of Angelina's, Millie realized. She and Chuckie strolled through the store and out the front door. Not a soul glanced their way. They joined the murmuring crowd, moved through it, and crossed the street. The Silverado was parked about forty yards away. One clean base hit and we're home.

She said to Chuckie: "Take the bag. It'll look more natural for you to carry it." They walked together, her hand tightly gripping his arm. To keep him from flying away. The people on the sidewalk didn't look at them. Too busy gawking at the four cop cars parked across the street, blue lights flashing the color of burning propane, the white lights a piercing stab of electricity . Millie kept her eyes on the crowd, on the cops checking out the crowd, listening for any stir of excitement. The cops were asking questions, nodding their heads after a few seconds, and then moving on.

She watched one uniformed policeman detach himself from a group a few yards away and walk toward her and Chuckie. "I'll do the talking, Chuckie," she said. "He's just asking routine questions."

The cop signaled to them with his index finger. Come here. He wasn't exactly bored, she saw, but he wasn't expecting inside information from the sightseers, either. After all, what was there to see if all the mayhem had taken place earlier inside the coffee shop? Though you never know.

"What happened here?" Millie said. "Heart attack? Looks like there was a fire over there, Jerrone, what do you think?"

"Huh? Umm." This from Chuckie, who then shrugged his shoulders. So far, so good.

"You kids seen anyone suspicious hereabouts?" the cop said, his voice a rasp of sandpaper on stone. "Men running down the street, guys in a hurry? Maybe they jump into a car and speed off? Maybe a guy carrying a gun? So on. Anything might be helpful."

"Uh-uh," Millie said. "Nobody like that. Have we, Jerrone? No, we sure haven't, sir. What did they do? Somebody get shot? God, right here with people out walking and stuff? Where's the ambulance?" All the while keeping her face half-hidden in Chuckie's hoodie.

"We're just gathering information. Talking to everyone here. So you didn't see anything unusual?"

"Not a thing, sir. No, hmm-umhh. I'd remember," Millie said.

"No, sir, we ain't seen nothing like that," Chuckie said, "like, you know, men shootin' each other with guns, nor either lightin' off bombs, you know, crazy shit like that? A few blocks back we heard somethin' like gunshots, or either firecrackers, like that, but not around here. Huh-unh! Why folks . . ."

"Jerrone," Millie said, "Let's . . ."

" . . . walkin' in the street here, somebody crash they car? Any dead out there on the street? I don't wanna see. I seen enough today. Goddamn! Good thing you here with them cars flashing they lights. Help folks get settled in they mind, you know? Police settle things down for us. Maybe go home now, get supper, best thing for everybody."

Jesus Christ, Chuckie, what are you doing? And wouldn't you know it—he was smiling that gone-to-heaven smile of his.

"Jerrone," she said, "stop running your fucking mouth, will you? The man doesn't want to hear you jabber like an idiot. If you have something to say, say it. Otherwise, what the fuck? I've told you about that a million times."

"Is he OK?" the cop said.

"As OK as he's ever going to be."

"What's in the gym bag?"

"Huh?" Chuckie said. "Which?"

"Oh," she said, "well, supper, sir, and some clothes we found."

"In the gym bag?" he said. He looked at Chuckie. "Your supper's in there?"

Chuckie shrugged his shoulders. Said nothing. Finally following instructions, now that it's too late.

"Mind if I take a look?" the cop said. He reached for the bag. Chuckie didn't move. "Show him, Jerrone, he won't take it," Millie said. The policeman unzipped the bag, Chuckie still holding it close. Looked in. "My god, have you kids been dumpster-diving? Stealing pizza from trash cans? Jesus. I wouldn't have believed it. OK, all right, move along." He zipped the bag closed. "Just a minute," he said. "Here." He reached for his wallet. "Let me give you a couple of bills. At least buy a fresh burger."

"No, sir," Millie said, "it's against our religion. But thank you. And bless you. Let's go, J-boy, your mother will be worried sick, you know how she is." He shrugged his shoulders, twice. Don't overdo it, Chuckie.

Then they were in the Silverado. Millie pulled a roll of twenties from her cross-body bag. "Chuckie, take this. There's extra for the hoodie. Now get out of my truck and out of my life, and forget you were ever here. You've been lucky twice today. Third time you won't be." She started the engine. "Why didn't you keep your damned mouth shut back there? I told you not to talk, remember?" A beat. "Don't answer. Just leave."

"Man, I can't hardly talk no how. I was nervous, that's why. That police looking right through me, you know? Damn. This whole day gone crazy. Joey and them dead, me too, almost, you shootin' guns like a cowboy. Don't know what to think. I'm done, done talkin', done trying to think. Lemme aks you a question, OK?"

"No. Get out."

"Why didn't you keep that money? You don't want it, give it to me. I give you half. Where we ever goin' see that much cash-money again? I feel like goin' back in that alley, wait till the police gone, see is it still there. Stick it down my shirt. Ain't goin' hurt nobody if I spend it, will it? Don't belong to nobody, now Mr. Joey dead. Just a waste, all that fresh money in the garbage can. Somebody goin' find it, sure as trouble, and then they be rich. Should be me and you gets rich. We the only ones left. Man, my head hurts, right behind the eyes. You ever get one like that?"

Millie reached across his chest, opened the door, and pushed him out—not hard, but firmly.

"Your mama will be worried about you, Charlemagne." She pulled the door shut. Locked it. Gunned the engine. Gave him one last look through the glass.

He managed a leaky grin, turned, and jogged slowly into the shadows.

She slipped the Silverado into gear and drove off. At 3:00 a.m. she climbed into bed and cuddled against Mandy's back. Mandy was warm and smelled of something citrusy. She didn't open her eyes, but her long left arm reached straight up. "*Tes*, she said, "I left some pizza for you. Italian sausage. Your favorite. Did you find it?" She dropped back into sleep as her arm drew Millie closer.

Chapter 29

From *The Brooklyn Daily Eagle*

GANG VIOLENCE SHOCKS CITY
THREE KILLED
IN SHOOTOUT, BOMBING

By Nick Grgich, Special to *The Eagle*

Three men with reputed Mob ties were found dead last night after a bombing and gun battle at Caffe Angelina, a coffee shop near the corner of Bay Parkway and 85th St. Authorities believe that the violence, which took place from about 7:30 until 8:00, was probably related to the struggle over drug turf in that area of the city.

Dead are Joey D'Angeli, owner of Caffe Angelina, Salvatore ("Cannonball") Luccio, and Vincent ("Coach") Coccimiglio. All were long-time residents of the neighborhood.

The police have not identified any suspects but have been questioning store owners and witnesses who were near the crime scene. Several witnesses heard the gunfire and explosions and called 911. However the police and ambulances were delayed by traffic jams on two of the major thoroughfares leading to the area. Fans returning home from a basketball game between the Brooklyn Nets (6-40) and the Cleveland Cavaliers (40-6) also contributed to the delay.

Authorities have informed the *Eagle* that the nature of the murders suggests gang-style executions. The theory emerging is that two or three experienced killers entered Caffe Angelina at about 7:30 and quickly overcame the victims. Evidence at the scene indicates that two of the three victims used firearms.

In a statement read this morning at a press conference, Chief of Police Andy Papko urged citizens to remain calm. "We do not believe this incident to be the work of terrorists. We see it as a typical take-over attempt on the part of criminals in our city who are battling for supremacy in the drug trade. Mr. D'Angeli has long been known as a Mob boss who traffics in drugs, money laundering, and loan-sharking.

"Two months ago he was brought to trial for murder in New York, but on the second day of the trial Federal authorities failed to produce their key witness, who has since disappeared and is believed dead. Mr. D'Angeli was subsequently released from custody. The Justice Department was said to be preparing a case against Mr. D'Angeli for money-laundering."

In his statement Chief Papko said that the police will pursue every lead in identifying and questioning suspects. "We have developed an extensive database on the workings of the crime world of which Mr. D'Angeli was a member. Sooner or later, somebody out there is going to talk and we will crack this case. In the meantime, let me remind you that the leaders of the notorious D'Angeli crime family have all been eliminated. That's one less major criminal enterprise in our midst."

Asked to elaborate on the extensive damage done at the crime scene, Chief Papko replied, "Our present mind-set is that the level of force employed, while perhaps excessive, was in line with previous gang-related assassinations."

In addition to the firearms, two explosive devices were used. It appears that Mr. D'Angeli, after being shot twice in the arm, attempted to escape the premises in his car, which was blown up by a remote device seconds later. The back door of the coffee shop was also bombed.

No explanation has been offered for that bombing, since the killers apparently entered through the front door. Additionally, it is unknown why approximately two dozen bullets were fired into the walls and floor of the café. Forensic experts have identified the spent cartridges from the bullets as coming from weapons known to be popular among underworld figures.

A third unanswered question in this bizarre case was addressed by a source close to the Police Department who wishes to remain anonymous. "At this point in time, we have not as yet determined why harmless colored smoke bombs were part of the lethal arsenal of these men. I myself, personally, think they were a signal sent by an ambitious gang laying claim to D'Angeli's drug territory. They're flexing their muscles. Don't be surprised to see a gang war in the near future among their competitors."

Editor's Note: Shortly after the above report was filed, the Eagle learned from a trusted source that more than $1,000,000, mostly wrapped in bundles of $100, was found in a trash can in the alley two doors away from the coffee shop. Further investigation will be needed to determine whether the money has any connection to the murders.

Chapter 30

Follow the Money

A couple of days later, Millie, Mary Michael, and Ralph are in his kitchen sitting around the antique oak table that Sheila left him. Late morning, sun streaming through the windows. Millie back from her five-mile run and thirty-minute shower. She's in jeans and a Pats sweatshirt. Ralph's wearing a cream-colored polyester leisure suit that nose-dived out of fashion with Sonny and Cher, white patent-leather belt and shoes, and black socks with flamingoes. Millie's eyes meet Mary Mike's. The two women refrain from commenting.

Mary Mike has on an ankle-length, black-and-white-stripe, mock-turtle-neck, long-sleeve, plus-size cotton dress with black boots. Her hair a tsunami of gray waves flecked with white. Millie notices that Mary Mike has put on a few pounds recently.

Two boxes of Dunkin' Donuts, warm and fragrant, sitting on the counter by the stainless-steel sink. The aroma of fresh coffee. Ralph watering his plants and whistling tunelessly. He has a new money tree from Harry and David. The tree has a braided trunk. Life's good.

Mary Michael pours the coffee, stacks a dozen do-nuts on a bright yellow Fiesta platter, and sets it on the table.

Millie's just given them the rundown on recent events in Brooklyn. The postmortem on Joey Angels.

"Yeah, I see how it went, Mil," Ralph said, "but Christ, why throw the fucking money in a trash can? It's all over the news, you know? 'Rival gang members slay—that's the word they use, "slay"—big-time Mob guy that the Feds been after for years and can't get him. Killers ditch $1,000,000.' And we don't like publicity for our business, you know, but here it is every time you turn on the TV or pick up a copy of the *Globe*, a million fuck-ing dollars covered in tomato sauce and stringy cheese, in a stinking trash can in the alley. And of course Joey Angels blown up in his car, which half the businesses in that alley got their windows shattered in the explosion. And Joey's goons inside, full of bullet holes. But it's the money that's got everybody talking."

"What publicity?" Millie said. "I see the news too. Nobody's talking about the removals business."

"You know what I mean, Mil. It's just bad for the business environment."

"I don't understand why you're saying that, dear," Mary Mike said. "Especially when no one knows who took out Joey and who dumped the money. Or even if the two things are connected."

"You know, Ralphie," Millie said, "when I took this job, I never dreamed that one of the best things about it would be these—what can I call them?—after-parties with fresh donuts and coffee. I'm going to start with a couple of old-fashioned today and absolutely drown them in coffee. And then move on to crullers. But first I have a little surprise for you guys." She reached into the brown paper bag she'd carried in with her and pulled out a rectangular white pastry box. "Here, Ralphie, open it."

He did. "Huh," he said. "Cannoli? See that, Mary Mike?"

"Oh, that's lovely, hon,'" she said. "I haven't had cannoli in, oh, I don't know how long. My nephew's graduation from welding school? I think that was it."

"Just the other day," Ralph told them, "I was telling Stuart over at Dunkin' there, 'Stuart, you know, I'm not complaining, 'cause I'm in here every day and I eat everything you got—the donuts, the egg and ham McDunkin' or whatever, even muffins, which are not for some reason high on my list,' I said. 'But why don't you add cannoli? You could do it, easy, right?' And he says to me, 'Ralph, how long you been comin' in here now? You know this store better than me, and you know I don't sell cannoli. They didn't come with the original franchise, and I'm not lookin' to change. We're donuts, period, on that side, plus we got sandwich items, like you say, but cannoli? Huh-uh.' 'You ever hear,' I ask him, 'you ever hear about the guy in New York invented the donnoli?' 'The fuck's that?' Stuart said. 'It's like a donut,' I tell him, 'a donut plus cannoli. They shape a donut like a cannoli and then squirt the cream inside.' 'And you think my customers'd like that, Ralph?' he says. 'I couldn't give 'em away,' he says. 'And you know why? Let me explain to you why,' he says. 'They want the Cadillac of donuts, period. Same thing every day. Gives 'em a sense of stability, you understand?' he says. 'People need that, the state the fuckin' world's in. You go innerducing donnoli, for Chrissake, and it makes 'em upset. You know what, Ralph,' he says. 'They don't want a million choices when they have the primo item already. They like what they got. And that's what I give 'em. Does that answer your question?' 'Yeah,' I tell him. 'I just thought for a little variety, you know?'"

"Millie, dear, what made you buy cannoli?" Mary Mike said.

"I saw a tray of them in Angelina's and I thought, what a waste, because no one's going to buy them after I settle the bill with Joey. I couldn't get them out of my mind. Fresh this morning from Antoine's over on Watertown. Ever been there? You can put them in the fridge and they'll still be good tomorrow." She had now eaten two old-fashioned and was reaching for another. Starved after her workout. No mystery there.

"Which brings me back to the money," Ralph said. "You coulda got away with it, couldn't you? Who'd wanna check a lousy gym bag that some young woman was carrying?"

"If the young woman's clothes were spattered with blood," Millie said, "then any cop on the scene would have checked the bag. I'm wearing an Army jacket, Army pants, combat boots, and I'm covered in blood. Plus I'm carrying a holstered pistol and another in my waistband. They're concealed but it doesn't take an Einstein to see the bulges under my jacket. In other words, I'm a walking neon sign flashing the word 'Suspect,' Ralphie."

"OK," Ralph said, "but you could take off your jacket, fold it, and carry it over your arm, couldn't you? That'd work. And keep the million dollars in the bag. Or the kid carries the bag, looks like he just came from the gym?"

"Except that he's a liability, he's shaky after passing out cold on the floor with Joey's pistol in his ear, and I couldn't trust how he'd react. You saw how he went motor-mouth when that cop asked us a question. I wasn't sure that Chuckie could play the scene if he had to carry the money. I couldn't take the chance."

"A million fucking dollars," Ralph said.

"You know, Ralphie," Mary Mike said, "Millie's right. It's just money, after all, and we have plenty. Also, we've got more contracts in the pipeline. So why take a chance?"

227

"Yeah, sure, who gives a damn about the money?" he said. "But that much fucking jack? There had to be a way, that's all I'm sayin'. Just my opinion, I know nobody's askin' for it."

"It's a grand opinion, Ralphie," Mary Mike said. "It shows you're paying attention to things. But Millie's the one had to figure it all out on the spot."

"OK, then," he said to Millie, "but why couldn't you at least slip the kid a few bundles? He needed the money. He could of stuck 'em in his pocket and nobody's the wiser." He paused. "OK, yeah, I know he tried to hold you up earlier that day, but then he didn't really mean it, you said."

"He meant it, he just wasn't any good at it."

"But you weren't going to shoot him, so you coulda given him a few bucks instead."

"I did, but it was my own money."

"Yeah? How much?"

"The point, Ralph," Millie said, "the thing to keep in mind, is that some of the money might have been tagged. I couldn't take the chance. And the truth is, I needed the gym bag to hide my bloody jacket in. I never really thought about keeping the money. For a minute I did, but then I realized it could be funny money."

"You decided this ahead of time?"

"To hide my field jacket in the bag? Yeah," she said. "And also I realized that the money wouldn't be safe for us to spend. And for Chuckie? A total disaster."

"How's it a disaster?" Ralphie said. "Because what the hell good is the dough if you don't put it into circulation? And like the kid said, who's it going to hurt? The guy who took out the contract on you is dead. He's not going to complain."

"See, Ralphie, here's the thing," Mary Mike said. "The Feds are all over Joey from way back. They know he washes money. They know he's a loan shark. Does dirty business of all kinds. After the murder trial goes off the rails, they go back to those other things to get him. Money-laundering. Tax evasion. Racketeering. Drugs, the papers say. Bribing union bosses. It adds up."

"Uh-huh." This is Millie.

"And so you can't tell if the money in the bag is marked or not. It could be a set-up by the Feds. Anyone trying to pass those bills would show up on their radar," Mary Mike said. "So why take the chance?"

"Where did you learn all this stuff, Mary Mike?" he said.

"You remember that banker I whacked because he cheated on me?" she said. "That's not all he taught me. He showed me how to launder money. How to set up off-shore accounts and dummy corporations. Some of the stuff is legal. Some of it, you know, mezza-mezz. Some of it flirts with prison time. But it's easy to beat the system. Banks do it all the time. I told you this before, sweetie."

"The one he cheated on you with his wife," Ralph said. "Right?"

"Yeah, the son-of-a-bitch."

Millie got up for more coffee. Poured her cup full. Topped off Ralph's cup, then Mary Mike's. Began to brew a fresh pot. "So if it's risky for us," she said, "think of the exposure for a kid like Chuckie Favors trying to spend it."

"No, I get that," Ralph said. "He's in deep shit. Black kid, drops out of school." Ralph holds up his left thumb. "Has no job, does this and that for a Mob guy, pick-ups and deliveries—a bag man, in other words." Now Ralph extends the left index finger. "So, he's—what?—'a known associate,' right?"

"That's right, 'a known associate' of gangsters," Mary Mike said.

"Known locally," Millie said, "but not yet by the Feds. Still, yeah, he'd be grabbed."

"Plus," Ralph said, tapping his middle finger, "put that together with Joey being a shylock and a money-washer. Guy that handles a lot of cash. OK, where are we?" he said. He has now reached the ring finger of his left hand. "Oh, yeah, and then Joey and his bozos end up dead, the known associate starts waving hunnerd-dollar bills around, and bingo, the cops like him for the murders. He's the primo suspect. Only he's innocent, but he's the only one they pull in, right? And the cops try to sweat a confession out of him."

"They couldn't hang it on him in the long run," Millie said, "but they'd pick him up in a heartbeat and try to squeeze something out of him. He might even confess, because the kid gets a little flustered under pressure. It wouldn't stick, but Chuckie's life would be derailed. Pass the donuts, would you, Ralph?"

"Something else about those bills," Mary Mike said.

"What now?" Ralph said.

"You'd be drawing attention to yourself if you used them for everyday buys, even if they were clean. You can't order a burger and hand the McDonald's girl a hundred-dollar bill. Buy toothpaste and you're gonna give the CVS clerk a hundred? Or look at your friend Stuart there, at Dunkin' Donuts, he's gonna start wondering why you hand him a crisp bill every morning when you buy fresh donuts. Or does he still give them to you free gratis?"

"You guys don't get it," he said. "Once in a while you hand a guy a C-note, maybe when you load up on groceries at Star Market, OK? It's easy to spend fifty, a hunnerd on groceries. No one's gonna notice. Or you ask 'em to break the bill at the customer service they got there, over at Star's, give you five twennies. Or listen: You go out to a nice restaurant some night, spend two or three bills, that's nothing these days."

"And, if the bills just happen to be funny money?" Millie said. "Sooner or later somebody's going to trace them back to Star's or wherever, and the cashier or the waiter's going to remember Mr. Ralph Klammer, and eventually the cops—the Feds, not the locals—are going to want to talk to you. They'll have interesting questions, too, you'll enjoy them. Like, 'We're interested, sir, in where you got these hundred-dollar bills. You mind telling us? Did ja notice that the serial numbers on a lot of 'em all run in sequence?' You'll be in a room downtown at one of the law-enforcement buildings, Ralphie. Or maybe in a cop's office in Waltham or Brookline, if you go out on a long trip, and you'll be sitting at a metal table that's screwed to the floor. These guys'll say, 'Like you to explain that, where this money came from, if you can, Mr. Klammer. It's OK, take your time.' And since when do you go out to high-end restaurants, Ralphie, where you spend two or three hundred? You're a burger and pizza guy."

"Here's another question they're gonna ask you," Mary Mike said. "They're gonna say, 'Where'd you get that leisure suit from, Sir? From that "Antiques Roadshow" there on TV? Because they sure as hell don't sell 'em any more in the stores around here, far as we know, though me and my partner here, we ain't up to the minute in fashion. Or did you lift that from some old geezer in Dedham or Melrose that's keeping it to scare the bejesus out of the little kids come Halloween?'"

"C'mon, for Chrissake, Mary Mike," he said. "let me up. I bought it online. It's got a tradition, see. That's what the ad said. Then I remembered it looked good on this guy in an old dance movie my mom used to watch all the time. So I thought, try it, Ralph, maybe it looks sharp on you too. Grab a little style, you know. It was cheap."

"Have you ever seen one of those?" Mary Mike asked Millie.

"Not a live one, no."

"You know what they used to call them?"

"Huh-uh."

"Full Cleveland. You wear your polyester leisure suit with white patent-leather shoes and belt, that's a Full Cleveland."

"OK, you guys are real fuckin' funny. We're all laughing at Ralph Klammer the dope, now, right? Who by the way buys the donuts and coffee for you out of his own pocket, sometimes. It's an old-fashioned suit, yeah, but like anything with a little history it makes a statement."

The women glance at each other again. Eyebrows go up. Lips press tight. Not a word. A little time passes.

"So, then, look at it this way," Ralph said, "we could just fence the money, get something for it, anyway."

"Ralphie," Mary Mike said, "we don't know any fences. We never had any use for them. You got me to keep the money clean and invest it legitimately when we need to."

"But we could get a fence, right?"

"Sure, but could we trust him not to talk when the marked bills put him in the pokey?"

"'The pokey'?" he said. "The hell're you saying? Is this another joke?"

"She's just saying it's not worth the trouble," Millie said. "This fence we hire, he'll be at risk. He knows that already, that's his job. But with this kind of cargo he'll raise his usual take and we'll be lucky to get forty percent, max. And M's right: you'd never be able to trust the guy. If he gets caught, he'll give them our address and phone number, Social Security numbers, high-school references, everything. Ralphie, we have a nice, profitable business going here. Why risk it?"

"Yeah, OK, I was just thinking."

"Besides, I told you: I wanted the gym bag for my field jacket. I had one thought, and one thought only, when I punctuated Sal Luccio: where to dump the damned jacket after he'd bled on it. Afterward, when Chuckie and I were outside in the alley, I thought of the rest: ditch the money, hide my jacket in the bag, throw something over the jacket to cover it up, and wear Chuckie's hoodie to shadow my face."

"'Punctuated.' I like that, Millie," Mary Mike said.

"I thought you would."

"You did some quick thinking there, in the alley," Mary Mike said. "You were excited, pumped up a little I bet, to have a plan and know you're going to get away with it right under their nose."

"Um-hmm, you know how it feels. You're sailing."

"And the money's the last thing you want right then, isn't it, hon'?" Mary Mike said. "What's a bag of cash worth if you're snagged by the police? They'll know that you killed those bozos for their money. Which you didn't, but you still whacked them, and now you're holding the proof in your hand. Proof that it was done for the money, I mean. Hard to sweet-talk your way out of that, sweetheart. Not to mention the blood all over your clothes."

"So let me ask you," Ralph said, "why'd you cover your jacket with the garbage from a pizza joint? That's a sensible question, isn't it?" He looked at the Fiesta plate. Empty. He hadn't been paying attention. He took the plate to the counter and piled more donuts on it. Chocolate-covered, crullers, glazed, jelly, Boston Kreme. Another full dozen. He filled their cups with the fresh-brewed coffee.

"The pizza?" Millie said. "Nearest thing I could grab. I was improvising. Running on automatic. A pizza box and pizza scraps turned out to be a good choice. It was so dumb it worked."

"Yeah," Ralph said. "Good. Inneresting job all the way around, Mil, I gotta say that. And at the end you send Chuckie home and you drive back in your truck, and everything's hunky-dory, right? The whole operation wrapped up. No chance that this kid blabs, is there?"

"Blabs? Ralphie, Jesus, we've had this conversation before, remember? Why would he say anything? Who is he going to tell it to? He'd just implicate himself."

"Chuckie's story, Merciful Mother of God," Mary Mike said. "I can just see it. The cops pick him up. They start questioning him. Two cops, a veteran and a rookie, plus the kid in a smelly, dreary little room, that's the way I imagine it. Couple of dim lights hanging from the ceiling over a metal table."

"The hell're you saying, Mary Mike?" Ralph said. "This never happened, so what're you . . . ?"

"So just listen, Ralphie, I'm telling a story. 'All right, Charlemagne,' one of them would say. That's the older cop, the one asking most of the questions. 'Just tell us what happened,' he says. 'Use your own words. Clear up some of these discrepancies we have.' And poor Chuckie, scared enough to fill his drawers, says, 'It was this lady, see, I didn't do nothin'. Mr. Joey want to shoot me, but this lady shoot Mr. Joey instead.' By now the kid's also sweating bullets.

"'Yes, so you said,' the cop says. 'A white woman. But Chuckie. OK I call you Chuckie? Who is this mystery woman? We don't have any information on a woman at the crime scene. You see my problem? Who the hell is this female assassin that you claim to know?'

"'She didn't give me no name, man. Truth. I just, like, saw her that one day. It was a accident.'

"'But you said you were with her when she canceled Joey's check. And you saw her take out the Sicilian Bull, Sal Luccio, which I don't think anyone here's going to swallow. But: that's what you told the police officers who grabbed you off the street. So then, Chuckie: were you her sidekick? I'm curious to know that. You didn't just walk into this coffee shop for a hit of cappuccino and accidentally happen to see all this shooting, did you? Help me here, Chuckie.'

"'Naah, huh-uh, I never see her before, like I tole you.'

"'OK, how did you meet this interesting lady? Let's start there.'

"'Oh, man, see, I was goin' rob her, like. Take her money. Only I didn't do it. Change my mind.'

"'Really.' Not a question. The detective sits straight up. 'Um-hmm. Changed your mind. What do you think, Detective Shirley?' He's talking to the other cop, the younger one, who's taking notes," Mary Mike said, "Detective Beverley Shirley. Only one thing she can think of, so she taps her forehead with a forefinger: maybe this kid is a mental. You following me, Ralphie?"

"Yeah, yeah, I'm right there. The kid isn't making sense to the cops, so maybe they think he's a little—I don't know—defective."

"Good, Ralphie, you knocked it over the Green Monster." A tiny pause. "All right, where was I? The cop leading the choir, he probably says, 'Take your time, son. We just want the facts. The honest-to-god truth. We're here to help you.' He realizes that Chuckie could be bonkers with this story. Though the cop thinks maybe there could be a grain of truth in it, so he'll keep fishing for a while. He also thinks it's possible that Chuckie might just be a good liar, for a young guy. In other words, the cop's not one hundred percent sure what to think.

"'See, what I did,' Chuckie says, 'it's bad, but I didn't do it, I mean the robbery, see?' The officers stare at him. 'OK, then, lemme try an' think in my mind what-all went down. See, what happened, I step in this lady's truck and point my uncle's gun at her. Scare her so she give up her money, understand? But she already waiting for me—man, don't ask me how—and she has her gun pointing at me 'fore I can get settled on the seat and explain.'

"'Let me think a minute, all right?' the older cop says. He's still looking to put his feet on solid ground. He doesn't have a roadmap here. But he comes up with something. He says, 'Ah, Chuckie, have you been sick lately—you know, dizziness, headaches?'

"'Got one right now.'

"'No, but I mean in recent weeks. Are you on any meds? Prescription drugs?'

"'My mama says don't take none them medicines, they make you a addick.'

"'Um-hmm? Detective Shirley, any questions at this point?' He's trying to find a path in the darkness, hoping his partner has a GPS, or at least a flashlight.

"'Yeah,' the younger cop says. 'You said you decided not to rob this woman, after all. Why? You had a weapon, she had a weapon. This is a little strange, to my way of thinking. I don't see how this plays out. I can't understand why she'd have a weapon ready and waiting. Or if she did, why she didn't shoot you when you got into her vehicle pointing your own weapon at her. So help us understand this little scene, Charlemagne, will you? Way I see it, she got you to change your mind, would that be right?'

"'I got scared, see, after this guy Ray, on the lady's telephone, he tell me put my gun down before she shoot me.' Chuckie by now probably sees that it's hopeless: no one's going to fall for this insane story. But maybe in a way that's a break for him, he thinks.

"'Jesus Christ, son, you expect us to believe this horseshit?' That's the older cop. 'Goddammit! Answer the question!'

"'Which?'

"The older cop pauses. Squeezes the bridge of his nose with his thumb and forefinger. In his mind, he's watching a bartender pour him a double Glenfiddich in a dim, quiet bar. 'Where are we, Detective Shirley? I'm starting to lose the thread.'

"'Explain the phone call, will you, Chuckie,' Detective Shirley says, 'and maybe that'll clear up one or two things. Just stick with what happened. You don't have to hurry.' Beverley Shirley is calmer than her partner. They've worked together before. Detective Shirley knows how to bring the older cop down.

"'Ahhh, OK.' Chuckie takes a big breath. Gulps warm water from the plastic bottle on the table. 'What happened, I jimmy the lock and slide into her truck with my uncle's gun pointing at her, but she already has her gun up against my ribs.'

"'Whoa, wait a minute,' the older cop says. 'You already told us about her weapon. You jimmied your way in? With her in the goddamned truck? Christ Almighty! Do you expect anybody to believe this cockamamie story? Try to have a little respect for my fucking intelligence, Goddammit! Do you have any idea the kinda deep trouble you're in, son? We're investigating multiple murders here. Jesus Christ! Get back to this business with the phone call, you think you can?'

"'She on the phone when I get there,' Chuckie says. 'Man name Ray. She say Ray want to talk to me.'

"'OK, the fucking interrogation is over,' the first cop says. He slaps his hand on the metal table. 'Detective Shirley and I have reason to believe that your story is a complete and utter fabrication, don't we, Detective Shirley?' The other cop nods. 'But we think you might be suffering from some sort of traumatic kind of issue from those headaches, and we're going to have someone from our behavioral science unit look into your medical history before we proceed further.'"

"You nailed it, Mary Mike," Millie said. "What do you think, Ralphie?"

Ralphie with his arms crossed, brooding. He lifts his shoulders about a millimeter. "Yeah. Dynamite."

Jesus Christ, Millie thinks. "For god's sake, Ralphie, lighten up. We were just kidding, the leisure suit's great. Retro style is probably a big thing now, you know? You're out in front of the trend."

"Yeah? Why didn't you just tell me that?"

"Hell, Ralphie, I don't know. I was eating donuts, all right?"

"What do you think, Mary Mike?" he said.

"What's not to like?" she said.

"What about Mandy?" he said.

"She hasn't seen it, Ralphie," Millie said.

"Yeah, but what if?"

"She'd scream," Millie said.

"You think?" he said. "Is that good?"

"So all I'm saying," Mary Mike said, "I'm just saying that Chuckie couldn't give 'em anything to chew on."

"Yeah," Ralph said, "but the cops can't question him without a lawyer or somebody there, can they? The kid's under age."

"Sweet Jesus, of course not, Ralphie, but that isn't the point. Pay attention, dear. This is a hypothetical, see? I'm telling you what'd probably happen regardless. Chuckie could have the whole Harvard Law class of twenty-and-aught-two representing him, that's not the point. If he's a suspect, that's the only story he's got to offer, if you think about it. But Chuckie's never gonna be a suspect. Capeesh? I was just showing you how nuts it is to think he'd be a blabbermouth in the first place, just like Millie said."

Nodding, holding both palms out toward Mary Michael: "'Kay, OK, it was just a question."

"And," she said, "Millie won't appear on the grid either because no one's going to pull together a story from the facts, which nobody at this point even knows what they are. One of which is the money: you say everybody's thinking about the money some guy dumped in a trash can. That's good for us. You see why? Because nobody in their right mind throws away twenty-two pounds of hundred-dollar bills, either dirty or freshly laundered. So then, it'll always be a mystery why the killers did it. If they killed Joey and his pals, why not take the money too? They wouldn't be risking a longer prison sentence, that's for sure."

"Yeah, yeah, I see that," Ralph said. "Twenny-two pounds. I didn't know that."

"And if it was somebody else besides the shooters that dumped it, why would they? Who would these guys be? How did they ever get their hands on the money? Were they just hanging out in the alley, with all the shooting, the door being blown off its hinges, and Joey's car exploding like the Fourth of July? What're the odds?"

"I already said," he said, "it was a good idea to dump the goddamned money. I just needed Millie to go over a couple details."

"So here it is, Ralphie: we're the only ones who know the real story," Mary Mike said. "And it'll die with us. End of story."

"Can I ask a question, Mil?" Ralph said. "It's been botherin' me. Why didn't you just whack that fucking Joey while you had him in the shop there, after you clipped him in the arm? I don't see why you go and send him out so you can blow him up in his car. What's the deal? You could have been done in two seconds, *pow! pow!*, he's dead, you're outta there with the dough, and you're way ahead of the cops."

"Holy Mother, Ralphie," Mary Michael said. "You haven't been listening."

"Yeah, I could have, but it was personal, Ralphie, OK?" Millie said. "Not just another hit. I decided to give Joey Angels the VIP send-off. He deserved the best. So I gave him a history lesson, and then I blew him up. Another thing: I didn't want anybody finding that C-4 and accidentally lighting themselves up."

"History lesson. Jesus, I can't keep up."

"Yeah, I told him a few things about Sheldon and Ray."

"All this time in the business, Mil, starting with my

mom showing me the ropes, I never saw such a fucking mess."

"Wheels within wheels," Mary Michael said. "Sister Immaculata—boy was she right. You can't beat a good Catholic education, Ralphie."

"My mom told me. I didn't get one. Anyway, what the hell, it's all over and done. We can close the books, right? Funny, but that bozo Joey even paid for Millie to ice him. Though he thought he was contracting out a hit on Millie—that's the big joke. Though he didn't actually know you personally, Mil, he just happened to make a call that ended up with our guy in Philly. Jesus, I can't even remember how this fucking mess all started, can you?"

"The mess. The mess, Ralphie, since you asked," said Millie, "started when you and the fucking client, who turned out to be fucking Joey Angels, insisted that I had to ice Sheldon even after Sheldon's original plan had changed. You remember that, don't you?" Millie taking a newish tone here. Not easy to tell if she's angry, just jerking Ralph's chain, or bouncing his head off the floor for some reason.

"I told you on that very day, 'Ralphie,' I said, 'we need to postpone this hit. Explain to the client that circumstances have changed, we have to do the hit tomorrow or the next day, what's the fucking difference? Let's keep it professional.' I said, 'Tell this hot-dog client that he isn't in charge of the operation, I am—me, the one in the field—and I don't like it.' So, OK, Ralphie, you call him and then get back to me, and you say we have to go ahead, we can't cross this guy, he's scary, plus he'll now pay us double. That's where it all began, Ralphie, when the Mob guy stuck his foot through the phone to step on your shark. That and offering you double."

She had more: "Pardon my French, Ralphie, there are ladies present, but all of the bat-shit things that came afterward, if you look at them, you can see a line going straight back to that fucking phone call." A different tone of voice, definitely.

"You're mad at me, right?"

"Mad? At what? You almost got me killed. Twice. So why should I be mad at you? Actually, it was my own fault. I should have canceled and told you and the client to go to hell in the first place. But I made the choice to go ahead. I'll tell you when I was a little mad at you: when Ray told me that day in the motel that Joey'd taken out a contract on the shooter who iced Sheldon. Which was me."

A pause, then: "Set up the dominoes in a certain way, Ralphie, and they all fall down, *click click click click click*. You tumbled first. I didn't want to get knocked over somewhere down the line. So, yeah, I might have been a little upset then, but I decided it would be better to whack Joey than you. He was the guy I was really mad at."

"You're aces, Mil. Thanks."

"Just don't fuck with me in the field again."

"Like I said, Mil, never again." He held up his left hand, palm out. "Scout's honor."

Most of the donuts were gone. Three of the cannoli had been eaten. The sun was somewhere overhead, starting to slide down the other side of the sky. Millie stood up and stretched. Started to make a ham and cheese sandwich from Ralphie's fridge.

Ralph left the room. He returned a couple of minutes later wearing khakis and a mint-green, long-sleeved polo shirt. One of only two remaining in captivity. L. L. Bean slippers on his feet. Mary Michael was poking around in the cabinets for something alcoholic to sand down the edges of the looming afternoon. Her trained hand soon found a fresh bottle of Noah's Mill. "Ralphie, my goodness, sweetie," she says. "Where did you get this lovely bit of drink, now?" She held up the bottle: "Time for my medicine. What do you think? It's past noon."

"Sure. I'll have one myself. You, Millie?" Millie stuck her arm around the fridge door and raised her thumb. Ralph brought three Manhattan glasses to the table. Poured an inch or so of Noah's Mill into each. "*Salud!*" he said. "Drink to a nice tidy job, no loose ends."

"Not quite, Ralphie, there's still one loose end," Millie said, sitting down at the table with her six-tier sandwich. It had grown from a simple ham and Swiss cheese sandwich to a ham, Swiss cheese, lettuce, pickles, American cheese, and turkey sandwich. Plus Dijon mustard and pepperoncini.

"The hell do you mean?" he said. "You got more guys out there you gotta clip? Who's still alive?"

"The bent cop in Kansas City who started this whole damned thing."

Chapter 31

Jimmy Twist

Southwest Airlines flight #641 landed precisely on time, at 3:10 p.m., a fat lazy bird softly settling on her nest. Millie had been reading a crime novel called *Settling Scores*, by Cody Boy Stark. Looking inside, she found that the author's real name was Clarence Dooley, Ph.D. She figured the work of earning his fancy degree didn't include writing courses. The murder scenes bored her.

Millie was once more traveling as Japonica Lake. She had only a single carry-on and her Linea Pella crossbody, where her Epipens and a few other necessary tools of the trade snuggled patiently. She'd have to return to locker #33 at Union Station to pick up her Sig Sauer. Yesterday Mr. Moustakas had sent an overnight package to his nephew in Kansas City. The nephew's job: deliver the package to Union Station. Mail it back if the contact doesn't use it.

She walked through the concourse at Terminal B and met her driver at the pick-up area that divided the street in front of the concourse. She tossed her wheelie-bag on to the seat in back. Opened the front door and slid in.

"Whoa, girl, you don't look like you did last time, huh-uh. You sure you the right one?" said Jauncey Chambers.

"I won't look the same next time either, Jauncey, if you ever see me again." She was wearing her new smoke Tom Ford Elise sunglasses. They went well with her gray slacks, black Valentino Garavani rockstud boots, and Tom Ford black leather moto jacket.

"Oh, yeah, that the voice, all right. You know, I almost call you back. Goin' say to you, 'Lady, the taxi cheaper, and you don't have to bother the driver with all you torment, neither.' But you phone didn't work."

Same old Jauncey.

"I use burners, Jauncey."

"Mm-hmm, I figured. You throw 'em away after you use 'em once. That way nobody traces the call."

Bright sunny skies today. Cool but pleasant. Millie felt relaxed and easy. Though with Jauncey, sure, there's always the chance of bubbles rising from the bottom of the lake.

"It's a nice day, Jauncey, let's take a ride to Union Station."

"I need to know somethin', girl. What you and me goin' be doin' together later today? Or maybe you just here to pay me for my car that you shoot Mr. Kukich in." More of his jive.

"I see that you're driving a new Navigator," she said, "just like Sheldon's. Did you steal it? Where's Sheldon's car? Steal it too, sell it for parts?"

"Steal the man's car? How you goin' steal a car from a dead man? Car don't belong to nobody. That one done gone away. Don't exist no more. Parts, like you say. This one mine. Bought it myself."

"I didn't know felons could swing that much credit, Jauncey." The ride was smooth, the new-car smell reassuring. It gave her the peace of mind to think ahead to the next step, and the step after that.

"Damn, what you sayin'?" he said. He was holding the steering wheel at the bottom with his left thumb, guiding the car from his lap. "Them dealers want to sell cars, girl. How you think Lionel got his fancy wheels? Man had a longer sheet than you got time to read. And anyway, my cousin Earle he co-sign 'cause I got a good job."

"Doing what?"

"What I'm doin' now, takin' people to the airport. Work for You-ber three, four days a week, help Earle when he got a double burial, then I drive You-ber some more. Do odd jobs when they come up. This and that. Man, I put money away. Be rich by now if my old car didn't get used up by you and Lionel." Jauncey enjoying the talk, now with two thumbs at the bottom of the steering wheel, the captain steering his ship through calm seas. "You still don't say what kinda new business we got. Don't want to lose this car, girl, you follow me? You goin' shoot a man, do it someplace else. My insurance don't cover homicide."

Jauncey pulled in front of Union Station. "Stop right here," she said. "I'll be back in a couple of minutes. I want you to be at this spot when I walk out. I don't want to wait around."

Five minutes later they're driving away, Millie carrying a shoebox-size package. "Now let's get something to eat."

"Man, who you know send you presents in Kansas City?" he said. "You want a gun, all you have to do is let me know, hear me? Don't use 'em myself, but they easy to get in this town. Send 'em in the mail, you lookin' for trouble." She opened the package—the Sig Sauer, three extra magazines. Mr. Moustakas making sure I won't run out of ammunition. Does he think I'm going to be in a gun battle? She put the pistol and magazines into her bag. Fingered the Epipens, just to make sure.

"Did you search the house again?"

Jerry Masinton

"Top to bottom. Found what you want, too."

"I was pretty sure it had to be there."

"Um-hmm, you right. First two times around I don't know where to look. Tap the floorboards and walls. Look behind pictures. Tear up the closets. Look in the vents. Man, nothin' nowhere. Then last night I go downstairs to the basement, look behind the furnace, and I see the steel ring in the floor. Pull on the ring, you see they's somethin' hidden under there. But I never lift it up, see what's underneath."

"Why?"

"Somebody in that house with me, upstairs, sneakin' around, lookin' here and there, tryin' to be quiet. Not wake the neighbors, see? After a while, I hear somethin' glass hit the floor and break. The man run into somethin' he can't see. Minute later he on his way downstairs, still real quiet. 'Goddamn!' I thought. 'You in big trouble, Jauncey.'"

"And you decided to hide." They were entering the downtown area. Millie checked her iPhone for a good restaurant near her hotel.

"Hide? Hell, yeah, girl. Ain't suppose to be there in the first place. House still under police watch, too. Signs out front say go away, know what I mean? I find a place underneath the stairs, get down behind some big boxes there. It's dark, the man shine his flashlight everywhere, and I'm gettin' scared. Think to myself, why you doin' this, Jauncey, you want to end up dead?"

"Did you get a good look at this guy?"

"Good enough. He's police. That's all I got to know. Stopped breathing for ten minutes straight, till he go home. Seen the man somewhere, but I disremember where. Too damned nervous to think about it. Another reason I should of called you—tell you the cops involved and I got a sudden need to retire from the crime business."

246

"Where did you park your car?"

"Up the street, another empty house with a For Sale sign on the lawn."

"Is that where you parked the other times?"

"Um-hmm, yeah. Figure no one pay attention to me that way," he said. "Hmm, still tryin' to think where I see that cop."

"You saw him at T-Bone Charlie's."

"Huh? Whoa! You mean we see him that day we there with Lionel?"

"Yeah."

"How you know that? Damn! The way you work, girl, I can't keep my feet steady on the ground. You way ahead of me here. You and that police know each other?" Jauncey's hands were now at ten and two o'clock on the steering wheel. The captain preparing for choppy water ahead.

"You ever see him at Sheldon's house before that?"

"No, but I see a police car two, three times in front, so I don't go in. Couldn't figure why they there at night."

"Same reason you broke in—to find Sheldon's safe."

"You don't have to tell me that now. But how the man know Mr. Kukich have a safe to rob? Wait a minute, back up. How you know about the safe, or either this police? You makin' me nervous again, you know that?"

"I thought you liked the excitement, Jauncey." She checked her iPhone. "Slow down, will you?" He did. "Turn here." They drove for a block and a half. "OK, find a parking spot. We're going to get something to eat at this place." They were at the BRGR Kitchen & Bar on East 14th Street. It was almost five o'clock. I could eat the entire cow, Millie thought.

"You want hamburgers, you get 'em cheaper at Mc-Donald's," Jauncey said. "Can't beat the fries, neither. Me and my boys, every Friday we used to eat at McDonald's, then go to a movie-show. Man, those boys come to see me, all we do is cook and eat. Pulled pork, ribs, dirty rice, grill wings. Man, I'm gettin' hungry. Who told you about this place?"

"Nobody. My hotel's not far from here. I hope it's fairly quiet. We need to discuss our plans for the evening."

"Now we gettin' round to it. But you never aks me have I got plans of my own, girl, you know that? Like, you need to drive folks around tonight to make money, Jauncey? Or maybe, hey, Jauncey, you and Sharilla got plans for tonight, go out to the Blue Room, say hi to Andre, hear some jazz?"

They were in the restaurant now, the smell of burgers and fried onion rings like a cloud they were walking through. My clothes are going to smell just like this place, Millie thought. I don't even want to think about my hair. They sat at a booth, a large cylinder of light hanging down over them.

"You and Sharilla are still together, then?"

"Not living-together together, but she can't do without me, know what I mean?"

"I thought she was mad at you for chasing a white woman."

"That's another thing you got me into, girl. You call me on the phone that day you break Lionel's finger, Sharilla know I'm talkin' to a woman. She figure you the same woman I didn't have nothin' to do with in the first place. But Sharilla got it in her head I be chasin' this woman, so nothin' I say change her mind. When you call, I say, 'Yeah, Lionel, how you doin', man,' but that don't fool her. Man, I had to do a lot of fancy talkin' later on."

They ordered burgers, sweet potato fries, and Cokes, with a separate order of tire-sized fried onion rings. Her burger was a Juicy Lucy, his was a Big Mock. I hope he doesn't eat his share of those onion rings, she thought.

"Later after what?"

"After I get home from that place you left me to walk all the way home."

"The parking area of that old diner."

"Yeah. Earle, he finally show up and take me home. Then Sharilla, she say, 'Get out the house! I ain't livin' with no two-timin' dog!' Try to explain what happened, only that make it worse. Can't say, 'The woman and me go to this place to see Lionel, she break Lionel's finger, and then we barely get away 'fore the cops kill Lionel.' No way I could come up with a story to turn her mind away from me and you."

"And now you're trying to get back with her because she hasn't closed the door all the way."

"That's it."

"But you don't have any plans for tonight."

"Not exactly per se, huh-uh, but I got lot of stuff goin' on, know what I mean?"

"What you've got going on, Jauncey, is what you signed on for when I called you. You're going back into Sheldon's house again, only this time I'll be with you. You and I are going to see what he kept in that safe in the basement."

"I knew it, I knew we gettin' back to that damned basement. Was me, I just leave it alone, now that I see that police." He paused. "Why you come back to this town lookin' for trouble?"

"We'll wait until ten or eleven. Starting at about seven, we'll drive past the house a few times to see whether your friend is there."

"If he is, then we can go home, forget all about it, that what you thinkin'? You aks me, that's a plan we can vote on."

"No. I need to talk to him."

"Man, it's like the movies again, ain't it, like when you shoot Mr. Kukich? I'm here, but I don't believe it. You plannin' to shoot that police?"

"I don't know."

"You put me in a puzzlement, you know that? Tell me why you here, anyway." Jauncey said. "Nobody know what happen that time in my car. That cop ain't lookin' for you. If he want to rob the safe, what do you care? Ain't your money."

"He's a loose end, and I don't trust loose ends," Millie said. She looked at the onion rings. Only one of them left. Technically it was Jauncey's since she'd already sucked down her three. "Are you going to eat that onion ring?"

"Huh-uh. Don't want no more. What loose ends you mean, if he don't even know 'bout you?"

"Let's start with this, Jauncey: the cop is the guy who set Sheldon up to be killed."

"You tellin' me this policeman was in the basement with me pay you to shoot Mr. Kukich? Don't see how that happen, if you don't know the man. You done lost me, girl, I'm in the woods."

"No, he doesn't know me. He was in Sheldon's house looking for anything that might tie him to the kill. He's afraid that Sheldon might have left evidence that points to him."

"Don't see how if the man didn't shoot Mr. Kukich."

"This cop is an interesting guy, Jauncey. He had already helped to set up three other men in Witness Protection before Sheldon. The other murders went off clean. The victims were quickly identified. Sheldon's body was never found. That's a problem for him."

"Whoa, you runnin' ahead of me, gal. This policeman killin' people in a Federal program?"

"Uh-huh. He's not the shooter, though. He locates the victims and sells them out to somebody in the trade. But yeah, same thing as shooting them."

"And he's nervous 'cause Mr. Kukich body disappear?"

"That's right. He's looking for something that might point to him in that house. Incriminating evidence that

Sheldon could have squirreled away—that's what's eating him up. You remember that Sheldon's ID was planted on the dead black guy in your car, don't you?"

"Um-hum, I ain't forgot."

"That alone would have given this guy heartburn. He'd think: 'Is somebody out there's fucking with me?' And then when Sheldon's body never surfaces? To Jimmy, that's no coincidence. Are you with me, Jauncey?"

"Yeah, maybe, but I still don't see why you need to do anything. Or me neither. We driving down another separate road."

"Here's the way I see it, Jauncey: Sheldon's case didn't come off as planned. The other Witness Protection guys testified, thinking they'd be safe in their new locations. But they weren't: they got whacked. Sheldon didn't testify. Why? Because he found out that he'd be killed if he testified, so he backed off and flew back to Kansas City. He didn't realize it, but the contract on him had already been put out. He was already a dead man."

"Way you know this," Jauncey said, "you the one got the contract on Mr. Kukich. You do the others too? Man oh man."

"Huh-uh. I don't know who did them."

Just then the waitress came to their table. "Hi, everything good? Can I getcha guys anything else?" Her name badge said Heather.

"We're fine, thanks," Millie said.

"Can I take those plates? Give you some extra room there." She gathered up everything but the drinks.

"I'll be back to fill up the drinks," Heather said.

"No, we're all right, thanks," Millie said.

"I just love those jumbo onion rings," Heather said. "Did you guys like 'em?"

"Heather," Millie said. "Heather. I'm going to say this once and once only. We're fine. Peachy keen, in fact. We don't want company. We're planning an assassination, and we'd like some privacy, OK?"

"Oh, sure," Heather whispered. "Thank you." She backed away from their table with a tiny lopsided smile.

"Ooooh, you cold, lady, you know that?"

"Yeah. Now listen. This cop has to know that Sheldon bailed on the prosecutor because he'd figured out the set-up. Maybe Sheldon even followed the string back to the contractor. Sheldon was a former Mob guy, so he'd know how these guys think. The cop can't take a chance that Sheldon identified the players and then set a trap. You see where I'm going, Jauncey?"

"Sure, I got it. Maybe Mr. Kukich wrote some stuff down on paper and put it in a safe place, people's names and shit. That what the policeman lookin' for."

"Yeah."

"Them papers I gave you from Mr. Kukich suitcase?"

"Yeah."

"Damn! You right! But I saw you take that envelope from Lionel that day. The papers, they inside it, not in Mr. Kukich safe. They got this policeman name on 'em, right?"

"No, but they led me to him. His name is Jameson Twist. Jimmy Twist. He's a detective in the Kansas City Police Department. And Officer Jimmy's behaving the way a guilty man behaves."

"How you be sure that policeman thinkin' the way you say? Maybe somethin' else goin' on in his head?"

"Think about it, Jauncey. Jimmy Twist knows why Sheldon refused to testify against the crime boss. Jimmy knows this because he and somebody in the Witness Protection Program report directly to the Mob. Bottom line: Jimmy's afraid that Sheldon connected the dots and left evidence behind, either before or after the trial began. Why else would he be sniffing around Sheldon's house?"

"The money. You said so yourself, he after the same thing we are."

"I said the safe, Jauncey, not the money."

"Damn! Now you got me thinkin' this cop is bad dangerous. He tryin' to stay out of jail for killing people. If you and me get in front of him, ain't goin' make any difference to him. Good reason for us to stay away, then. I know you good with a gun, lady, but that don't help me none."

"If we drop it and go home, that won't help you either."

"Why not? From now on I just stay away from Mr. Kukich house, forget about that safe, bury bodies with Earle."

"After last night, Jauncey, Jimmy Twist is after you too, not just any papers that might be in that safe."

"Whoa, girl. What you sayin'? He didn't see me last night, otherwise I wouldn't be here havin' this conversation."

"You forget that he's a cop. Any cop with eyes would have noticed the car parked three times in the driveway of an empty house near Sheldon's."

"Goddamn! You think? Maybe he didn't see it. It was night."

"By now Jimmy has used the license plate to trace the registration of the car. He knows who you are, Jauncey. He's got to kill you."

Chapter 32

Red Buttons

The restaurant was filling up. Rising chatter of voices, scraping of chairs against the floor, eau de burger filling the air. Millie and Jauncey had been in the place for an hour. They needed to move fast, she knew, now that Jauncey was in Jimmy's crosshairs.

"Ready to go?" she said. She slipped on the Tom Ford leather jacket she'd carried in from the car.

"How you know this police be there at Mr. Kukich tonight?" he said. Still maybe a little hesitant about this operation. "Could be any night."

"He knew you were there last night. He saw your car. So he has to speed up his timetable. He'll be there. And he'll be expecting you to keep him company."

"How you come around to all this?" He leaned over the table toward her.

"I worked it out from what you told me. And something else: he might have put a tracker on your car. We can't rule it out."

"So he can sneak up on me, you sayin'. We suppose to sneak up on him, what you said before. Take him down before he see us. Now he goin' follow me. Man, I'm jittery in my stomach. Too many ways this damn thing go wrong."

"We've gone over it twice, Jauncey. You want to walk it through again?"

"Me? Hell no, I know what to do. I'm just restin' on the idea, you follow? Steal cars, I'm all alone, they no one pointin' a gun at me. But this here bother me, thinkin' this police goin' have a gun on him that he like to use."

"I'm going to leave now. I'll go to the ladies' room and then find my way out the back. Follow me in fifteen minutes. Get in your car and wait ten minutes before you leave. I want to see whether you're going to have a visitor. Here, pay the bill." She laid four twenties on the table. "Give Heather a good tip. We don't want to leave a bad impression."

When she walked out of the ladies', the Sig was snugged against her right hip. An extra mag in its pouch on her left hip. She left by the rear door and rounded the corner back to the parking lot, staying in the shadows between cars. The lot was about half full. Good enough cover, she thought.

A Honda minivan pulled in parallel to Jauncey's Lincoln Navigator, two spaces away, leaving an extra slot on his driver's side. A woman and two teen-age kids got out and walked to the restaurant. "Mom, can I have. . . ?" from the girl as they drifted toward the door.

An unmarked gray Ford sedan was cruising between the parking lanes. Millie watched it. A cop car. Might as well put Christmas lights on it. After a while it slid into a space behind the Lincoln. The driver doused the lights. He sat in the dark, waiting. Millie screwed on the Sig's silencer. She moved into the shadow of the mini-van, about ten or twelve feet from Jauncey's car.

Five minutes later Jauncey appeared. Walked to his car and pinged open the lock. The guy in the Ford was quick and quiet. He slipped behind Jauncey and said something to him. He shoved Jauncey face-first against the car, hard, and held a pistol to the back of his head. The guy was very efficient.

"God Jesus damn! You scare the shit outta me, man. What you want?"

Millie had no trouble hearing what they said. The guy's back was to her, but he had a high-pitched voice. He sounded tired.

"Where's your girlfriend? Didn't you invite her to the party?" He turned Jauncey around to face him.

"Ain't no girlfriend. I give her a ride for You-ber. You want to rob me, you don't have to point that gun at me, understand? I give you what I got, then you leave outta here, OK? Gun make me nervous." Fear was leaking into his voice.

"Who is she?" He jabbed the pistol into Jauncey's ribs. "Uber drivers don't have meals with their fares." It was early evening, getting dark now. Another car entered the parking lot at BRGR, the lights brushing past the two men before turning away. "I need to talk to her," the guy said.

"Why you need to talk?"

"None of your fuckin' business, pal. Who the hell is she? That's the last time I ask you."

"Name Miss Honey, or maybe Druilda somethin'. I disremember. Say she in town on big business. Didn't understand a word about it." Chauncey skating on the razor's edge. A little swag returning to his voice.

"Wise-ass." The guy slapped the side of Jauncey's head with the pistol. Jauncey groaned. Gasped. Began breathing rapidly through his mouth. Dropped his car keys.

"You lying piece of shit. I know who you are and what you're up to. And you're gonna tell me sooner or later about that woman. But first you and me are going to take a little ride." He moved a half-step back. "Pick up the fucking keys and hand 'em to me." His pistol was pointed at Jauncey.

"OK, don't hit me no more." Millie saw Jauncey glance her way in the shadow behind the gunman. He picked up the car keys, held them out, and let them fall just as the guy reached for them.

Suddenly, without sound, Millie was there. She shoved her Sig under the gunman's right ear, pressing hard. She grabbed his hair and pulled his head back. "Hand it over, Jimmy, and don't fuck around or you're dead." She twisted the barrel against his neck. "I'll kill you before you can squeeze the trigger," she told him, "so play nice."

Jimmy tried to shake his head yes. A couple of seconds passed. He was still holding his pistol. A tell. He tried to swing it around in her direction. Millie shot him in the left knee. She grabbed his weapon before he could react. The silencer had helped, muting the report down to a *pap* sound. She looked around the parking lot. No one close enough to have heard.

"Whoa! Damn!" Jauncey said, Jimmy groaning "Aaaahhh!" at the same moment. "Jesus," Jauncey said, "I barely see you coming." Jimmy slowly collapsed. He made strangled groaning sounds and seemed to have trouble catching his breath.

"Get in, Jauncey. Start the engine. You heard the man, he wants to go for a ride. Where to, Jimmy?" She pulled him to his feet. "You're going to ride in the back with me." Millie opened the door and shoved him into the car. He had to drag his left leg after him. She followed, pushing him to the passenger side. He was sucking in air through his teeth, his breath hoarse.

"Jesus," Jauncey said, "what you doin' to my car? This just like that last time with Mr. Kukich. Man goin' bleed all over the back seat."

"Just drive, Jauncey," she said, "forget about the damned car."

Jimmy was breathing hard. She could see the sweat on his forehead. "You dumb bitch, do you know that you just shot a police officer?" Squeezing the thigh above the knee with both hands. "You're dead, you know that?"

"I bet you want to visit Sheldon's house again, don't you? You know the way, Jauncey. Let's get there before Jimmy here changes his mind." She looked at the knee. "I don't think I hit an artery, Jimmy. You're lucky. You can still make it to the party. You did invite me, didn't you? Buckle up, don't want to take chances, do we?"

"Who the fuck. Are you?" Jimmy said. "You're in over your head, lady, whoever the hell you are." He slumped against the door, but didn't pass out. Breathing fast through his nose now. The groaning in rhythm with his breath. Would he go into shock? she wondered.

Jauncey again: "Damn! Have to get Earle help me clean up the blood. They got these detail places too, maybe one of them do it. Good thing you didn't shoot no bullet holes this car." Jauncey was starting to levitate.

"The sooner we get there, the less blood he leaves in your car."

In minutes they were on State Line Road heading south. "Sit up straight, Jimmy. It's not fatal." Millie pulled him upright. She held the Sig firm against Jimmy's gut. His groans were now raspy whistles from the throat. A man trying to gargle and sing at the same time. Still holding the shot-up knee with both hands.

"What did you think would happen here, Jimmy? You'd take Jauncey to Sheldon's house, kill him, make it look like a bungled burglary? Only first he'd help you find whatever you're afraid Sheldon had hidden away, right? Then you'd shoot him."

"You don't know what the fuck you're talkin' about. But you're dead, you stinking bitch, I can promise you that, even if you kill me."

"Language, Jimmy. Tell me why I need to die. Make it a good story."

"I like to hear it too," Jauncey said. "Why you want to kill this woman. And me either." Traffic was heavy on State Line. Friday evening. People starting their weekend. Happy times ahead.

"How close are we?" Millie asked Jauncey.

"Four, five minutes. We goin' park at Mr. Kukich house? The man can't walk far."

"Park where you always do. The walk will do Jimmy some good. Give him a little fresh air."

"Girl, like I told you, you cold." He sounded more amused than sad.

"How's your head, where he hit you with his pistol?"

"Oh. Yeah. Gotcha. Make him remember what he done to me. He goin' need help, though."

Jimmy suddenly lunged forward, grabbed the steering wheel with his left hand. Turned the car hard to the right, pulling the car off the shoulder and down toward the ditch, Jauncey fighting him for control. Millie clubbed Jimmy's hand with the Sig, fired twice as he tried to grab the pistol, and slapped him across the cheek with it, all in one motion. Jauncey breathing hard, now controlling the steering wheel, steering left to get back on the road, overcompensating and heading into oncoming traffic, then back to his lane. "Goddamn! God damn! You got him? I damn near die of a heart attack. You OK?"

"Jimmy, you're one dumb son-of-a-bitch. Now you've got a headache to go with your bad knee."

"Time we get there, my car ruined, what I think," Jauncey said. "You shoot out my screen and radio. Should've picked you up in Earle's truck."

He turned west off State Line and pulled into the driveway of a house in the middle of the third block. No lights in the house or in the three running west of it. No cars parked along the street. A little spooky, Millie thought.

"OK, party time," she said. She got out of the car, the Sig pointing at Jimmy. Stepped to his side of the car, opened the door, and yanked him out. He fell, groaning loudly, "Christ, oh, Christ!"

Jauncey helped her to pull Jimmy to his feet. Jimmy slumped down, a dead weight between them. "Fuck you! I'm not going," he said. "I can't."

"We'll have to park in front of Sheldon's house," Millie said.

Jauncey moved the car: "How we goin' get him in the house?" he said. They were at Sheldon's front walk, half-carrying, half-pushing Jimmy. "Can't shove him through the window I used." Jimmy was panting.

"Remember the key ring?" Millie said. "One of those keys will fit the front door, I think." No cars had driven by. A few lights blinked on down the street on the other side of the block. A perfectly peaceful suburban evening.

The third key fit. She and Jauncey helped Jimmy in and closed the door. The journey to the basement was tricky. Jimmy offered no help. Millie pointed the way with her LED flashlight. They sat Jimmy down on an old wooden chair. The darkness almost palpable.

"Jauncey, stay here with Jimmy while I find the electrical panel. Maybe we'll get lucky. Slap him if he moves."

A few minutes later the basement lights came on. The rest of the house stayed dark. A small light bulb dangled over Jimmy, illuminating only his upper half. He seemed to be floating in a pool of darkness.

"All right, Jimmy. It's your party."

"You fuckers. Why don't you just kill me?" Jimmy now singing a different tune. "I'm bleeding bad."

"No, you're not, Jimmy," Millie said, "but we'll wrap that knee so you can explain a few things. That's why you're still alive."

Millie found some old sheets draped over a couch and an easy chair. She tore one of the sheets in strips. With a few quick motions she wrapped Jimmy's knee tight while Jauncey held the flashlight and pressed the Sig against his temple. She used another strip to tie his right hand to a rung of the chair.

"Be careful, Jauncey, it's got a hair trigger."

Jauncey sniffed. "I don't trust guns none," he said. "This thing goin' go off, ain't it? First time I kill a man with a gun. Put a few in the ground, though." His bounciness returning in this unlikely setting.

"See if our friend has a phone."

Jauncey handed her Jimmy's phone and the Sig. She dropped the phone on the concrete floor, stomped it with her boot heel, pounded it with the butt of the Sig. Kicked it out of her way.

"Now see if any of these keys fit the safe you found."

Jimmy's head snapped up. "OK, I got you wrong, you know something about this case," he said. "Maybe I read you wrong. But you can check my wallet, see I'm a cop. I'm investigating a murder—Sheldon Kukich, a stinking thug. A killer. Just doing my duty. So you help me, I'll help you. Who are you? What's your angle here?"

"Lately everybody wants to know who I am. I'll have to print up some business cards."

"Kukich had information I need," Jimmy said. "To take down some big Mob guys. Fucking animals, those goons. I looked for the safe, couldn't find it. See, we can work together on this. Nobody has to get hurt." He was having trouble holding his head up. The talking had worn him out. Millie pointed the light directly at his face. He was sweating, blood oozing from the damaged knee. Maybe more serious than I realized, she thought.

"Son-of-a-bitch!" This was Jauncey a few feet away, behind the furnace. "What the hell is this shit?"

He came toward her holding a sheaf of paper, maybe thirty sheets with fancy engraving. He had also found half a dozen rolls of $100 bills, each wrapped with a rubber band. There was nothing else. No hand-written notes or letters. Not a thing.

"Man, you see this shit? They's serious money here. I be damned! What're these papers? You think they any good?"

"What's there?" Jimmy said. "Lemme see it." His voice coming from far away.

"You're tired, Jimmy. Tell me what you wanted to find. And why. Then you can see it. I know you set up Sheldon's murder, you and some pals of yours from the Witness Protection Program. You're killing people who turn state's evidence. Guys who testify in the trials of Mob figures. Wanna tell me why?"

"I don't know what the hell you're talking about." His voice was a whisper.

"Yeah, you do. A friend of mine did a little research and found your footprints all over these cases. Your Fed buddies too. Local cop and Feds working together to execute mobsters? That's a good story. Tell me the rest."

"You figure it out, you know so much." Stubborn.

"What, you didn't have enough to do playing detective? You're in bad shape here, Jimmy. The sooner you explain things, the sooner we call a doctor."

Jimmy was rocking from side to side, making the chair creak and moan. "A cousin of mine was killed a few years back after he testified against a Mob guy in New York. He resettled in Omaha, this cousin. What they did to him wasn't pretty. They wanted to send a message."

"So why didn't you go after the Mob? Why are you selling out the informants?"

"OK, lady, try this on. My cousin was a scumbag. A made guy from New Jersey. Hot-shot for the Lucchese outfit. I was a cop. I didn't give a shit what happened to him. He got what he deserved."

"But then you got an idea, right? You and the others. Help me out here, Jimmy," she said.

"These guys, these savages, they're killers. New Jersey. New York. Toronto. The Feds turn 'em. Promise immunity and a new start if they snitch. That's how you nail the bosses, you get one of the soldiers to talk." He stopped. Rested his chin against his chest. Closed his eyes. Going into shock?

"What else, Jimmy?"

"Why are we here? Jesus, I don't have much left, I'm passing out."

"It's your game, Jimmy. Finish up and we all go home." She was holding the Sig across her stomach, the flashlight on Jimmy. Jauncey flipping the pages of the documents he had found. Trying in the faint light of the LED to count the money in the fat rolls of bills.

"You oughta be glad somebody's tending to business," Jimmy said. "Otherwise these fuckers would get off with not even a knuckle rap. 'Here,' the government says, 'here's a nice house in the suburbs. A new name. Life-time security. Courtesy of the U.S. taxpayer.' Me and two guys I know in Witness Protection decided fuck that shit, we're gonna make 'em pay."

"And you made some money on the side, didn't you?"

"The money came from the Mob, what do you care? We just ID'd the informants after they resettled. Their guys did the rest."

"One more question, Jimmy. How many people have you killed to protect this scam? Plus you planned to whack Jauncey here. And then me, after I entered the picture."

"No, you're wrong. I just wanted to see if I was in the clear. That's all. Kukich's body was never found. So I couldn't take a chance somebody knew something." His voice arrived from a deep cave.

"That's what I figured," Millie said. "But it turns out you didn't have any worries. Show him the stuff, Jauncey."

Jimmy stared at the documents and the rolls of bills. "Money? What's that other stuff?"

"Bearer bonds, Jimmy. A lot of them. But that's it. Nothing that'd point to you. The stuff you wanted was in his suitcase when he died. He never had a chance to plant it or show the Feds."

"I don't . . . I don't see . . . "

"You did all this for nothing, Jimmy. That's what you don't see."

Jimmy bent slowly sidewise to his left, a grin forming, saying something like "huh" or "hih." With his left hand, he slowly reached down and pulled a small pistol from an ankle holster. Didn't think of that one, Millie thought, as she swung the Sig and put three rounds into his chest—three red buttons.

Later, riding with Jauncey, she told him about the bearer bonds. "They belong to the person who holds them. They're as good as cash. But you need to hire a good lawyer before you try to use them. Same with the money. Your lawyer can sort it out for you."

"And he keep my secret, right?"

"Yeah, client confidentiality. You're a rich man, Jauncey."

"But I still got to get rid of the man's body in the back seat."

"You and Earle. Find Jimmy a place near Sheldon. And ditch the car this time. You can afford a new one."

"Man, I never believe what happen if I didn't see it. You save my life, girl, you know that? But, damn, I don't see how everything fit together, know what I mean? Let me aks you a question." He was driving under the speed limit, careful, deliberate. "Why you leave them papers from you pocket on the basement floor back there? And the man's wallet?"

"It was the stuff from Sheldon's suitcase—newspaper articles and the things he wrote down on hotel stationery. The cops will figure it out, see what Jimmy and the two Witness Protection guys were up to. The wallet? What do you think, Jauncey?"

"Me? Hmmm. Show that the man was there and got killed. His blood on the floor. But then they got a mystery when they can't find his body."

"That's right."

"And them police never know who-all done him. Nor neither why. They never goin' put the right story together."

"Um-hmm."

COMING SOON:
Who's Who Among the Dead

Book #2 in *The Millie Henshawe Series*

by Jerry Masinton

Do you like badass women who shoot guys for a living? Read *Who's Who Among the Dead* and fall in love with Millie Henshawe all over again. She's tough, gay and smart as hell.

In *Who's Who Among the Dead,* Millie gets caught between rival gangs of the Russian mafia in Boston when she is asked to whack a guy who has already been declared dead. She investigates, only to find herself in the embalming room of a run-down mortuary discussing who's who among the toe tags with Anton Poliakov, an émigré with a dangerously high level of free-floating anxiety and mangled English.

ACKNOWLEDGMENTS

Warm thanks to the members of the Write-On group who read *Wrong Man Down* as it was being written. Your superb critiques and useful suggestions helped more than I can say.

Big thanks also to Maureen Carroll, editor of Anamcara Press, who not only read the manuscript with an eagle eye but also guided me through the minefield of the publication process with good humor and expertise.

Good books need good editors, and in my case I had a truly great editor—my wife, Martha Masinton, who helped me from the very beginning to shape the book, clear out the debris, and tell its complex story clearly. Without you, this would have been only a poor orphan of a novel. And as much as anything else, it was your encouragement that made the difference.